I0658728

A Gangsta's Pain 3

J-Blunt

Lock Down Publications and Ca$h
Presents

A Gangsta's Pain 3
A Novel by *J-Blunt*

J-Blunt

Lock Down Publications
P.O. Box 944
Stockbridge, Ga 30281
www.lockdownpublications.com

Copyright 2023 by J-Blunt
A Gangsta's Pain 3

All rights reserved. No part of this book may be reproduced in any form or by electronic or mechanical means, including information storage and retrieval systems without permission in writing from the publisher, except by a reviewer who may quote brief passages in review.
First Edition January 2023
Printed in the United States of America

This is a work of fiction. Names, characters, places, and incidents either are products of the author's imagination or are used fictitiously. Any similarity to actual events or locales or persons, living or dead, is entirely coincidental.

Lock Down Publications
Like our page on Facebook: Lock Down Publications @
www.facebook.com/lockdownpublications.ldp

Book interior design by: **Shawn Walker**
Edited by: **Sunny Giovanni**

Stay Connected with Us!

Text **LOCKDOWN** to 22828 to stay up-to-date with new releases, sneak peaks, contests and more...

Thank you!

Submission Guideline.

Submit the first three chapters of your completed manuscript to ldpsubmissions@gmail.com, subject line: Your book's title. The manuscript must be in a .doc file and sent as an attachment. Document should be in Times New Roman, double spaced and in size 12 font. Also, provide your synopsis and full contact information. If sending multiple submissions, they must each be in a separate email.

Have a story but no way to send it electronically? You can still submit to LDP/Ca$h Presents. Send in the first three chapters, written or typed, of your completed manuscript to:

LDP: Submissions Dept
P.O. Box 944
Stockbridge, Ga 30281

DO NOT send original manuscript. Must be a duplicate.

Provide your synopsis and a cover letter containing your full contact information.

Thanks for considering LDP and Ca$h Presents.

Acknowledgements:

Here we go again! I love what I do so I'ma keep on doing it. Shout out to everybody that's been rocking with me and supporting me throughout my fight with this injustice system. A special thank you to the fans and supporters of J-Blunt. Thanks for the feedback and the reviews. Connect with me on Facebook @ Author J-Blunt

J-Blunt

PROLOGUE

D-Ray turned onto 9th and Wright, checking all the mirrors on the Jeep Trailhawk to make sure he wasn't being followed. Shit had been rough on the young gunner for the last few days, and he had to move smart. His niggas had been dying at an alarming rate as of late and he didn't to be next. His niggas Kevo, Deonta, and Tweezy all died within a few days of each other. BGM niggas were being hunted and knocked off one by one by some niggas from Parklawn. 40th and Center, BGM headquarters, had become a ghost town. Nobody was safe. Until the heat died down, D-Ray was playing it safe. He changed cars, putting away the BMW and pulling out the Trailhawk with five percent tint. He relocated to stay with his lil vibe on 9th Street. Nobody knew him on the low end, so he planned to lay low until the heat died down. And when it did, he was going to gather his squad again and blow down every building in Parklawn. When he turned onto Tranay's block, he immediately noticed the white Range Rover that sat idling at the curb. He knew who the truck belonged to, Cushy Chris. He was a local hood star. D-Ray was sure that he fucked Tranay, but she denied it.

"Cushy Chris." D-Ray grinned, shaking hands with the Range Rover's owner.

"D-Ray, what it do, nigga?" Cushy grinned, flashing his diamond and gold toothed smile.

"Shit. I see you shining in the buffs!"

"Yeah. Spent a light ten on these," Cushy said, taking off the expensive Cartier glasses to wave them in the air. "Fucking the city up and all these bitch ass niggas! You see them pointers."

"You fucking it up!" D-Ray laughed.

"I know. That's what I do." Cushy laughed as he slid the glasses back on. "What you on, though, my nigga? You know I got that super loud on deck. Straight from Russia, my nigga. Them crackers got that fiya over there. This what Vladimir Putin was smoking when he told his niggas to drop them missiles on Ukraine."

"Fool ass nigga." D-Ray laughed. "But is that shit really smoking?"

Cushy looked offended. "Is the diamonds in my Presidential real?" he asked, showing the iced out watch on his left wrist. "You want me to grab the diamond tester for you, nigga? Everything I got is *really* what I say it is."

D-Ray took a look at the young hustler's wrist, wishing he wasn't standing in Cushy's hood. Had they been anywhere else, Cushy would be stuffed in a garbage can with a bullet in his face and D-Ray would be flexing the Rover, the buffs, and the Rolex. But the situation was in Cushy's favor so D-Ray played his role. "I know how yo' bitch ass do it out here. Yo' hoe ass stay flexing. Let me get a half ounce."

"Yo' bitch ass just made a good choice cause I'ma knock off a hunnit because I fuck with you." Cushy smiled as he walked back to the truck.

The men made the transaction before shaking hands and D-Ray headed for Tranay's house. As soon as Cushy Chris hopped back in his Range, he made a call.

"Cushy, what it do, fool?" Junior answered.

"You ain't gon' believe who I just ran into, my nigga."

Junior paused. "Don't say that bitch ass BGM nigga."

Cushy smiled. "He just copped from me and went in the house. I think he locked in all night. What you want me to do?"

"Don't do nothing. Sit on that nigga and make sure he don't leave. I'm on my way."

"Ay, you know this ain't free, right?" Cushy asked. "You gon' do what we talked about, right?"

Junior laughed. "I'ma drop the price for you and throw you one. That's my word.

***

"Why Cushy parked outside?" D-Ray mugged as he walked by Tranay and into the living room.

"I don't know. He wasn't up in here. I didn't even know he was outside," she sassed, irritated by the accusation.

D-Ray looked over his shorty, weighing her words and demeanor. Tranay was a short and thick, brown skinned shorty with an expensive wig habit and an insatiable sexual appetite. Nympho was an understatement. She also had a fire shot that he knew didn't belong to only him. And she was a terrible liar.

"Nigga, you think I'm stupid?" D-Ray asked, raising his voice. "All I'm saying is don't be having these niggas over here while I'm ducked off. You know I'm laying low. You tryna get me killed, bitch?"

"On my mama and my baby that nigga wasn't up in here," Tranay said, losing some of the attitude. "I just told you I didn't know he was outside. I'm not lying."

"Keep on playing with me and I'ma buss yo' shit, nigga," D-Ray threatened before heading to the bathroom. After draining the snake, he went back into the living room where he found Tranay watching TV. He sat next to her and pulled out the weed he got from Cushy along with a wrap. "What you watching?"

Tranay rolled her eyes. "Why? It ain't like you care."

D-Ray let out a chuckle while rolling the blunt. "You mad because I checked you about yo' lil boyfriend, for real?"

"That ain't my boyfriend. I already told you that. The only person I'm fucking is you. Need to be asking who *you* fucking because you leave my house early and don't come back until late at night. How many hoes you fucking?"

"You a cold bitch the way you flipped the script like that." D-Ray laughed again. "But I didn't mean to come at you like that. My bad. You know you got that wet wet and I don't want no nigga sticking his fingers in my cookie jar."

"Whatever, nigga." Tranay smirked, trying to hold in the smile. She liked being complimented. Especially, about her sex game. She knew her pussy was fire. She had whipped a few niggas, D-Ray included. It made her feel good to know that her pussy could damn near control a nigga's mind.

D-Ray slid close to her, gripping one of her thick thighs. "I said I'm sorry, baby. You know I fuck with you the long way and I'm just tryna make sure that what's mine stays mine."

"Who said it's yours?" Tranay asked, pushing his hand from her leg.

D-Ray took a long puff on the blunt before sliding a hand between her legs and rubbing her pussy through the black leggings. "If it ain't mine, who's is it?"

"It's mine," she breathed, liking the feel of his hand stroking her kitten.

D-Ray took one more puff of the blunt before passing it to Tranay and sliding to his knees. He spread her legs apart and started licking her pussy through the thin black fabric.

"Ohh!" Tranay moaned.

"You want me to eat *my* pussy?" D-Ray asked.

Tranay blew out a thick cloud of smoke and nodded. "Eat yo' pussy, baby."

D-Ray grabbed the blunt and took a couple of puffs while Tranay stripped off the spandex and sat back on the couch. When she was comfortable, she grabbed the blunt and puffed while D-Ray dined between her legs. He slipped his tongue between her pussy lips, licking her from top to bottom.

"Oh yeah, nigga," Tranay moaned, gripping the back of his head, and pulling his face into her pussy.

D-Ray buried his nose in her pussy and thrust his tongue deep inside. After a few wiggles, he found her clit and began to stroke it. That drove her wild. She began to buck her hips and leap beneath him like a wildcat. Suddenly, her body went stiff. For a long moment, her thighs held his face firmly and her pussy held his tongue. Then, she gradually relaxed as the orgasm passed.

D-Ray stood and ripped off his clothes while Tranay looked up at him like he was a God. When he was naked, D-Ray grabbed the blunt to take a couple of puffs, before throwing it in the ashtray and kneeling between her legs. He slipped the head of his swollen knob against her lips before easing all the way in her tight pussy. She rocked her pelvis steadily against him as he pumped in and out of her. After they were moving at a steady rhythm, he lifted her shirt to kiss her breasts and suck her nipples. When he felt her pussy spasm, it was enough to make him explode.

"Awe shit," D-Ray moaned as his body went stiff and his dick jerked inside her. A few moments later, he lay back on the couch and reached for the blunt and lighter.

"Nah, nigga. We ain't done yet," Tranay said, not ready to quit. She knelt between his legs and took his dick between her moist lips and bobbed her head up and down. D-Ray closed his eyes and puffed the blunt while getting his dick sucked. Right when it got good, there was a knock on the door. Tranay stopped sucking and looked towards the door.

"Fuck who at the door," D-Ray said, trying to push her head back down.

"Wait. That might be my mama with Drayquan," she said before calling out. "Who is it?"

"It's Cushy. I need to holla at D-Rat."

"Damn! What the fuck this nigga want?" D-Ray cursed as he put on his pants and stomped angrily towards the door. He snapped the locks and fussed while snatching the door open. "Nigga, what the fuck—" He stopped speaking and froze when he seen the pistols and three niggas wearing masks.

The nigga closest to the door slapped D-Ray with the pistol, making him fall as the killers rushed into the house. One kept a gun on D-Ray, the other went to Tranay.

"Who all in here?" One of the men barked while closing the door.

"It's just me and him. Please don't kill me!" Tranay cried.

"I'ma look around," one of the men said before taking off through the house.

"We the only ones here and ain't nothing in here," D-Ray said from the floor.

"Shut the fuck up, bitch ass nigga!" One of the gunmen said, stomping D-Ray in the face.

"Please don't shoot me! I don't got nothing to do with this." Tranay continued to plead.

The men ignored her, staying on point and waiting for their nigga to come from checking the house. He appeared a few moments later.

"Ain't nobody else here," he confirmed.

Without another word, the intruders turned their guns on Tranay and D-Ray and gave them headshots.

Pop, pop, pop, pop!

CHAPTER 1

Junior sat on the bed staring at the ceiling trying to make sense of everything that was going on around him. An hour ago life was good; he was getting money, had killed the last of his enemies, and two bad bitches were in a hotel room with him ready to fuck his brains out. Before he got the phone call, his biggest problem was figuring out how to bring all the major hustlers in the projects into one fold. He wanted to bring everybody onto one team: Parklawn Grinders. That's what he was thinking about, and what bitch he was going to stick his dick in first, before he got the call.

"I love the suite, Junior. This bitch is the shit but what about the party, nigga? Is we fucking or what?" Lisa asked, ready to get it popping.

"You said you can fuck for two hours straight," Meeka added. "I want my pussy licked and fucked, nigga. In that order."

Junior looked towards the women sitting on the couch. Both of them were bad and boujee. Lisa was a bad ass lil vibe from Parklawn that loved fucking niggas with money. She was a light skinned cutie with big lips and dollar sign tattoos above both eyebrows. She also had and banging ass body that she was showing off in a white jumpsuit and red bottoms. Meeka was her bad ass friend. She wore a rainbow colored wig along with a purple body suit that showed every curve of her slim, fine frame.

"I'ma have to get with y'all another time," he said while getting up from the bed. "Matter of fact, I gotta get ghost. Y'all can keep the room for the night."

Lisa stood in his way, concern lighting her eyes. "Hold on, baby. Is you good? You need some help?"

Junior stared into her sparkling eyes for a moment, then down to her beautiful lips. He wished he could stay and fuck her brains out, but the call had changed everything. "Nah. You can't help me with this one. I'ma get up with y'all later. IOU."

"Yeah, nigga. You definitely owe me," Meeka said. "I want my two hour fuck."

Junior left the suite and the bad bitches, sulking all the way to his Lexus truck. Quitta was in jail. According to Rakisha, Quitta had sold a white girl some dog food and the bitch died. What he didn't understand was where in the fuck Quitta got some heroin and why she was selling it? She could've asked him for money. The shit didn't make sense. On top of that, Quitta was wanted in connection with Fredo's body. It was only a matter of time before the Milwaukee Police made their way to Lacrosse for the interrogation. Would she remain true to him even though he left her? That question had been echoing in his head ever since he got the call from Rakisha. He jumped in the SUV, turning on Moneybagg's *'A Gangsta's Pain'* album. He turned a couple of corners when his phone rang. The area code was from Lacrosse.

"Hello?"

"Junior, I'm in jail! They charging me with murder!" Quitta cried.

When Junior heard his baby mama's voice and terrified tone, he knew shit was all bad. "How are you calling me? Is this call being recorded?"

"No, I don't think so. I'm on the desk phone. This is my one call. I need a lawyer," she cried. "They said I sold her some drugs and they asking about you."

Junior thought fast. "Don't say nothing else on this phone. We gon' talk later. I'ma call a lawyer as soon as I get off the phone. But don't call this number no more. I'ma get rid of this line and get another number for you to call. I'ma get the new number to yo' brother or Rakisha."

"Okay. You gotta get Mooka. He with Rakisha."

"Okay. I'ma get him. Just remember what I told you. Don't tell them muthafuckas nothing. Only talk to yo' lawyer, okay?"

"Okay. I'm scared, Junior. I don't want to go to prison," she cried, breaking down.

"You not going to prison. As soon as you get bail, I'm coming to get you. I told you I got you. Trust me."

"Okay," she sniffled. "They want me to get off the phone. I love you."

"I love you, too. I got you, Quitta. I promise."

Junior's body went numb after ending the call. Their worst nightmare had come to life. Quitta fucked around and caught a body and now they were asking about him. The situation was bad. The worst thing that could've happened had actually happened. If he didn't move carefully, he would end up in a cell next to Quitta and their kids would grow up without parents. He couldn't let that happen. He had to figure out a way to get Quitta out while keeping his own freedom. After snapping out of the mind numbing zone that Quitta's call brought upon him, he called Michael Henrik. Michael was the lawyer street dudes called when they needed a Hail Mary. He was the king of defense attorneys. He charged a bag for his services, so guys had to have their money right to hire him to defend them.

"This is the Law Office of Michael Henrik. How may I help you?" A secretary answered.

"My name is Junior Steward. My girl is being charged with a homicide and I need a lawyer."

"One moment, Junior. I'm going to put you through to Michael."

***

"How the fuck Quitta catch an OD body?" John asked from the passenger seat of the Lexus truck.

"I don't know. I couldn't talk to her about it and Rakisha acting like she don't know shit," Junior mumbled as he drove along the highway. "She don't even fuck around with no kind of drugs so how she end up selling some shit to a bitch that OD'd is a mystery. But somebody gon' tell me something when we get to Lacrosse."

"Damn, my nigga. It seem like if it ain't one thing, it's another. It might be time for you to take a vacation."

Junior looked over at John, mugging him. "Fuck that's supposed to mean? You think I should go to jail, nigga?"

John looked surprised. "Jail? Fuck you talking about? I said a vacation, not jail."

Junior calmed a little. "Oh. I thought you was talking about jail. Some niggas call that a vacation."

"Yeah, some clown ass niggas," John laughed. "You been kicking it with Dazè too much."

Junior shook his head and laughed. "Man, this shit just got a nigga stressed. I'm tryna stay sane but I'm worried about Quitta. This a lot of pressure to have on her. Plus, she pregnant."

"Sis is a soulja, brah. I think she gon' be aight. Plus, you got *Henrik* to represent her. You know he the damn near the best lawyer in Wisconsin. She gon' be straight."

"I hope so," Junior breathed.

After a three and a half hour drive on the highway, Junior parked in front of Ron and Rakisha's house. They had moved from the house that the Folks shot up and into a big ass five bedroom house on the Southside. Since it was past midnight, Junior sent Ron a text before he and John climbed from the car. When they walked up on the porch, Ron was opening the door.

"Junior, what it do?" Ron grinned, happy to see his nigga again. "It seem like forever since the last time I seen yo' ass."

"Ron! What's good?" Junior smiled as the men embraced. "This my lil brother, John."

"What's good, John?" Ron asked, looking up at John like he was a giant.

"What up, fam?" John nodded as they shook hands.

"Y'all come in," Ron said, stepping aside to let them in the house. "If you the little brother, what y'all big brother look like? And why all the little brothers taller than the big brothers? My lil brother 6'4". How tall is you?"

"I'm 6'6". Putting on for the big lil brothers." John laughed.

They stepped in the house and greeted Toogie, Melody, and Rakisha.

"Where Mooka?" Junior asked, looking around for his son.

"Nephew upstairs sleep," Toogie said. "You want me to get him?"

"Nah. Let him sleep for right now. I'ma probably have to spend the night so I can grab my Corvette from storage. Is that cool?" Junior asked, looking towards the woman of the house.

"You already know you good. Them niggas ain't still looking for you, is they?" Rakisha asked, being cautious. She didn't want her house shot up again.

"Nah, that shit squashed. I had to send niggas to Chicago to deal with it. We good now."

"Good. Y'all can sleep on the couches. Quitta probably call in the morning anyways. Did you talk to her?"

"Yeah. I got her a lawyer. When she get bail, I'ma go get her. How the fuck she catch an OD, Rakisha? Where she get some dog food from?"

Rakisha paused before answering. "Uh, it wasn't even her shit. You know Quitta don't fuck with drugs. It was Steph's."

Junior frowned when he heard the name. "Steph in Lacrosse?"

Rakisha and Ron nodded in unison.

"Who is Steph?" John asked. "Is that the nigga that took the hunnit from you?"

"Yeah, that's that bitch ass nigga," Junior answered before turning his attention back to Rakisha. "Why was Quitta with Steph? And why the fuck did she get some work from him?" he asked, his insides burning with jealousy.

"It wasn't like that, Junior. We all ended up at my friend's birthday party. They talked and I guess the girl kept interrupting their conversation because she wanted some Diesel. Quitta handed her the dope, but it came from Steph. The dumb bitch overdosed and somehow it got mixed up and they told the police that Quitta gave her the drugs."

Junior shook his head as he looked towards his little brother. John wore the same look as Junior. "That shit sound stupid as fuck," Junior said, expressing his thoughts.

"You know these white people don't give no fuck. A white girl died, and a black girl gave her the drugs. That's all they need," Ron said.

"Okay." Junior nodded. "I got her a good lawyer and when she get bail, I'ma get her out. Ron, let me talk to you outside for a minute."

When they stepped onto the porch, Junior got right down to business.

"How long Steph been back?"

"He been in and out of town for the last month or so. He stay ducked off though. He ain't really out there like he used to be."

"You know where that bitch ass nigga staying at?"

"Last I heard he was with Brenda that live over there by the Elderberry Apartments."

"How long ago you hear that?"

"Earlier today. He might be there right now. He driving a blue Porsche."

Junior nodded, revenge burning a fire in his eyes. "Can you get his phone number?"

Ron recognized the look in his nigga's eyes and smiled. "I can get whatever you need."

"I need his number and me and my brother need some dark clothes."

"Say less."

***

After getting Steph's number and changing into a black Balenciaga jogger, Junior drove to Brenda's house, parking a block over before calling Lisa.

"Hello?"

"Lisa, this Junior. Remember when you asked me if you could help me out earlier? I need yo' help and you the only one that can do what I need done."

"Okay. What do you need me to do? You know I got you, baby."

"I need you to call this nigga, Steph, and tell him that yo' name is Shawna and you Quitta big sister. Tell him that you talked to Quitta, and you need to meet with him right now. It's an emergency. Tell him she locked up. You might have to convince him that you ain't on no police shit or other bullshit if he get suspicious. I need you to get this nigga to meet you somewhere right now. Let it be his choice for the place to meet. Can you do that for me?"

"I run game on niggas for a living, Junior. This shit easy. I'ma have the nigga meet you there with a big bag of money if you want me to."

"Whatever you gotta do to get the nigga out of the house, do it. I owe you forever if you can do this for me."

"Get ready to owe me, nigga."

"What she say?" John asked after Junior hung up the phone.

"She said she got it. I'm finna slide. Keep the car running. Make sure you call me if you see anything that don't look right."

John gave Junior an up and down look. "Nigga, I ain't no rookie. Go fuck that nigga up. I'ma be here."

***

Junior hopped out of the Lexus, walking quickly down the street, and disappearing between a yard. After crossing an alley, he paused near Brenda's garage to take in his surroundings. It was after midnight, so nothing moved. Most of the houses in the neighborhood were dark, the occupants sleep or occupied for the night. When he was satisfied that everything was still, he found a dark place to hide near the side of Brenda's house. A few minutes into the wait, his phone began vibrating. It was Lisa. "Talk to me, baby?" He whispered.

"He meeting me at the gas station across the street from Taco John's in ten minutes. You owe me forever, nigga."

"I'm forever indebted. Thanks, baby."

Adrenaline surged through Junior as he clutched the 9mm Beretta waiting in anticipation to put a bullet in Steph's face. He didn't want the money back. It was no longer about that. This was a principal murder. Street justice. A combination of breaking in his house while he was out of town and getting his baby mama locked up on a stupid ass overdose. Yeah, this nigga had to go.

The front door of Brenda's house opened a few moments later and Junior made his move. He walked from the side of the house just as Steph was walking down the porch steps. Steph sensed Junior's presence and turned just in time to see the gun being lifted.

"Wait a—" Steph was saying when the gun started talking. *Bocka, Bocka, Bocka*

***

Quitta lay on the hard mattress in the holding cell, rocking her legs, unable to sleep. It was late but she didn't know the exact hour because the only time she got to see a clock was when she was taken to the interrogation room. The last time she'd been questioned by the detective was around 11 o'clock. That was at least an hour ago. It seemed like the later it got and the longer she stayed in the cell, the more scared she became about her future and freedom. She was desperately trying to hold on to Junior's words. He promised that he would get her a lawyer and that when she got bail, he was coming to get her. She held onto the promise with everything inside of her. It was all she had to believe in at that moment because her situation wasn't looking good. She'd talked to Detective Washington twice and he knew Quitta didn't sell Amy the drugs. He wanted her to snitch on Steph. That required a recorded statement and probably getting on the stand to testify against him if the case went to trial. Then, there was Terrance's murder. They knew Junior did it but didn't have any evidence to connect him to it. She was the only one that could give them what they needed. There was also Fredo's murder. She was seen with him in the club right before he died. They had video of Junior in the club with her but the images of him were grainy and low quality so they couldn't positively identify him. But she could. Detective Mark Washington promised her immunity if she told them the truth about all the cases they were building against her. If she snitched, she would walk. It was that simple.

Movement outside the holding cell interrupted Quitta's thoughts. A key being inserted into the lock made her sit up. When the door opened, a heavyset white man with gray eyes and a big black beard called her name. "Marquitta Ware. Can I have a word with you?"

Quitta hadn't seen him before and looked him over, trying to judge his intentions and whether he would bring good or bad news. "Who are you?"

"I'm Detective Russo. I know the beard is a lot but I'm a professional. I just want to ask you some questions," he said in a low and gentle voice.

Quitta gave him another long look before getting up from the bed and following the detective through the police station. She glanced at the clock on the wall. It read 12:47 AM. "I asked for a lawyer. I don't know if I supposed to be talking to you."

The detective paused to face her. "It's totally up to you, ma'am. If you don't want to talk, you don't have to. I can take you back to the holding cell if you want. You have the right to remain silent. I'm not gonna pressure you to tell me anything. You already know you're in a lot of shit and I want to help you sort it out. I just want to talk. Can we?"

Quitta searched his gray eyes again, looking for his intentions. She didn't see anything evil in his stare, so she agreed.

"Okay." They walked in the interrogation room where a Subway meal and drink was sitting on the table.

"I heard you were pregnant, so I brought you some food," the detective said, motioning for her to have a seat.

Quitta eyed the food reluctantly as she sat down. "Thank you."

"No problem." He smiled, sitting down across from her. "So, what are you having? Boy or girl?"

"I don't know yet. I'm only two months."

"Where is the father?"

Quitta gave him a look that let him know she seen what he was doing.

He lifted both hands in an innocent gesture, palms up. "None of this is being recorded. We're just talking."

"I don't know. Getting me a lawyer, I hope."

"If I was married and my wife ever ended up in a situation like this, I would want her to cooperate and do everything necessary to get out. Especially, if she was pregnant with my kid. The stress of all of this is bad for you in the early stages of pregnancies. It could contribute to you losing the baby. You have to get yourself out of here for the baby's sake. Is the father of your kid the kind of man that would do anything for his family?"

Quitta thought about his words, looking for the trap. He spoke true about what stress can do to an early pregnancy, but she knew it was because he wanted her to break and start spilling information.

"I'm not trying to trick you," the detective said, reading her body language. "This is just a conversation. And you should eat the sub. It's a steak and cheese with extras. Got some fries in there too. And cookies. Don't let it get cold and go to waste."

Quitta reached into the bag and pulled out the food while the detective spoke.

"I see that you're from Milwaukee. How'd you end up in Lacrosse?"

"I have family here," she answered in between bites of the fries.

"Hopefully, they will be here to support you through this. Fighting a homicide charge can be rough on a family. And expensive. Lawyer fees for this is probably going to start at about fifty thousand for a halfway decent one. Your family got that kind of money?"

Quitta nodded. "I think so."

The detective watched her for a moment, evaluating her. "Do you think he'll turn himself in to get you out?"

Quitta looked up, locking eyes with him. "He didn't do nothing."

The detective nodded. "We can't prove it, yet. But people talk, Quitta. Everything in the dark has to come to the light. The question is If your gonna save yourself and jump off of the sinking ship. Junior is gonna get caught eventually. Let's just say that maybe he gets away from us this time. Then what? Do you think he's going to suddenly change his life? I don't think so. I think he'll get more involved in whatever he's in, and one day it will all catch up to him. The question is, what side will you be on? Are you going to continue to let him drag you and your children into his shit or are you going to do the right thing and distance yourself from a man that is destined for a cell or grave?"

Quitta tried not to let the cop's words the affect her, but truth be told, she felt them in her soul. Junior was a street nigga that wanted to rule a drug empire. Nothing good could come from that. All of the money would bring more problems and she didn't want his problems to fall upon her and their kids. She didn't want to be shot at again or end up in another jail cell. But she didn't tell the cop that.

"It doesn't seem fair that I'm the one doing all the talking," Detective Russo laughed, trying to get Quitta to talk.

"I don't have anything to say."

"How about you tell me about your upbringing. What was it like growing up in Milwaukee?"

Quitta searched the detective's face, trying to understand his angle. Why did he want her to talk about her life? "What does that have to do with anything? Why do you want to know about my life?"

"Because we're talking. I want to know more about you. I think you're an interesting person. You are in a world of shit and all you have to do is tell us the truth and walk, but you would rather keep your honor than be known as a snitch. I respect that. I want to know more about you as a woman so I can understand why you operate the way you do."

Quitta considered his words, certain that he had some kind of angle but unable to see his true intentions. "I don't know if I should be talking to you about my personal life."

"Okay." He laughed. "I see that you don't trust me. I'm a cop. I get it. I just wanted to bring you out of the cell for a little while. I know those rooms can do tricks on a person's mind. But if you would rather be in a cell than out here eating Subway and talking to an old farm boy, then I'll respect your desire. I'll take you back as soon as you finish eating. I just want you to know that I think you're special and if you ever want to talk, I'm here."

"Okay." Quitta nodded, unsure how to respond to what the detective said. She wasn't sure if he was flirting with her, being nice, or trying to trick her into confessing.

"How about you tell me about your relationship with Steph," he asked, knowing that he was violating her Miranda Rights. Once she had asked for a lawyer all questioning was supposed to have ceased.

"He is my ex."

"I know that. And I also know that you didn't sell Amy the drugs that killed her. We heard that Steph was there, and I think he gave her the drugs. How your name got mixed up in this is still a mystery to me. And unless you tell us something, you're going to be charged with her death. I understand why you're helping your kids father. Why are you protecting Steph?"

Quitta shrugged. "I don't know. I want to talk to my lawyer first."

"I don't think you do. It's as simple as saying what happened and getting one serious charge off of you. I think—"

The detective's words were cut short by the door opening. In walked a female police officer wearing a serious look. "Excuse me, Detective. I need you for a moment," she said, glancing at Quitta.

"Sure," the detective said as he walked towards the door. "I'll be back in a moment."

When the door closed, Quitta began listening hard, trying to hear what the police were talking about on the other side of the door. She could hear their voices faintly but couldn't understand what they were saying. But the look on the female officer's face said that something serious was going on. Quitta just hoped the news wouldn't affect her situation.

Detective Russo walked back in the room a few moments later. Quitta searched his face, looking for a sign of what was to come. The detective's face remained flat as he sat at the table. Then, he looked at Quitta, staring into her eyes without speaking.

"Did something happen?" Quitta asked.

The detective ran a hand over his beard before speaking. "Steph is dead."

The words made Quitta jerk in her seat, mouth drop open, and eyes pop. "What?"

"Yeah. Happened about twenty minutes ago. This isn't good for you, Quitta. You should've told us he gave Amy the drugs. Now there is nobody to connect to her death but you."

Quitta dropped the fries as the weight of the detective's words fell upon her. Steph was dead. The responsibility of Amy's death fell solely on her. She couldn't tell on him if she wanted to. He was dead. "Oh shit! Oh my God!" Quitta panicked, as tears began to spill.

The detective reached out to grab her hand. "I'm sorry," he said.

"What happened? Who did it?"

"We don't know yet. It just happened."

Quitta lowered her head and continued to cry as thoughts of a prison cell filled her head. There was no way out now that the person that actually sold Amy the drugs was dead. She wondered who killed him. Was Junior in Lacrosse? Did Rakisha tell him what happened and he went to kill Steph?

"Are you going to be okay?" Russo asked.

Quitta nodded.

"Do you know of anybody that would want to kill Steph?"

Quitta shook her head, keeping her head down.

"Did him and Junior have problem?"

Hearing the detective try to connect her baby daddy to the murder gave her chills. She was about to respond when the door opened again, and a male police officer walked in along with a skinny well-groomed white man in a suit.

"Don't say another word, Quitta. I'm your attorney, Mark Whistler," the lawyer blurted before turning to Detective Russo. "She already requested a lawyer, why are you talking to my client? Did you take any statements? I want whatever she said to be turned over right now!"

Russo stood and lifted his hands. "Somebody had way too many fucking energy drinks."

Mark gave the detective an angry leer. "I want a moment with my client right now. If you've violated any of her rights, I'll make sure to write it in my motion to get this case thrown out!"

"I didn't take any statements, Red Bull," the bearded detective laughed.

"C'mon, Russo. Let's give them the room," the other cop mumbled, leading the way from the room.

When they were gone, Mark turned his attention to Quitta. "Did you give them any statements?"

Quitta shook her head, still tripping on how the lawyer barged into the room and took it over. "No. I told them I wanted a lawyer. They tried to get me to talk but I didn't say nothing."

"Good. Very good. I'm not the lawyer that will be representing you in court, but I'm an associate. Your actual lawyer, Michael Henrik, will be representing you. He's still in Milwaukee and will be here in a few hours. I'm just going to ask you some questions and make sure that none of your rights were violated."

CHAPTER 2

The booking room in the Lacrosse County Jail stank. Quitta lifted the neckline of her T-shirt over her face, covering her mouth and nose from the pungent odor. The cause of the smell lay on the floor a few feet away. A chubby blonde haired white woman lay passed out on the floor. Her clothes were filthy, shoes dirty, hair wild and greasy and she stank. Like shit, piss, and vomit.

"Guard, can somebody come and get this bitch? She might be dead. And she stank," Quitta complained to the police officer behind the desk.

The officer looked up from the computer screen for a moment to see what Quitta was talking about. "Melissa is a regular in here. That's what homelessness, drugs, and alcohol do to you. Just say no," the officer cracked before turning his attention back to his laptop.

"Nasty muthafuckas," Quitta mumbled, turning her attention back to the television that was hanging from the ceiling. An old episode of Judge Mathis was showing but Quitta couldn't focus on the popular Detroit judge. Her mind was on being in jail again. Her lawyer had gotten her out of the interrogation room and in to the booking room. Now, she would be held in the county jail until she could be seen by a judge and given a bail.

The bathroom door opening made Quitta glance across the room. A brown skinned woman walked out wearing a black half top, leggings, and heels. What made the woman stand out, besides the bright yellow wig she wore, was the missing teeth. Her two front teeth were gone. She lost them while fighting a trick that tried to rape her. Her name was Tiffany. She was also from Milwaukee. She had come to Lacrosse to strip at a club but fucked around and got locked up for almost killing a trick when she went upside his head with a twenty pound dumbbell.

"How much longer do I gotta be in this booking room, Jamie?" Tiffany asked the officer, covering her mouth as she spoke. "Hopefully not too much longer. Normally takes a few hours to get all the paperwork situated."

"It's already been a couple of hours. And why don't somebody do something about this stanking ass bitch?" Tiffany complained, kicking the drunken woman in the rib as she walked by.

"Shouldn't be that much longer," officer Jamie said, paying more attention to what was on that computer screen than the women.

"I knew I shouldn't have brought my ass out here with these stupid ass crackers," Tiffany spat before sitting on the bench. "How the fuck a muthafucka attack and try to rape me but I end up in jail?"

"Because you black," Quitta answered. "They doing me the same way. They know I didn't do nothing but they charging me because I didn't snitch."

"Some dirty muthafuckas," Tiffany snarled. "My baby daddy need to hurry up and get his ass up here and bail me out."

Tiffany's words made Quitta think about getting bail. "How much is your bail?"

"Twenty five hundred. What about you?"

Quitta shrugged. "I don't know. I don't have one yet. I gotta see the judge first. Hopefully, I see him in the morning."

"Damn, girl. Why you gotta see a judge to get bail? I didn't. It should be on the computer already. Jamie can look it up for you." Hope flashed in Quitta's eyes.

"For real? My lawyer said I gotta see the judge first."

"Girl, I don't know who yo' lawyer is or what he talking about, but I didn't see no judge and I got a bail. You better ask Jamie."

Quitta got up and made a beeline for this officer's desk. "Jamie, do I got a bail?"

The officer gave Quitta an irritated look. "Why do you guys need so much? Why can't you just sit down and wait to be taken upstairs?"

"Because if I got a bail, I won't be going upstairs. You can go back to looking at your tranny porn as soon as you tell me how much my bail is."

Jamie mugged Quitta. "Just for that, I'm not looking up shit. Go have a seat."

"C'mon, Jamie. I'm just playing. I need to know how much my bail is so I can get the fuck outta here. I'm pregnant."

He gave her a long look, his eyes pausing on her lips and breasts. "Since you're kind of cute and have a nice rack, I'll forgive you." He smiled.

"Now, I definitely know you watching porn. Let me see your screen," Quitta teased.

"Shut up. We can't even watch porn on these computers. What's your full name?"

"Marquitta Ware."

The officer typed her name on the keyboard and began surfing through information. "Uh oh." He frowned

"What that mean? What you mean, Uh oh?" Quitta asked, becoming worried.

"It says you don't have a bail."

Quitta's heart dropped to her feet. "Stop playing, Jamie. What do it say?"

"I'm not kidding. I swear to God you don't have a bail. It says you have to see a judge for bail. What the hell did you do?"

"Some bullshit," Quitta sulked, all of the hope that she approached the desk with disappearing in an instant.

Jamie clicked the mouse a couple of times and his eyes lit up. "Whoa! They're charging you with murder. That's why you don't have a bail. They don't give bails for charges as serious as this without a judge."

"That's some bullshit," Quitta mumbled, lowering her head, and walking away.

"Damn, girl! They charging you with murder?" Tiffany asked.

"A bitch overdosed, and she told her friends I bought the dope for her. Then, the mu'fucka who the dope actually came from got killed yesterday. They tryna get me on some shit that don't even got nothing to do with me."

Tiffany shook her head. "These some dirty ass crackers."

"All right, ladies!" Jamie said, getting the women in the booking room attention. "Listen up for your names to be called because you'll be heading upstairs."

***

THE NEXT DAY

Quitta sat in the holding cell nervously awaiting her moment before the Judge. She spent one night in jail before finally getting her day in court. Now, she would go before the Honorable Kevin Gaston to see if the state had enough to charge her with Amy's death and set a bail. Her eyes were heavy with dark bags from sleep deprivation and crying all night. She hadn't slept much since she got arrested. The stress of everything that was happening kept her mind racing and sleep far away. She still couldn't believe that she was about to be charged with murder. The only reason she bought Amy the drugs was that so that she could talk to Steph. She had no idea that the girl would overdose. And to make matters worse, Steph was dead. How? Was it Junior? Did he kill Steph because he found out it was his drugs that killed Amy? And now that the person that was actually responsible for selling Amy the drugs was gone, what did that mean for Quitta? Would the Judge and District Attorney believe her if she told the truth? All of these thoughts and questions had Quitta worried sick. But there was hope. She talked to her lawyer and found out that she was going to get bail. Junior had kept his word that he would get her a lawyer. She knew her baby daddy wasn't going to leave her fucked up. Now, she was scheduled to go before the court commissioner to see what she was being charged with and how much her bail would be. Whatever it was, she knew that Junior would pay, and she couldn't wait to get the fuck out of jail.

"Marquitta Ware?" The bailiff called as he opened the holding cell door.

Quitta stood and walked over. "Yeah."

"It's your turn to go before the judge. Let me put these cuffs on you."

After getting handcuffs on her wrist, Quitta was led down a hall and into the courtroom. The first person that she noticed was the Judge. The older white man sat behind a polished oak bench, radiating authority. She looked around the gallery quickly, scanning the courtroom for her supporters. She had been talking to Junior five times a day since she got access to the phones and was anxious to see him. He wasn't hard to find. He sat in a pew near the back of the gallery along with Ron, Toogie, Rakisha.

After a smile, Quitta went to sit next to her lawyer, Michael Henrik. Michael was a well-dressed forty-seven year old white man with a sharp face and short salt and pepper hair that was slicked to the back. Michael also had clout in the legal world. He was very well respected, and his reputation often proceeded him.

"Hi, Quitta. How are you doing?" He asked as she sat down.

"I'm nervous and ready to get out."

"Don't be nervous. This is just an initial appearance. They will say what you're being charged with and set a bail. Shouldn't take any longer than ten minutes. I already talked to Junior, and he said that he'll put up the money to get you out. I'll argue to get the bail as low as possible."

"Okay." Quitta nodded.

"We're ready to proceed, your honor."

The court reporter, a short blonde woman, began reading from a computer screen. "State of Wisconsin versus Marquitta Ware, 22FF05110, charged with first degree reckless homicide. The case is assigned to Judge DiMotto, Branch 25. This is the initial appearance."

"Steven Milan for the state," the District Attorney said.

"Michael Henrik on behalf of the defendant who appears in person subject to jurisdictional objections. We wave the reading of the criminal complaint."

"I don't have one," the judge frowned, looking towards the District Attorney.

"Sorry about that, your honor," Steven apologized. "I have an amended one. I needed to have a chance to file it."

"Are there new additions?"

"Your honor, I make a motion to dismiss the criminal complaint," Michael Henrik spoke up. "The initial complaint, which I have a copy of, doesn't provide sufficient evidence or probable cause to charge my client with homicide. Even the detectives that investigated the case all agree that my client is not a drug dealer and did not sell the deceased woman the drugs that killed her. Why she was even arrested is beyond me. Again, I argue for the criminal complaint to be thrown out and my client released."

Quitta wasn't sure about everything that was happening or being said, but she knew that her lawyer was putting up a good argument to have her released. And that gave her hope.

The judge smirked at Michael's argument before turning to the District Attorney. "You want to explain what's going on?"

"Your honor, this case is very complicated and fast moving. Things are changing by the moment, and we are trying to keep up. Mr. Henrik is right that there are questions surrounding Marquitta and Amy's drug exchange. Marquitta was involved in the transaction with another man, Steph Fielder, who was murdered yesterday. We've also recently learned that Marquitta is being investigated for her connection to a homicide that happened in Milwaukee and the investigating detective is in the gallery looking to question the defendant after these proceedings. I amended the complaint to reflect these changes and ask that the court accept the new amended complaint as well as take into consideration all of the aggravating factors and influences surrounding Marquitta Ware."

The judge looked at Marquitta while reaching a hand out to the District Attorney. "Bring me the complaint so that I may take a look. The record will be clear that with the filing of the new compliant, Mr. Henrik can raise his objections and jurisdictional challenges for whatever reason," he said before taking a moment to read over the new compliant. "Having read the new compliant, I find probable cause for the homicide charge. Ms. Ware, you are being charged with first degree reckless homicide. If convicted, you face fifteen years in prison. Do you understand that?"

"Yes, your honor," Quitta mumbled. Devastation washed over her. She couldn't believe that she was actually being charged with homicide.

"You have a right to have a preliminary hearing on this case. State, as to bail?"

"We recommend no bail," Steven said. "This is based on the seriousness of the offense as well as the homicide investigation involving her that is going on in Milwaukee."

"I object to no bail, your honor!" Michael Henrik yelled, jumping to his feet. "I was not made aware of any investigation in Milwaukee. Furthermore, she is not being charged with anything other than the first degree homicide in this court. I ask you to not take into consideration the allegations made by the state with regard to my clients bail involving this case."

The judge took a moment to think, his eyes darting back and forth from Quitta to her attorney. Quitta felt like she was about to throw up. The suspense from the judge's decision seemed to hold the entire courtroom in suspense. "I will take into consideration the information presented by the state. I can see with my own eyes that there is an officer in the court waiting to question the defendant," he said before addressing Quitta. "Ma'am, I don't know what all you're involved in, but I cannot ignore you being charged with a homicide while under investigation for another. Those are aggravating factors which, taken into consideration, leaves me no choice but to deny bail. This case will be moved along to a preliminary hearing at the earliest convenience."

***

Quitta sat in the interrogation room watching her lawyer's mouth move but unable to understand what he was saying. Her mind was still in the courtroom trying to comprehend why and how the judge had denied her bail. She thought bail was guaranteed. Her mind had been so consumed on getting back to her man and son that she never considered the possibility of not being allowed to go home. But the judge had ruled that she wouldn't get a bail. That decision was about to drive her crazy.

"Do you understand what I just told you, Quitta?" Michael Henrik asked.

Quitta focused on her attorney, snapping back to the moment. "I didn't hear nothing you just said. I can't stop thinking about not getting bail. I don't want to be in jail. I thought I was getting out," she whined, barely able to hold back tears.

"Quitta, I'm going to be honest. I didn't see things going the way they did. I didn't know about the detective from Milwaukee or that you were a person of interest in a homicide until just now in the courtroom. I'm going to get a handle on this and get you outta here, but that might take time. You're involved in very some serious accusations. I need time to get all the evidence and create a defense."

Quitta didn't have a choice but to accept her new reality. As much as she wanted to throw herself on the floor and cry, she knew that wouldn't do her any good or get her out of jail. She had to accept what was happening because there was nothing that she could do about it. "Okay. I understand. Am I at least going to get a bail soon?"

"I'm working on it. This Milwaukee allegation is swaying the judge's decision. If we can figure that out, we might be able to request another bail hearing. We're going to have to talk to the detective to see what they have. I have history with Detective Johnson. I'll make sure you don't do or say anything that will incriminate you. Answer him truthfully unless I tell you otherwise. Are you ready?"

Quitta shrugged. "I don't really got a choice, right?"

Michael shook his head. "Not really."

The attorney left the room and came back a few moments later followed by a tall dark skinned man with a big mustache, wearing a blue suit. Detective Johnson smiled as he sat across from Quitta, wishing her lawyer wasn't present so that he could really interrogate her. Threatening a woman with taking her kids was a trick often used by cops. Especially the young and inexperienced. But he wouldn't be able to do that to Quitta. Detective Johnson had history with Michael and knew that he had to keep everything on the up and up.

"Marquitta, this is Detective Johnson. He wants to ask you some questions about a homicide," Michael said before giving the detective the floor.

"I'm not going to bullshit you or play around, Quitta," the detective said, pulling out his phone and showing Quitta a picture of her and Fredo in the club. "This is you in this picture, right?"

Quitta looked towards her lawyer. Michael nodded.

"Yeah. That's me," she admitted.

"And who is the man in the picture and how did you know him?" Quitta paused to glance at her lawyer. When he didn't interject, she continued. "I think his name was Fredo. I had just met him that night."

Detective Johnson frowned. "You said his name *was* Fredo. Why did you say that?"

"Knock it off with the bullshit, man," Michael spoke up. "We know he's dead. Ask your questions."

Johnson gave a smirk before continuing. "You left the club with him. Where did you go?"

"He dropped me off at my mother's house."

"How long were you with Fredo after you left the club? Did you go right home? Did you stop somewhere? At a gas station, maybe?"

"No, we didn't make any stops. He took me right home. I was only with him for fifteen or twenty minutes. I never talked to him after that."

"Did you know if you were being followed? Did you have any altercations with anyone that night? Did he?"

Quitta shook her head. "No. Not that I know of."

The detective showed her another picture in his phone. It was a blurry picture of Junior. "You didn't have an altercation with the man you came in the club with?"

Quitta gave her lawyer a panicked look.

"Let me see the phone," Michael said, trying to gain control of this situation. "The picture is blurry, and you can't make out who he is."

"She knows who she went to the club with," the detective said nodding to Quitta. "You were seen entering the club with this man. Who is he?"

Quitta looked to her lawyer again. Michael nodded.

"That's my kids father, Junior."

"What did you and Junior get into an argument about?"

"He seen Fredo talking to me when he went to get us drinks. We had some words and he left."

"He and Fredo had words too, right?"

"Not really. He told Fredo I was his girl and to leave me alone. I guess Fredo really wanted me because he didn't stop trying to get at me. Junior got mad and left."

Detective Johnson gave a look that told Quitta he knew she was lying. "So, your baby daddy got mad that you were talking to another man while he was at the bar and then leaves you in the bar with the same man that disrespected him? That doesn't make much sense. Why didn't he take you with him? Has something like this happened before? Is he a jealous man?"

"No, he's not jealous. I walked out of the club with Junior and tried to leave with him, but he was too mad and wouldn't let me in the car. I went back inside to get a ride home. That was it. When I got home, he was still mad."

"So, Junior was at home when you got there?"

"Yes."

"Was there anybody else there that could back this up?"

"Yes. My mom, her husband, and our son."

Detective Johnson gave her a long look. "You were the last person seen with Fredo while he was alive. Right after he dropped you off, he was ambushed and killed at a gas station. Are you sure that you don't know anything about this or who was involved?"

"No, I don't. He dropped me off at home and that was it."

"You knew we were looking for you, right? Why didn't you come and talk with us? Do you realize that hiding makes you look guilty?"

"Okay. That's enough with the questions," Michael interrupted. "She answered your questions. Fredo dropped her off at home and she never heard from him again. Do you have anything else?"

Detective Johnson gave the attorney the same searching look that he gave Quitta. "Yes. I have one more question for your client," he said before turning to Quitta. "I'm going to get what I need to convict you and your baby daddy but if you cooperate right now, I'll get the district attorney not to prosecute you. This is your one opportunity to walk away from this without being charged with anything. Will you cooperate?"

Quitta searched the detective's eyes, reading the seriousness of the moment in his dark irises. Then, she looked towards her attorney. "I don't have anything else to say."

"You heard her," Michael said, signaling the end of the meeting.

Detective Johnson looked at Quitta like she stunk as he stood. "You gon' be sorry that you didn't take the deal," he promised before leaving the room.

J-Blunt

CHAPTER 3

Renae sat on the bed next to Dazè, smoking a blunt while he slept. She thought about the fast pace of their relationship and how crazy she was about a man that she barely knew. In less than a month, she had become obsessed with him. She wanted to talk to him all the time, be around him every moment, and she thought about him non-stop. She wasn't in love with him, yet, but he had a hold on her. There was something about him that drove her crazy and made her want to do things. Freaky things. Like wake him up to morning head and a blunt.

She peeled back the sheet revealing his naked flesh. Dazè's complexion was a light brown. It was like the color of coffee with milk and creamer. He had muscles in places that she had never seen on someone she was with. Sculpted shoulders, chest, arms, abs, and legs. And she couldn't forget about that magic stick. His morning wood stood up like a rocket about to take off from a launch pad. It was the perfect size and shape for her walls. And her mouth. She lowered her head to flick her tongue across the slit, watching Dazè for a reaction. When he didn't move, she used her tongue to lick from his balls to the tip of his head.

"Mmm," he groaned, thrusting his hips but not waking up.

Renae smiled, loving the sex game, wanting more. She took a long drag on the blunt and blew the smoke around his dick before slurping the head in her mouth. Dazè moaned again, thrusting his hips, pushing more meat into her mouth. Renae went down even more before coming up slowly, sucking hard.

"Awe shit," Dazè groaned, opening his eyes, and palming the back of her head. "Damn, girl!"

Renae smiled, moving the blunt to his lips. After Dazè took the blunt, she turned all of her attention to getting breakfast. She took more of him into her mouth, slurping, licking, and sucking while her hands teased his balls and thighs. Dazè puffed the blunt and kept eye contact with Renae while she served up morning head. He loved the way she seemed to know his body. Even though they just met,

41

she knew what he liked and how to do it. And she gave it to him any time he wanted it.

"You look so good sucking my dick."

Renae smiled again, lust flashing in her eyes. She took Dazè further down her throat, trying to swallow the whole thing. When she came back to the tip, she paused to watch his reaction. The look on his face said it all. He felt everything that she was feeling. They were connected on all levels. This was supposed to happen. Ride or die. She went down on him again and didn't come up until she had swallowed his seed.

"I want you to wake me up like this every morning." Dazè grinned.

Renae began working her way up his body with kisses, pausing at his neck and whispering in his ear. "You can get whatever you like, baby. One hand washes the other one, right?"

"That's right," he agreed. "So let me show you how a real nigga return a favor."

Dazè flipped Renae over and gave her some gangsta loving. When they were done, they lay back and puffed another wood.

"Do you think reincarnation is real?" Renae asked.

Dazè gave her a look. "That's one of those, *Nigga, I'm high as fuck questions*," he joked.

"I am high as fuck." Renae laughed. "But I'm serious. Do you think that we lived before and that we can come back?"

Daze gave her words some thought. "That's what Buddhists believe. They believe that when you die, you go to Purgatory, Hell, Heaven, or get reincarnated. But in order to be reincarnated, your good gotta outweigh the bad. I was raised to believe in Christianity, but I learned other shit while I was locked up."

"I think I might believe in them Buddhists because I feel like I met you before. I just feel connected to you. It's crazy."

Dazè laughed.

"Why you laughing? I'm serious."

"I'm laughing because I felt the same thing. I was just thinking about that when you was sucking my dick. It feel like we did this before. Like I already knew you."

The star crossed lovers stared at each other for a moment.

"You think this is meant to be?" Renae asked.

Dazè shrugged. "I guess it's only one way to find out."

"And what's that?"

"By staying together. I got you if you got me."

Renae smiled, understanding the true meaning of his words. "You want me to be your girl?"

Dazè shook his head. "Nah, I don't need a girl. I need a woman. I want you to be my woman."

Renae's smile grew wider. "Okay. I got you. I'm your woman."

He leaned in for a kiss. Renae accepted his tongue, tingling on the inside.

"Ay, do you know how to send a nigga that's locked up some money? I gotta get my nigga, Cee-Cee together."

"Yeah. You do it through accesscorrections.com. I sent Junior money when he was locked up, so I already got an account. You got a debit card?"

"Nah, I don't. But you do, right? If I give you three hundred, you can send it to him, right?"

"I got you. I just need his prison number. You know it?" Renae asked, grabbing her phone.

"Yeah. 567330."

Renae logged onto accesscorrections.com and sent the money.

"I'm done. Who is Cee-Cee? I heard you mention him before."

"That's my nigga. One of the realist niggas I met. Most times niggas get locked up you don't go in looking for friends. You come in by yo'self and you leave by yo'self. But I fuck with this nigga because he solid. Whenever I made a move, he was right next to me. He put it all on the line for his niggas and I'm the same way. If I fuck with you, I fuck with you the long way. He coming home in a couple months, and I want you to meet him. Matter of fact let's take some selfies and send 'em through Textbehind. You know how to do that?"

"I got you, baby."

They were taking pictures, about to send them to Cee-Cee when Assassin began barking.

"Y'all dog going crazy downstairs," Dazè commented.

"I know. Let me see what the fuck she barking about."

After throwing on some clothes, Renae left the room and headed downstairs. She could hear her mother laughing as the dog barked and growled.

"Get him, girl! Get his ass!" Gail laughed.

Six stood in the middle of the living room wrestling with the big German Shepard. They jumped on the couch and rolled around before falling to the floor.

"It's way too early to be making that much noise," Renae said, not sharing the same enthusiasm as her mother and the dog at seeing her older brother.

"Its 9:00. Most people with some business out taking care of it. What's yo' excuse?" Six said, calming down his play with the dog and sitting on the couch.

"I work second shift, nigga. I got business," Renae sassed before turning her attention to Santana. "Hey, girl. You should make him take a shower after wrestling with the dog. Don't let him touch you."

Santana laughed. "You crazy, Renae."

"I want to talk to y'all about moving," Six said. "It's getting dangerous out here. It was a miracle that didn't nobody get shot the other day."

"I know you just looking out for our safety, son, but I don't want to move," Gail said. "I raised all of my kids in this house and just because somebody shot at your brother don't mean we gotta leave."

"But ma, y'all not safe here. If it happened once, it can happen again. Me, John, and Junior in the streets, mama. Niggas gon' hate or we might have drama and if you still in the hood, that makes us vulnerable. I don't want this to happen again. I want to buy you a house in there suburbs. Mequon or Waukesha."

"I ain't going to no suburbs, bro," Renae spoke up. "You need to tell your brother to stop doing dumb stuff out here. I heard him and fifty robbed those niggas. That's why they came over here shooting. It was your brother's fault."

"What do you think I'm here for," Six said, giving his younger sister a long look. "But it don't matter who did what or why. What matter is y'all vulnerable being here. Anything can happen."

"The same thing can happen in the suburbs too," Gail spoke up. "If somebody want to do something to us because of something one of my kids did, ain't nothing I can do to stop it. Moving to Mequon or Waukesha won't stop it. Plus, we don't know nobody way out there. I ain't tryna live in nobody's boonies."

Six let out a frustrated breath. "I'm tryna keep y'all safe. Why y'all want to live in the hood if y'all don't got to?"

"Because the hood raised us. You too, nigga," Renae said.

Movement near the door leading upstairs got everyone's attention. Dazè stepped into the living room a moment later. He and Six stared at each other for a moment, recognition flashing in the men's eyes.

"Dazè?" Six questioned.

"Yeah, this me, fam. What's good, my nigga?"

"Oh shit! Nigga, what's hannin?" Six yelled, going over and giving Dazè a hug. "I heard you was out, nigga. Damn. What's good?"

"Man, just loving this freedom, my nigga. Tryna get a bag and enjoy life."

"Hell yeah," Six agreed. Then, he thought for a moment. "Who else upstairs?"

"Nobody. He spent the night with me," Renae spoke up.

Six looked from his sister, to Dazè, his mother and then back to Dazè and Renae. "Y'all messing around?"

"I'm grown, bro. Why is you in my business?" Renae asked.

"Because I want to know," Six said before turning to Dazè. "You and Renae?"

Dazè gave a nervous laugh. "Yeah, brah. I'm feeling yo' sister."

"Okay. Y'all grown." Six nodded, unable to conceal his surprise or mixed emotions about the relationship. "So, what you doing? How you eating?"

"I'm with Junior. I'ma Grinder."

"I can love that." Six nodded. "Come take a ride with me. I need to holla at you."

"Let's do it."

"Let's take a ride, baby." Six nodded to Santana. On the way out the door, he turned to Gail. "We gon' continue that conversation later."

"I'm staying, son. Ain't nothing you can say to change my mind."

When the trio stepped outside, Six stopped to look at the bullet holes in the house left from the guns of the BGM niggas. "I can't figure out why they don't want to leave."

"Y'all have a lot of memories in this house. You can't put a price on that," Santana said.

"But the whole point of success is to take your family from the hood. That's why I do it. If you can get out, you supposed to leave."

"Not everybody think like that, brah," Dazè chimed in. "Some people want to die in their hood."

Six turned to look at the friend that he hadn't seen in more than a decade. "Why die in the hood when you can live a good life?"

Dazè shrugged. "I can't answer that because I want to live good. When I get the chance to get out, I'm gone."

"Me too." Six laughed, nodding towards the white Bentley Continental parked at the curb. "Let's take a ride."

"Damn, this bitch is phat!" Dazè commented as he climbed into the backseat of the luxury whip.

"Yeah. These muthafuckas have a nigga pulling up like he the president," Six said as he climbed in the spacious backseat next to Dazè. "I wanted to holla at you about Junior and my mama house getting shot up. But before I do, I want to ask you about my sister. What's going on with that?"

"Man, the shit just happened, fam. She went to The City with me to holla at the folks for Junior and we just clicked. Been kicking it ever since. To be honest, I don't know what we doing. We just vibing right now I guess."

"So that was you that helped Junior out that jam, huh?"

"I'm on count in The City. My name in the books. Junior my nigga so I got involved. If I fuck with you, I fuck with you."

"I'm the same way. If I fuck with a nigga, I'm all in." Six nodded, liking the real nigga vibes he got from Dazè. "But I gotta be a buck with you, Dazè. I know we go way back like zips for six hundred but I don't like my niggas fucking with my sisters. That shit can get messy, and I don't want to be in a position where I gotta choose because I'ma always ride with my blood."

Dazè understood Six's position. "I wouldn't expect a real nigga to do nothing less. I got two sisters and if it came down to my nigga or my sister, I'm riding with mines. But like I said, shit just happened so fast, my nigga, and now we vibing. But I also want you to know that I got so much love for y'all family that I wouldn't put y'all in a situation where people would have to pick sides. Before it came to that, I would end it and walk away. That's on everything that I love."

Six gave Dazè a searching stare, judging the weight of his words. "I hope it don't ever come down to that because you a real nigga and I love being around real niggas. Now, tell me what happened with my OG house getting shot up."

"Some bullshit that Junior got in with some BGM niggas. We was in the club on Sam born day and them niggas was there, but we didn't notice them cause we was having a good time. Fucked around and had to fuck some fuck boys up, but that didn't have nothing to do with them BGM niggas. Anyway, the way we was putting on that night let everybody know we was from Parklawn. They put two and two together and came through with the heat."

Six shook his head. "That's exactly the kind to shit that we don't need. It's hard to beef and get money. You can't do both. Y'all niggas out having a good time and some bullshit pop off over some old shit. This is what the fuck I be tryna tell lil bro."

"I ain't tryna make no excuses for lil bro, but that shit was fluky. Junior is focused on the bag, fam. That's my nigga and we chop it down about everything. He focused on taking over Parklawn. He just gotta clean up all the shit that happened before he started fucking with the heavyweights. But them BGM niggas is a wrap. We fucked them niggas like good ass pussy."

"That's good to hear. Everything you said. When do you think this lil nigga coming back to the city cause I got some words for him?"

"He was supposed to go to Lacrosse to get Mooka and bail Quitta out, but I think I seen something on Facebook about her not getting bail."

As if on cue, Dazè's phone rang. He looked at the screen and smiled. "This that nigga right here," he said, putting the call on speaker. "What up, fam? I was just talking about yo' ass."

"What's good? Where you at?"

"I'm in the Bentley with Six."

"Six in Milwaukee?" Junior asked, sounding surprised.

"Yeah, nigga," Six spoke up. "We need to holla. Where you at?"

"I just got off the E-way. I'm pulling up to mom's crib right now."

"We right around the corner. Santana turning around right now. We need to talk."

***

Junior, Mooka, and John were standing on the porch when the white Continental pulled to the curb. Six, Santana, and Dazè hopped out a few moments later.

"Uncle Six!" Mooka yelled, running to greet his uncle.

"What's up, lil nigga? See you got the fresh braids," he said, playing with the ends of his nephew's shoulder length corn rows.

"My aunty Rakisha braided my hair."

"She did a good job, man. You looking like a young playa," he said before turning to his brothers and giving them hugs. "What's good with you niggas?"

"Shit. Riding them muthafuckin highway for 3 hours in Junior Corvette got a nigga legs cramping," John said, stretching his legs.

Six turned to look at the red Z07 parked at the curb and then to Junior. "That's you, huh?" He asked in a mocking tone. "Always got time to shine, huh?"

"I had it in storage," Junior answered, picking up on his brother's tone and taking a shot of his own. "What took you so long to come check on the fam? It's been damn near a week since them niggas came through. That Vegas living was too good to check on yo' mama?"

Six cocked his head to the side, his upper lip twitching, eyes squinting. "Oh, you getting bold now, huh? We testing nuts, lil nigga?"

"You sent the first shot, brah. I heard it in yo' tone. It sound like you get something to say."

Six moved closer to his little brother with their faces a few inches apart. "Hell yeah, I got something to say. You moving reckless, nigga, and you got my mama house shot up because you fucking up. I brought you into a family of real gangsters. Niggas that don't kill mu'fuckas at a gas station for fifty racks. Real bosses that make power moves and think before they act. This what I'm tryna teach you but you won't listen."

Junior sucked his teeth, tired of being treated like a lil nigga. "Man, I know all that, bro. And you know that shit with them BGM niggas started before I met Mr. Chow and the rest of them niggas. It wasn't nothing I could do to stop them niggas from sliding through here. I'm in the field, brah. I ain't on private jets and kicking it in mansions. I'm still in the trenches."

"Nigga, I know what you doing and what you going through. We grew up in the same shit. But I'm also tryna elevate you to another level. Yo' problem is you just don't listen. I told you not to slide on them niggas, but you did it anyway because you still thinking like a soldier and not a general. Generals ain't on the front line putting in work. Generals sit back and call shots. Now, what would a happened if you got knocked off or locked up for sliding? Then what? We would have wasted bringing you into the family. The work that they gave you would be wasted. This is what I'm talking about, nigga."

Junior waved a hand at Six. "Whatever, man. I just told you that shit happened before I met them niggas. And I don't care what you talking about but I'm fucking up anybody that shoot up my mama house. I'ma kill any nigga that put my family in jeopardy. That's just how it is."

Six got angrier because Junior wasn't listening. "Nigga is you listening to anything I'm saying? It's a way to take care of yo' business without getting yo' hands dirty. The bullshit that you doing out here is affecting more than you. This what I been tryna tell you for years but you think it's a mu'fuckin game until niggas hit where you live. What if Mooka, Renae, or Mama got popped? Then what, nigga?"

"Didn't nobody get hit. And we took care of that shit. It's dead now."

"How do you know its dead? You stupid if you think y'all killed everybody. You can't kill everybody, nigga. Think, nigga. Use yo' head!" Six yelled, tapping the side of Junior head with his finger.

Junior didn't like the gesture and swiped at Six's hand. "C'mon, my nigga. Don't put yo' fucking hands on me!"

Six smiled at the aggression. "You really think you can fuck with me, nigga?"

"Ay, y'all chill," John said, stepping between his brothers.

Six and Junior shoved him out of the way.

"Move, nigga!" Six yelled. "This nigga think he can fuck with big bro. Try me, Junior. I'll show you. You ain't ready for me, boy!"

Junior knew that he couldn't hang with Six in a fight. His older brother had been doing Jujitsu training since he was a teenager and he'd seen him destroy niggas. But Junior also knew that he couldn't show fear or back down. If he did, word would get around and some of his niggas might think it was sweet. Six called him out and he had to take on the challenge. If it meant taking an L to prove his point, so be it.

He threw common sense to the wind and took swing at his older brother. Six seen the punch coming. Junior wasn't a trained fighter, so he telegraphed the punch before he threw it. And Six was ready. He blocked the punch easily, wrapping Junior's wrist under his armpit and locking his arm so that his little brother couldn't get away. Then, in the same instant, he stepped closer, sticking a foot behind Junior's heel while giving him a shove. Junior stumbled backwards and would've fallen if Six didn't have his arm locked. And just to show off a little more, Six wrapped a hand around Junior's throat and shoved him into the side of the house.

"Get off my daddy!" Mooka yelled, running over, and pushing Six.

"Come here, Mooka," Dazè said, picking up the kid so he wouldn't get hurt.

"You think you can fuck with me, nigga? I will fuck you over, boy! I do this shit for real, nigga!" Six yelled in Junior's ear.

Even though he was out skilled and over powered, the younger brother didn't want to back down. He lifted his foot against the house and pushed. The brothers stumbled from the porch and fell into the grass. After a few rolls, Junior ended up on top. Since he had no training, he didn't know how to keep the advantage. Six bucked his hips and lifted Junior in the air, tossing him to the side. A moment later, the older brother was on top, pinning Junior to the ground. But what Six didn't see was the pistol that fell from Junior's waist, a few inches from his reach. While Six was wrapping his hand around Junior's throat, Junior's hand was wrapping around the butt of the gun.

"Bro, chill!" John yelled when Junior grabbed the gun.

"Junior, stop!" Dazè added.

"Six, watch out!" Santana warned.

"I told you that you can't fuck with me nigga!" Six mugged, squeezing Junior's neck. When he felt something jab into his ribs, he froze. He looked down and seen the pistol.

"Get the fuck off me, nigga," Junior mugged, barely able to talk.

Disbelief, hurt, and pain filled Six's eyes as he stared down at his little brother. He couldn't believe that Junior pointed a gun at him. "You upped on me, nigga?"

"Get the fuck off me," Junior repeated more forcefully.

The disbelief, hurt, and pain that Six felt began to change into anger. He considered choking Junior until he passed out, breaking his neck, or trying to take the gun. A part of him also wanted to know if his brother would actually shoot him. But when he looked down in Junior's eyes, he got his answer. His little brother was a killer. If it came down to it, he would shoot his big brother. "That's the last time you gon' ever pull a heat on me, nigga," Six mugged as he stood.

"And that's the last time you gon' put yo' fucking hands on me, nigga," Junior promised, tucking the pistol while getting up from the grass.

"What the fuck you niggas on, brah! Y'all tripping. Y'all fighting over some bullshit that neither one of y'all can't do nothing about," John snapped at his brothers. "Junior, you can't be pulling no muthafuckin guns on yo' niggas. You tripping, fam. And Six, you know bro ain't finna take no Ls from nobody. What you think was gon' happen?"

Junior and Six ignored John. Their chests were heaving while sucking in deep breaths and mugging one another.

"John right. Y'all niggas tripping, fam," Dazè said, shaking his head. "Y'all brothers. Y'all can't let this street shit come between y'all."

"I ain't tryna hear that shit," Junior mugged. "Don't put yo' hands on me no more, nigga, or I'ma forget we brothers. C'mon, Mooka. Let's go."

***

Junior was still mad. After jumping in the Corvette with Mooka, he drove around aimlessly thinking about the fight with Six. For the first time in his life, he thought about killing his brother. Six hoed him in front of everybody. That shit didn't sit right with Junior. It was a bitter pill that he couldn't swallow. Nobody would ever get away with talking to him like that and putting their hands on him. He had shot niggas for less. But Six was his blood. They grew up together. Hustled together. Fought together. But for some reason this fight felt different.

"Daddy, when is mama coming home?" Mooka asked.

"I don't know, man. Hopefully soon."

"Why can't we go get her?"

"Because the police won't let her out right now. But I'm working on getting her out. She should be calling us soon."

A couple moments later, the phone rang. It was Quitta. Junior gave the phone to Mooka and let him answer on speaker.

"Hey, mama!"

"Hey, baby! What you doing?"

"Nothing. I'm riding in the car with my daddy. My daddy and Uncle Six had a fight."

"What?" Quitta asked, making sure she heard him right. "Yo daddy and Six had a fight?"

"Yeah. At granny house. Daddy pulled a gun out."

"Junior, can you hear me? What is Mooka talking about?"

"It wasn't a real fight. More like a wrestling match. Nigga tried to hoe me, and I wasn't going. I upped on that nigga and told him I'ma burn him if he ever put his hands on me again."

"Wow, Junior! Are you serious? What y'all fighting for?"

"Some shit that I can't talk about right now. Nigga tryna act like he my mu'fuckin daddy or some shit. Tryna check me in front of other niggas and shit. I ain't going. But fuck that nigga. What's up with you? How you holding?"

"I don't know. I thought I was coming home. I don't want to be here," she whined, her voice breaking. "I can't believe they denied my bail."

"Yeah, that was some bitch ass shit. Once I seen Detective Johnson bitch ass in court, I knew they was gon' be on some bullshit."

"I talked to him after court. He want me to flip on you."

"I know. Henrik already told me. All you gotta do is hold. They don't got shit on us. They gon' try all kind of shit to get you to fold, but don't do it. We gon' beat this. I got you."

"Okay." Quitta sniffled. "I'ma stay strong. I just don't want to have the baby in jail. I want to have it in a hospital and spend the night holding it like I did Mooka. I need that bonding time."

"You gon' be out before that. We good, baby." The phone went silent for a moment.

"Is we gon' be a family when I get out?" Quitta asked.

Junior didn't answer the question. Instead, he asked one of his own. "Why was you with Steph?"

Quitta let out a stressed breath. "I went to a party with Rakisha, and he showed up."

"He just showed up at a party the same night you get to Lacrosse?" He asked, not believing it was a coincidence.

"Yeah. I never talked to him until he came in the house."

"What was y'all talking about?"

"About what happened. He still mad that I got him locked up and gave you his money."

"And the white girl kept interrupting you while y'all was catching up, huh?"

"It wasn't like that, Junior. All we did was talk. Nothing else. I never wanted to be with Steph. I want you. I want us to be a family again."

"I hear you. But I don't want to talk about that right now. Let's just focus on getting you out. We gon' let the rest work itself out."

CHAPTER 4

Quitta wiped the tears from her eyes after hanging up the phone. Being pregnant while locked up was going to be hard as hell. Her emotions were all over the place. One minute, she was laughing and the next she was crying. And she couldn't stop thinking about what Junior was doing and who he was fucking. Even though she had a whole relationship with Steph and broke bad on him while he was locked up, she was hoping that he would play things differently. That he would give her a fresh start after she showed her loyalty and willingness to hold and not fold. Getting her man back meant just as much as having her freedom.

She was walking back to her cell when she seen Tiffany sitting at a table reading a book. Not wanting to be locked in a room with uncontrollable emotions, Quitta walked over. "What you reading?"

"Cum For Me. This muthafucka is off that chain too!" Tiffany said, sitting the book on the table. When she seen Quitta's red eye's, she got concerned." You okay?"

Quitta shook her head, feeling a bout of tears coming on. "Hell, nah. I keep on crying, and I want to go home but these muthafuckas denied my bail," she whined. "And this damn baby keep on making me cry."

"You gon' be okay, girl. At least you got a nigga that tried to pay yo' bail and got you a lawyer. My bitch ass baby daddy won't even answer the phone. I swear to God when I get out I'm going back to jail for cutting that nigga dick off."

Quitta bust out laughing. "Don't do it, girl. Don't let no nigga get you put back in jail. Get him back by getting a finer nigga with a bag. Or fuck his cousin or something."

Tiffany grinned, revealing her snagga tooth smile. "Ohh, I'ma fuck his cousin, Rock. This nigga is fine, and he been tryna get with me. My dumb ass tried to be faithful, but I'm done with that shit. And when I put that snagga tooth head on his ass, he gon' buy me a Hell Cat!"

The women broke out in laughter.

"Marquitta Ware, come to the desk," the C.O. called, interrupting their moment.

"Let me go see what this bitch want," Quitta said before walking up to the desk. A short, chubby blonde haired woman with big brown eyes sat at the officer's station. "What's up, McCormick?"

"You have a professional visit."

Quitta was surprised. She wasn't expecting a lawyer visit. "Right now?"

"Yep. Right now. The officer will come get you in a moment."

Five minutes later, an officer came and escorted Quitta to a small conference room. She was surprised to see Detective Russo sitting at the table.

"Thank you for bringing her, officer," Russo said politely.

"No problem. Just give me a holler when you're done. I'll be right outside," the officer said before leaving.

"Have a seat, Quitta. You look surprised to see me," he smiled, stroking his big beard.

"I am. They said I had a professional visit. I thought you was my lawyer," Quitta said, sitting down slowly and wondering why he was here.

"I have a confession to make," he laughed. "This isn't a professional visit. It's personal."

Quitta raised her eyebrows, not fully understanding what he meant. "What does that mean?"

He rested his arms on the table, leaning forward. "It means that whatever we say is between me and you. I don't have any recording devices or anything to write with. I came to see you because I want to talk to you. I told you that I think your special. I wasn't kidding."

Quitta's mind raced as she tried to comprehend what the detective was saying. She couldn't figure out if he was genuinely interested in her or if he was trying to get information to convict her and Junior. "What is you on, man? You the police. Why are you saying this shit to me?"

"I just told you. I'm here because I'm interested in getting to know you. Nothing that you say to me will ever leave us. I'm serious."

Quitta wasn't going. She knew it was a trick. "C'mon, Russo. What the fuck is you on, man? I don't believe that you just coming to see me to talk."

"Okay. I get it. I'm a cop. You have every right to be skeptical. Tell me what I need to do to convince you that I'm here for you? Anything."

Quitta gave him a long searching stare. "Okay. You want me to believe you. Give me a phone."

Detective Russo smiled. "I knew you were gonna say that. That's why I brought this." He pulled an iPhone 10 and charger from his pocket. "I can get fired and charged for this. If this doesn't show you that I'm serious, I don't know what else will. Its already fully charged and my number is inside."

Quitta was so surprised that she was stuck. She wasn't expecting him to agree to give her a phone, let alone have one ready. "Damn, Russo! I wasn't expecting this."

"I know. That's why I did it. Now you won't have to worry about watching what you say on the phone, or the calls being recorded. Tuck it in your waist and don't get caught. And call me Nate. That's my name."

Quitta cuffed the phone quickly, letting her guard down a little now that the cop had gone above and beyond to convince her that he was serious. "Why do you want to get to know me if you're trying to put a case on me and Junior?"

"I'm not trying to put a case on you guys. I'm not even the lead detective on this case. Detective Mark Washington is. I just got involved because of you. I really want to help you get out of here. I don't think you should be locked up. We know the drugs were Steph's but legally there is nothing I can do to help. So, I'm doing it illegally."

"You're really going to risk your freedom and job for me?" Quitta asked, wondering why she was so special.

Russo held her stare for a moment. "Yes. I know I don't know you and this might sound crazy, but I think you're worth it."

"But you know that I'm pregnant and want to be with my baby daddy?"

"For now." he grinned.

Quitta laughed and shook her head. "I can't believe this is happening."

"It's real. I'm here for you and I mean it. And If you don't mind, I'd like to see you again."

"Okay. You have my address," she joked.

"I sure do." He laughed. "And I also have some information that should make you smile. Steph was the informant that was giving us information about Junior shooting Terrance. Now that he's dead, that is one less witness that can connect Junior to the murder."

Quitta's eyes popped. "Are you serious? It was Steph?"

"Yep." Russo nodded." Make sure that you use the cellphone when you tell him. Don't need that being recorded. Now, ain't I the gift that keeps on giving?"

"You really are," Quitta said, thankful to have the cop on her side. "Man, you are just blowing my mind today."

"I'm just glad that I can make you smile. You have a really pretty smile, you know that?"

"Awe! Thanks, Nate," Quitta gushed.

"Okay. I have to get going. Do not tell anyone that you have a phone. Not one person, you hear me?"

Quitta nodded. "I won't. I put that on my son."

"Good. Give me a call later. I'll see you again in a few days."

***

The police gave Quitta a phone!

Junior couldn't stop thinking about that after ending the call with his baby mama. He was convinced that the police had the phone tapped and were recording the calls. Quitta, on the other hand, had complete trust in the cop. She honestly believed that he liked her and wanted to help her get out of jail. Junior didn't feel the same way. He was convinced that everybody in the Lacrosse Police Department was listening in on every call trying to build a case. But because he couldn't prove the police were listening, he would just watch what he said like he did when they talked on the jail calls.

One thing for sure was that he wasn't going to convict himself. Gail didn't raise no fool.

"Damn, yo' baby mama talk too fucking much," Lisa said, snuggling up to kiss Junior on the neck while reaching under the sheet to grab his dick.

"And why she calling so fucking early?" Meeka yawned.

"That's how it be when you locked up. You wake up early and its hard as hell to go to sleep. Yo' mind always racing, and you can't stop thinking," Junior explained, knowing from experience what Quitta was going through.

"Good thing we don't have them problems." Lisa giggled, flinging the sheet back and exposing their naked bodies. "I slept good, and I woke up early and horny. Which one of y'all want this pussy first?"

After a morning threesome, Junior and the women went to shower. When they were squeaky clean, the women went their way and Junior went to wake Mooka. He was gripped by nostalgia when he opened the door to Mooka's bedroom and seen him stretched out on the Marvel Superheroes sheets. He remembered when he and Quitta first moved into the house in the suburbs. To come from sleeping on the floor at his mother's house and renting a room in Quitta's mother's house to a big ass house in Wauwatosa was a big step.

He decided to move back in the house to give his son a sense of normalcy while his mother was locked up. Raising Mooka on his own while running the streets was going to be a challenge but he was determined to make it work. After feeding, washing, and dressing his lil nigga, they left for the hood. Today was going to be a busy day. The first thing he needed to do was find his little man a babysitter or daycare. And he knew just who to holla at to make that happen.

"Granny, wake up!" Mooka said, crawling onto his grandmother's bed and getting in her face.

Gail's eye's opened slowly. "C'mon, man. Why are you waking me up? What you want?"

"I need help with Mooka. I need a babysitter," Junior spoke up.

Gail looked past her grandson, locking eyes with her son. "That's yo son, Junior. Yo' responsibility. You better figure it out." "C'mon, mama. Don't do me like that. You know I'm finna be running through the jects. I can't take him with me. I can't be running around Parklawn with a four year old tagging along. I already gotta worry about these niggas and the police. I know you don't want yo' grandson around that life."

"You should've thought about that before you decided to start fucking without a rubber."

Junior gave her a dead stare. "You serious, mama?"

"Damn, Junior! Leave him here. But we not doing this every day. You better figure it out because I'm not about to be yo' babysitter."

"Thanks mama. I owe you. Can you enroll him in a daycare for me? I'll get you tickets to that Anthony Hamilton concert that you been talking about."

Gail sat up in bed to give him the *mother eye*. "Boy, you bet not be playing with me! I'ma find him a daycare and I want my concert tickets."

After dropping Mooka off with his mom, Junior stepped outside, about to do a trap check. He needed to gather the team for a meeting. It was time to begin the Parklawn takeover. He had just stepped onto the sidewalk when the white Continental pulled up behind his Corvette. He locked eyes with Six through the windshield and the brothers engaged in a long staring contest.

"You still got that gun on you?" Six asked as he and Santana climbed from the luxury whip.

Junior tapped his waist. "Like a blind nigga with a walking stick."

"Before you be a corpse, you'll a be a celly, huh?" Six grinned, quoting Yo Gotti.

"You already know."

Six turned to Santana. "Let me get a second with my brother, baby. I'll be in the house in a minute."

"Okay, baby. Hey, Junior." She waved before walking up the walkway.

He acknowledged her with a nod. The men remained silent as they watched her walk away.

Six turned to look at Junior. "Was you really gon' shoot me?"

Junior maintained strong eye contact. "I ain't taking no Ls, brah."

Even though he never said he would've shot him, Six knew that his little brother would have put a bullet in his ribs. And the truth left him feeling devastated. "So, you really willing to kill yo' own brother?"

Junior could see how the truth affected Six. Real pain showed in his brother's eyes, but he wasn't going to take back how he felt. "Six, you my nigga. I looked up to you my whole life. When you beat my ass when we was kids, I chalked that up to you giving me some type of correction or you tryna make me tougher. But we grown now, my nigga. Do you think I been out here laying all these niggas down to turn around and let somebody beat my ass and humiliate me? I'm a man before I'm anything. You know what mama told us when we was little. If we can't win with our fists, pick up a brick and knock they ass out. Only now niggas ain't playing with bricks. We reached that level where everything is for keeps."

Six gave an approving nod at the explanation. "When you put it like that, I get it. I just didn't think we would reach this level. I'ma always see you as my little brother. As Junior. But I hear you. We in the big leagues now. We got boundaries. Every action has a reaction."

"Every action has a reaction," Junior agreed.

"I really didn't mean for shit to get that far. I wanted to teach you a lesson and show you how to move. So, I'll be man enough to apologize to you. I'm sorry for taking it there with you, my nigga. I just want what's best for you. I want you to be the best version of yourself."

"And my bad for upping on you, brah, but you was fucking me up. I didn't know what else to do."

"Sometimes you gotta have a misunderstanding to get a good understanding," Six said as the brothers embraced. "But it's all love, lil nigga."

"Love, brah."

"So, what's up with Quitta? Last night, John was telling me that they denied her bail."

"Man, that shit so crazy, my nigga," Junior said, letting out a breath and shaking his head. "The same nigga that's investigating Nicole and Q is helping the police in Lacrosse. They denied her bail because of the shit he told the D.A. about the BGM nigga. They tryna link the body in Lacrosse with Fredo and come after me. That's why they hitting her with the OD even though they know she didn't sell the white bitch the boy. If she flip on me, they gon' drop all her charges."

Six's eyes grew as wide as two full moons. "What the fuck, Junior? Damn, my nigga. You sure she gon' hold?"

"I think so. She know they don't got shit. I got Henrik representing her and he saying the same thing. They don't got shit but the OD. If he can get that shit threw out, she good. Plus, I just knocked off one of the informants while I was up there. They don't got shit."

Six stared at his brother for a moment. "You just whacked a nigga while you was in Lacrosse getting Mooka?" He asked incredulously.

"That's the nigga that hit me for a hunnit racks. That shit was on sight. I owed him that. Plus, he was one of the niggas getting down and telling the police I knocked off Terrance."

Six shook his head. He wanted to get on Junior's ass for being so reckless, but he didn't want a repeat of yesterday, so he let it go. "Ain't nothing I can say to none of that, brah. You in a lot of shit. I just hope Quitta keep it solid."

"Me, too," Junior agreed.

"Switching subjects. What's going on with the takeover? How far you get with that?"

"I'm still working on it. I planned on getting Murda, RIP, John, and Dazè together with some of the niggas that's really out here eating with the work. I want to convince them niggas to shop with us. Once they see how good our shit is plus we got the lowest numbers, they gon' jump on board."

Six nodded approvingly. "I like it. It would be a gradual thing. Take your time and do it right. That's what I'm talking about, my nigga. Use your head and you will go far. I was a little concerned that you might just start burning niggas like State Property or Plug Love."

"C'mon, now." Junior laughed. "Give me more credit than that. I ain't stupid. If we start dropping niggas, that's gon' bring twelve and niggas ain't gon' be able to get no money. I'm tryna dead all the beef and focus on this paper. The only reason I'm still out here fucking niggas up is so I can wrap all this shit up. But it's damn near done. Now, I'm ready to lock up these projects and elevate."

"Here go a little game for you, nigga. You can thank me later. What you know about Black Wall Street?"

Junior looked puzzled. "What the fuck is Black Wall Street?"

"Back in the day, in Tulsa, Oklahoma, Black people owned millions of dollars of property. Banks, schools, stores, all that shit. This was one of the richest communities in America, my nigga. And it became a thing because niggas kept that black dollar circulating in black owned businesses and neighborhoods. This is what you pitch to the team. The power of the black dollar. Keep all the money in Parklawn and y'all gon' get richer quicker. Thank me later."

***

The white Audi R8, red Dodge Challenger Demon, blue 550 Benz, and pink convertible Cadillac XLR made the parking lot behind the project buildings on 46th and Congress look like a mini car show. Willow, Shamar, and Kanesha along with her best friend Ebony all leaned against their whips. Near them stood the Parklawn grinders; John, Dazè, T-Murda and RIP. They were all watching and listening to Junior.

"I brought everybody over here for one reason. The love of money. And I got something that y'all need in on. Trust me. What I'm proposing is that we all grind together under one flag. That we sew up the whole project, starting with the white then moving on to pills, loud, dog food, and whatever else we can sell out this muthafucka. We want to eventually make it so that ain't nothing moving in the whole project if it ain't coming from us. I grabbed y'all because not only have I known y'all since I was a pup, but also because I respect y'all hustle. Y'all know how to get it and that's what we need. Muthafuckas that understand the grind."

"So, how this supposed to work, my nigga?" D'Dre spoke up, leaning against the R8. "We all supposed to be working for you?"

Junior knew he couldn't tell the independent hustlers that he wanted them to be his workers, so he switched the wording. "My nigga, I wouldn't disrespect none of y'all by telling y'all to stop doing what y'all doing and come and work for me. All of y'all are y'all own bosses and that's how I want to keep it. All I want y'all to do is shop with us. Keep all the money in the circle. The same principal that the niggas who owned Black Wall Street used. Back in the early 1900s Black Wall Street was one the richest community in the United States. Remember what was happening back then. White folks had they foot on niggas necks. But the niggas on Black Wall Street understood the power of spending money with they own kind. That's how they made the neighborhood worth millions. That's what I wanna do to Parklawn. I wanna turn this muthafucka into Black Wall Street. Ain't no bosses and workers. We all bosses eating together."

"Black Wall Street." Shamar smiled, loving the concept. "I'm familiar with a lil bit of black history. That's some boss ass shit right there."

"I never heard of Black Wall Street, but I like the way you put that together," Ebony said.

"If yo' ass would a paid attention in school instead of always being in the bathroom fucking E-Money in them stalls then yo' ass would've knew about it," Kanesha cracked.

"Girl, E-Money fine ass was my nigga! But don't be putting my business out there for the whole projects. Damn." Ebony laughed.

"Ay Junior, the only thing that's gon' make this work is the numbers," Willow spoke up. "What kinda prices you working with and what the product like?"

"All we got right now is powder, but the shit is damn near the best shit in the city. And y'all don't even got to buy the first batch.

I'ma throw all y'all a half brick. Bring me back fifteen thousand. Do y'all want in?"

Shamar's eyes bucked. "A half of brick of snow for fifteen? And you saying it's the best shit in the city. What's the catch, my nigga?"

"No fuck boy shit. All I speak is facts. No cap."

"My nigga, you know pandemic prices is fucking the world up. Fifteen hundred for a zip of hard and it be bullshit. You telling us that you got a half of baby of flake for fifteen? That shit sound damn near unbelievable."

"I got a good plug," Junior smiled loving their skepticism.

"Why y'all keep asking all these questions?" Kanesha spoke up. "Y'all acting like y'all wanna get whacked upside the head. This nigga got the best shit and best prices in the city. That's good enough for me. I been knowing this nigga since we was twelve. If he say that's what it is, then I'ma take him at his word. Let's get this money, Junior."

"I'm with my girl," Ebony said. "I been waiting for an opportunity like this. I got a few more bitches that we can bring in too. Bad bitches that love the hustle. Count me in."

Junior gave the women a nod before turning to Willow and Shamar. "What y'all wanna do?"

"My nigga, you had me at Black Wall Street." Shamar grinned.

"And you had me with a half a book for fifteen. Let's get it."

"Let's get it!" Junior smiled, happy to have the hustlers on the squad. "One last thing though. When I talked about hustling under one flag, I meant it. We all Parklawn Grinders. I'm PLG Junior, that's PLG Dazè, PLG John and so on and so forth. Let's put Parklawn on the map. Let's fuck the city up and show 'em how niggas eating on Black Wall Street.

The newest members of the clique cheered along with the veterans, ready to run up a bag. During the cheers, Junior noticed a light skinned nigga named Chris riding his bike alongside a brown skinned woman that was so thick it would have been disrespectful not to look at her.

J-Blunt

"Damn, she thick as fuck!" Ebony said, also noticing the woman.

Everyone turned to look at the brick house. She wore a white tank top, tan pussy cutting khaki shorts, and retro Jordan 3s. Her multi colored hair (pink, purple, and blue) hung in curls to the middle of her back. She had a pretty face, nose piercing, and both of her full lips pierced.

"Who is she?" RIP asked.

"I don't know. But I'm finna go see if she got a sister," John said, going to intercept Chris and Thicky Minaj.

"Y'all niggas always thinking with y'all dicks." Kanesha laughed. "Junior, I need to take care of some shit. Hit me when you ready."

"I'ma hit you when I put that package together. Like thirty minutes. An hour tops," he said, allowing his feet to move towards John, Chris, and the big booty cutey.

"Y'all niggas all the same. Seen my ass and think I'ma thot. Ain't no touching for free, nigga," the woman was saying when Junior walked up.

"You talking like we fucked up out here," John said, pulling out a stack of cash. "We Parklawn Grinders! This shit light."

Dollar signs flickered in the woman's eyes. "That's what I'm talking about. Benji gon' be my baby daddy," she said, bending over and making her giant cakes jiggle.

"Dayum!" Dazè yelled, loving the sight of her booty rippling.

A few moments later, she was surrounded by all the Parklawn Grinders.

"Twerk for the Gram," RIP said, pulling out his phone.

"Ain't nothing free, baby. Somebody drop some cash if y'all want me to shake my ass."

Junior stood a few feet away, keeping silent and watching his niggas make it rain on her ass while she twerked. Everyone was so caught up in the show that they didn't see the baddie approaching until she started screaming.

"Mercedes! What the fuck you doing?"

Everyone turned to the sound of the voice and spotted a light skinned woman that was bad enough to be the lead actress in a Hollywood blockbuster movie.

"I'm out here getting this money, bitch," Mercedes said, sticking out her tongue while continuing to twerk for the camera.

Junior locked eyes with the newcomer and was immediately drawn in by her gray irises. Although, she wasn't as thick as Mercedes, she was definitely badder. A long braided ponytail hung down her back, just above her ass. Her light skin had a hint of red from being out in the summer sun. Her eyebrows and lashes were done up like she had a glam squad. Her face was beautiful. Slanted eyes, high cheek bones, beautiful lips. Her style of dress was classy and simple. Gucci sunglasses, black half halter top, designer jeans with rips in the knees, and a pair of spiked pumps. While his niggas was caught up in the ass shaking, Junior left the crowd to meet the Ghetto Queen.

"I can't let you walk by me without putting yo' number in my phone," he said, blocking her path.

She gave him a quick head to toe glance. Junior was fresh to death rocking Saint Laurent shirt and shorts, a Ferragamo belt, and red bottoms. "Does that actually work?"

"You would be surprised what some people would do for the president of Black Wall Street." He smiled.

A question shown in her beautiful grey eyes. "Black Wall Street?"

Junior lifted his arm and swept it across the project landscape. "This is Black Wall Street. I'm the president."

She laughed, showing a perfect smile. "Black Wall Street. That was a good one."

"My name is Junior. What's yo' name?" He asked, extending a hand.

She looked him over again like she was judging if she should tell him. "My name is Diamond. I'm a girl's best friend," she said before sticking out her manicured hand for a shake.

"That name fits you," he complimented while pulling out his phone and giving it to her. "Put yo' number in there."

She laughed again, cocking her head to the side. "What make you think I just give out my number to strangers?"

"I'm not a stranger. I'm the president and I'm choosing you to be my first lady. It all starts with yo' number."

They locked eyes for a moment. Their mutual attraction was undeniable. Then, she started typing on the keypad.

"Okay, Mr. President. This is my number. But I have a question. How are you the president when I didn't vote for you?"

"Only residents of Parklawn can vote."

"I'm a resident and I didn't vote for you."

Junior was surprised to know that she lived in his projects. "You live here? Since when?"

"Since two days ago. I would stay and find out more about how you were elected but I need to get my sister before your boys have her on one of them amateur porn sites. We got some things to do. She was supposed to get some weed and come right back."

Junior reached into his pocket and pulled out the half ounce that he bought yesterday. "Open your hand. You in luck."

Diamond took the weed graciously. "Thanks. What I owe you."

Junior shook his head. "Yo' money ain't no good with me. Just answer the phone when I call."

CHAPTER 5

Junior left the hood and went to the stash house to grab the work. He pulled two kilos from the refrigerator and grabbed the scale from this cabinet before sitting at the kitchen table to weigh and bag up the white powder. If everything went according to plan, the entire projects would belong to the Parklawn Grinders in no time. And then after the takeover, he might really name himself The President.

"Hell yeah!" He grinned, loading a Ziplock bag with eighteen ounces of flake before zipping it up and repeating the process. As he worked and thought about being president, Diamond's face entered his mind. She was super bad. On a scale of 1-10, she was an eleven. She would make a bad ass first lady. He had to have her. So, he called.

"Hello?" She sang.

"You only answer the phone like that for me, right?"

She paused for a moment. "Who is this?"

"The president."

"Oh yeah." She giggled. "The President of Black Wall Street."

"That's right. And I just decided that I want to kick it with you tonight. Cancel all of yo' plans. Tonight, you with me."

"Excuse me?" She asked, surprised by his audacity. "I think you taking this president stuff too literal. You don't know me like that, man."

He let out a chuckle, liking her assertiveness. "That's what I'm talking about, queen. I like a woman that speaks her mind. Don't hold no punches with me, aight? I'ma try it if you let me."

"Shit, you ain't know? My mama didn't raise no punk ass bitch."

"I hear you. But I still want to see you tonight. Fuck with yo' boy. I'm like Allstate, baby. You gon' be in good hands."

"What is you talking about, man? I had plans on going to work tonight."

Hearing that she worked at night made Junior pause and think. "Work? What do you do?"

"I'ma dancer at Gold Diggers. Today is Tuesday so it really ain't nothing popping. I was thinking about going in and seeing if I could make few dollars."

Hearing that she was a dancer made him smile. He was definitely fucking her tonight.

"I tell you what. Skip the club tonight and fuck with me. I'll make it worth it."

"Hold on, nigga. I ain't no hoe. I don't fuck for money so don't think that its gon' be that kind of night."

Junior bust out laughing. She was game conscious. "Why would you come at me like that, queen? I wasn't even on that. I just want to kick it and have a good time. Fuck with me."

"I was just letting you know in case you was thinking that, because niggas be thinking that just because you dance you automatically fuck for money."

"Nah, it ain't like that. Just be ready. I'ma slide through later."

After ending the call, Junior finished bagging the work and cleaned up his mess. He stuffed the half kilos in a Louis Vuitton book bag and left the apartment. During the drive to Parklawn, he called the newest members of the Parklawn Grinders and told them to meet him in the hood. He had just hung up from talking to Willow when the phone rang. It was Quitta's lawyer.

"Henrik, what's good?"

His tone was serious. "Hey, Junior. I'm afraid I have a little bit of bad news for you, buddy."

Junior immediately thought the worst. Quitta's phone was tapped. He knew it. He steeled himself to receive the bad news. "What's up, man? What kind of bad news?"

"I just finished talking with Detective Johnson. He's coming for you. I don't know when, but he's coming. Maybe some questioning to scare you."

Junior glanced at the bag in the passenger seat with the three half kilos inside. If Detective Johnson swarmed him now, it was a wrap. The panic rose inside of him, making his heart beat faster. Visions of cells inside the Milwaukee County Jail filled his head. "What did he say? Am I getting arrested?"

"No, he doesn't have enough to arrest you. Not yet. But he's looking hard."

"Fuck. What does he want? What did he say?"

"It's about Fredo's murder. They have video of you in the club with Quitta and he wants to know where you were when the guy was killed at the gas station. They have footage from the gas station too, but I haven't seen it."

"Fuck!" He cursed again, banging the Lexus's steering wheel. "So, what should I do, man? How do I play this?"

"You have a couple options. I can call the detective and arrange it so we can go in together and you can be questioned. Or, you can keep on doing what you've been doing and wait for him to find you. A third option is to get out of town for a week or two to clear your mind and put your affairs in order. That'll let some of the heat and dust settle. Then, when you come back, we can figure it out. Ultimately, it's your decision to make. I work for you."

Junior thought for a moment. He wasn't ready to face Detective Johnson. Not right now. He was panicked and not in the right frame of mind. He needed to buy some time and get his shit together. "Okay. Uh, I can't see him right now. I'm not ready. I think I'ma hit it out on town. Damn, this is fucked up."

"There is a silver lining in this. Quitta isn't talking to them, and they don't have anything to go on. They're just fishing. As long as things stay the way they are, you're fine."

"As long as things stay the way they are," Junior mumbled, shaking his head. "I gotta go, man. I need wrap up some things. I'll check with you later. Thanks for the heads up."

"No problem. Let me know if you in anything."

Junior stared absentmindedly at the road, driving on autopilot. As long at things stayed the way they were, he would be fine. But things didn't work like that in the streets. Niggas was always looking for a snake move. He needed to get out of town fast. So, he called Six.

"What up, brah?" Six answered.

"When you going back home?"

"We was thinking about leaving tomorrow, why?"

Junior let out a stressed breath. "My lawyer just called and said the police coming to snatch me up for some questioning. I need to get out of town for a little while."

"Say less, my nigga. We leaving tonight and we flying private. Stay low and I'ma hit you when we ready."

"Yep. Love."

"You already know," Six said before hanging up.

After ending the call with Six, Junior called John and told him to meet him at Jeff's house. Ten minutes later, he pulled up to the trap and hurried inside with the work.

"What's going on, man? You got that good shit for me?" Jeff asked eagerly, rubbing his hands together like they were cold. Junior sat on the couch heavily, closing his eyes for a moment.

Jeff noticed his young friend's demeanor and became concerned. "What's up, my nigga? You good?"

Junior opened his eyes and stared at the fiend for a moment. "The police want this question me about a body."

Jeff's eyes grew wide like he took a big ass hit from the pipe. "Seriously! A body?"

Junior nodded.

Jeff became animated. "Damn, nigga. What the fuck you still doing in Parklawn? You better get yo' ass on a train or airplane and get the fuck outta here."

"I'm flying to Vegas later tonight. I need to holla at my little brother so he can take care of shit while I'm gone."

The doorbell rang, interrupting the men. "That should be him right there."

"I got it, man. Sit tight," Jeff said before going to answer that door. He came back a few moments later followed by John, Mike, and fifty.

"My nigga." 50 grinned, happy to see his little nigga.

Junior didn't stand to greet his niggas. Just shook his head.

"What's up, nigga? Why you looking like the whole world against you?" Mike asked.

"Cause it is," Junior said weakly. Then, he looked to fifty. "12 want to talk to me about Fredo."

Fifty flinched a little, his eyes growing wide. "On what, my nigga? You serious?"

Junior nodded. "They got Quitta on a OD in Lacrosse and Detective Johnson, the same one that knocked Nicole and Q, went up there to question her about it. She told them that I was in the club with her and now they want to question me."

50, John, and Mike's mouths dropped open.

"Why the fuck would she tell 'em you was in the club with her?" 50 yelled.

"And how the fuck she catch a OD?" Mike asked. "You gave her some work?"

"Nah, I didn't give her nothing. She was talking to a nigga that was making the serve. All Quitta did was hand the bitch the boy. The bitch went in the other room and died. They charging her with the body because she won't tell on the nigga. And now the nigga dead."

"What that gotta do with her telling them fags you was in the club with her?" 50 asked. "I told you that you should've let me off her ass."

"C'mon, my nigga. You ain't killing my son mother. They got the video from the club, my nigga. They knew it was me. If she would a lied, they would've charged her with more shit, and she would've looked like she was guilty. Her lawyer told her to tell the truth."

"What you finna do, nigga?" John asked, concern for his brother's freedom written on his face.

"I'm finna fly out with Six tonight. This what I got to talk to you about. I'ma be gone for a week. Maybe two. I need you to take care of collection and distribution while I'm gone. Here go the key. I'ma text you the details."

"Damn, my nigga. That shit is fucked up," 50 mourned his little nigga's situation. "All you gotta do is stick to the script, though. You went home after the club. They can't prove shit."

"I know. I'ma have my lawyer in the room with me. He said all they wanna do is ask me some questions. I'm just going through

Vegas to get away for a lil while. When I come back, I'ma get with my lawyer and get that shit out the way."

Mike shook his head. "Ain't shit you can do but keep it solid and not tell on yo'self. You gon' be aight, lil brah."

***

"What the fuck?" Dazè questioned as he read the text message again.

"What is it?" Renae asked.

"John just texted me and said Junior finna be out of town for a while so we got to fuck with him."

Renae took her eyes off the road for a moment to give Dazè a questioning glance. "What?"

"That's what I'm saying. I'm finna call Junior right now. Fuck this nigga on?"

"What's good, Zae?" Junior answered.

"I just got a text from John saying we got to fuck with him while you out of town. What the fuck that nigga talking about?"

"It's all bad, my nigga. Detective Johnson looking for me about a body. I gotta dip for a minute. A week or two."

Dazè was at a loss for words. "Damn, my nigga. On what?"

"What happened?" Renae asked.

"The police looking for Junior," he answered quickly.

Renae's eye's grew wide with concern. "On what?"

Junior continued. "Yeah, my nigga. I already talked to my lawyer. We gon' figure it out when I get back. John gon' do the pickups and pass outs while I'm gone"

"Damn, my nigga. That shit sound fucked up but hopefully yo' lawyer got a plan. I'ma fuck with John on that shit. Be safe."

"Put the phone on speaker," Renae said before could Dazè hang up. "What the police looking for you for?"

"That shit with Fredo. They holding Quitta in Lacrosse for that shit."

"Whhaatt? Damn, bro! Is they finna lock you up too!"

"Nah, I don't think so. My lawyer said they just wanna talk. I just need to get out of town for a lil bit to clear my head. I'ma figure that shit out when I get back."

All she could do was hope for the best.

"Okay, bro. I hope everything work out for you. And sit yo' hot ass down some fucking where before you give me a heart attack, nigga. Damn."

"What the fuck you think I'm tryna do?" He chuckled. "As soon as I put this shit behind me, I'ma focus on the bag. But I gotta go. Quitta on the other line. I'ma fuck with y'all later."

"Damn, that shit fucked up," Dazè breathed after ending the call.

"I know. That nigga just got out and he already look like he finna go back. I hope he find a way out of that shit because if they get they hands on him again, it ain't gon' be good." The thought of her brother going back to prison made Renae's eye's water.

Daze could see the love for Junior in her eyes and hear it in her voice. "Hope for the best but expect the worst, right?"

"Yeah. That's all we can do, I guess."

The lyrics to Gunna's song *'Die Alone'* filled the car for a moment. Then, Dazè's phone rang. He looked at the screen and smiled. After answering, he pressed the number five. The robotic recording thanked him before allowing the call to be connected. "Cee-Cee, what up, nigga?"

"Daze, what's good, folks?"

"Shit. Riding with my baby. Just came back from eating at Benihana's."

"Ha-ha! Renae got my nigga nose wide open." Cee-Cee laughed. "Tell her I said what's up?"

"Cee-Cee said what up?"

"Hey, Cee-Cee!"

"I sent you three hundred yesterday. Did you get that receipt yet?" Dazè asked.

"Hell yeah. Good looking, fool. I needed that shit too. Nigga box was starting to echo."

"Never that. As long as I got it, you got it. You on yo' way out anyway. How many days you got left? Like thirty, right?"

"Hell nah, nigga! Twenty eight. Don't give me more time than I got. These five years was enough."

"My bad, fam. I'll never give another man something they don't deserve." Dazè chuckled as Renae parked in front of her mother's house. He wanted a private moment with his nigga, so he remained in the car after she got out.

"I can't wait to shake this bitch ass joint, my nigga. And I ain't never coming back. I'm holding court in the streets. This prison shit ain't for real gangsters."

Dazè nodded in agreement. "Talk that real shit, my nigga. But just know that I'm out here running it up. These Parklawn niggas out here eating. Renae brother is that nigga but he probably finna get knocked for a body. The niggas that he fucking with ain't ready to walk in his shoes. I'm looking at this shit like destiny, my nigga. I got a feeling all this shit finna fall in my lap."

Cee-Cee was eager for details. "What you talking about, fam? All of what?"

"I can't say too much right now. This shit recorded. But just know that I might inherit a position that's gon' change a nigga life. Bag so big that a nigga can't carry it. Shit, this whole project might be mine, my nigga."

***

After ending the call with Cee-Cee, Dazè walked around looking for his PLG niggas. He found John in T-Murda's trap, sitting on the couch smoking a blunt.

"What's good, Dazè?" John asked, passing him the wood.

"Shit. Out here tryna get it. What's up with you niggas?"

"Shit. Telling John fool ass them YSL Blood niggas finna get cooked," T-Murda explained. "He think they got set up, but I think them niggas stupid. Niggas get they rap checks and buy some dope and stay in the hood. That shit backwards as a muthafucka."

"Yeah, that shit do sound stupid as hell," Dazè agreed. "You supposed to get yo' money and get out that shit. Them niggas did the opposite and dug back deeper in the trenches."

John shook his head in disagreement while looking at his ringing phone. "Man, y'all niggas tripping. That shit don't work like that. You don't just get money and automatically invest in legal shit. They street niggas. They did what they know. But let me answer this real quick. My side bitch calling for that big black dragon."

"Fool ass nigga!" T-Murda laughed.

"You heard about Junior?" Dazè asked.

T-Murda gave a pained look. "Fucked up, ain't it? I hope my nigga come from under that shit because we need what he tryna do by bringing the whole hood together. That Black Wall Street concept is the shit."

"It is. He snapped with that one. I hope my nigga make it out that jam, but if he don't, we still gotta keep that concept alive. Put Parklawn on the map and keep my nigga name ringing."

"Hell yeah."

John hung up the phone wearing a confused look. "This bitch just called me and told me her nigga want a nine piece."

T-Murda and Dazè shared a look.

"So," T-Murda shrugged. "Go get that money, nigga."

"I don't know why, but I don't believe the bitch."

"Who is she?" Dazè asked.

"Lil vibe named Anita that I be dipping with. She stay in the same apartment building as my bitch, Nikki."

"Why you don't wanna serve the nigga? You feel some type of way about fucking with yo' side bitch nigga?"

John thought for a moment. "I don't know. Shit just don't feel right."

"Trust yo' gut, fam," Dazè advised.

"You tripping, my nigga," T-Murda cut in. "It sound like you finna let some pussy get in between you getting a bag. Get out yo' chest and go get that money, nigga."

Dazè shook his head. "All money ain't good money."

"Bullshit!" T-Murda yelled. "Old money, new money, and crypto-currency all spend the same. If Junior was here, he would tell you to get that paper. He gave you the keys for a reason. If you want to be a boss, you betta act like one."

John looked back and forth from his niggas. Then he smiled. "Yeah, I'm tripping. I gotta get to the bag. Aye, Dazè, I'ma go grab this work and come back through. I want you to slide with me while I make the serve."

"Aight. I'm finna be right here with T-Murda. I owe this nigga an ass whooping in Live."

John went to the stash house to grab the drugs before stopping to pick up Dazè.

"Where we going?" Dazè asked as he climbed into the passenger seat of John's blue GMC Denali.

"He over on East. One of them Buffum County Niggas."

"I hate them BC niggas. Niggas used to be on some bitch ass shit in The Bay. I had they smash a couple of them niggas. They shiesty as fuck."

"You ever heard of a nigga named JP? He drive an old school green Impala."

Dazè thought for a moment. "Nah, that don't sound familiar. I met so many niggas that I forget names. But I'll Never forget a face."

Ten minutes later, John turned onto Buffum. It was almost 6:00 in the evening and the block was busy with activity. People stood on porches enjoying the summer weather and kids played in the grass and along the sidewalks. John found the Impala in the middle of the block and parked the Denali behind it. Then, he sent JP a text to let him know he was outside. His phone rang a moment later and he read the text.

"Damn."

"What happened?" Dazè asked.

John looked towards the blue and white house they were parked in front of. "Nigga talking about his Bully having babies right now and want me to come in."

"What you wanna do?"

John thought for a moment. "I damn near want to go in and see if I can get one of them dogs."

Dazè shrugged. "I'm with you."

John tucked the dope in his waist and reached for the door handle. They walked upon the porch and knocked on the door. It opened a moment later and a skinny nigga with dirty dreadlocks stood in the doorway holding a black handgun with an extended clip.

Dazè's instincts kicked in when he saw the gun. "What's that about?"

The nigga with the gun gave a hostile look while eyeing the Parklawn Grinders. "What y'all want?"

John got impatient. "Where JP at?"

This dirty dreadhead gave John a lingering stare before nodding in the house. "You can come in. He can't."

John and Dazè shared a look, reading each other's eyes. John wasn't going in the house by himself.

"We gon' be in the truck. Tell JP to come outside," Dazè spoke up as the men took a step back.

Something flashed on the young nigga's face. He didn't want them to leave. "Hold on. Y'all can come in. Both of y'all."

Dazè and John shared another look before stepping inside the house. The first thing they noticed was the smell. Like someone had been cooking spoiled food in the microwave. The living room was filthy. Dirty blue furniture, garbage strewn across the floor, and the walls looked like someone had dipped their hands in mud and used the walls to try and clean them.

Dazè covered his face with his shirt. "What the fuck?"

The dreadhead closed the door and smiled. "He in the kitchen."

They walked in the kitchen and found JP sitting at a small table holding a chrome handgun. He was a short nappy headed nigga with yellow eyes and a chipped tooth. Surprise lit his dull eyes when Dazè walked in the kitchen with John. The hairs on Dazè's forearms stood up when he seen JP. It was a setup!

"What's good, John?" JP nodded, shooting the dreadhead shooter a quick glance.

"What's good? You got that paper?" He asked, ready to get the fuck out of the stanking ass house.

"You got the work?"

Before John could respond, Dazè cut in. "Where I know you from?"

He gave a nervous twitch, his eyes revealing the conflict. He wanted to know if John had the dope on him before they made the move. And while JP was trying to come up with an answer, Dazè was trying to figure out how to get an advantage and which one of them he would shoot first. The dreadhead was close. Too close. Literally, an arm's length away.

"Nah, you don't know me," he said before turning back to John. "What's up?"

John didn't realize it was a setup and reached under his shirt for the drugs. JP took his hand off the gun to take the drugs and that's when Dazè made his move. He took a quick step back and twisted, lifting his elbow, and catching the dreadhead shooter on the chin, copying the move he'd seen the legendary UFC fighter John "Bones" Jones knock his opponents out with in the octagon. The dreadhead's jaw made a crunching noise as he went down. Dazè recovered quickly and shoved John in the back, sending him tumbling into JP. The men ended up in a pile on the floor, giving Dazè the time needed to pull his pistol.

"What the fuck you doing, brah?" John yelled while scrambling to get up from the floor.

Dazè didn't answer. He let his gun talk.

Pop, pop pop

JP's forehead opened up as the bullets tore into his brain. Without missing a beat, Dazè spun around and put a bullet in the dreadhead's face.

Pop

"What the fuck you doing!" John panicked.

"It was a setup, nigga. They was finna leave us in here stanking. Get that dope," Dazè said before searching JP's pockets and taking his phone.

John looked at the dead bodies. "I know this nigga. We was good."

"Ain't no dogs in here, fam. He said that shit to get you in the house. I was in The Bay with this nigga. He knew who I was. It was a setup."

Realization shown in John's eyes. He didn't hear or see any dogs. "Let's get the fuck outta here!"

When they were in the truck, Dazè searched JP's phone. "What's the bitch number?"

"Uh, I think it's a 555 number. Why?"

"Because I want to see if they was texting. See what they was talking about." Dazè searched the text messages until he found what he was looking for. "Damn, my nigga. He found out y'all was fucking around and had her set you up."

John took his eyes off the road to look at the phone. "On what? Let me see." Betrayal ripped at his heart as he read the text messages. "I'm killing that bitch, fam. On my mama, I'm killing that bitch right now."

"Be cool, fam. We need to play this shit right. We want that bitch to think you dead so we can get her ass outside later and push her shit in. I'ma send her a text and let her know you dead."

When the sun went down, John and Dazè drove to Anita's apartment building. During the drive, Dazè sent a text from JP's phone telling her that he was on his way. After parking a block over, the men were about to get out the car when John stopped him.

"I got this, brah."

Dazè searched John's eyes, reading the nervousness. "You sure?"

"Yeah. Let me get the phone."

Dazè gave him a long look before passing the phone. "Get that bitch. And make sure you get her phone."

John pulled the black hoody over his head and mobbed out. His hands were clammy and damp as he clutched the black semiautomatic 9mm Keltec in the front pocket of the hoody. He had never killed before and was scared as hell. He wasn't very religious but believed in God and wondered if murder would be too much for God to forgive. He thought about calling it off several times, but the burn of betrayal fueled his fire for revenge. He couldn't let this bitch get away with setting him up.

When he was near the building, he sent a text telling her to come outside and waited next to a tree across the street. Anita stepped outside a few moments later and began looking up and down the street for JP's car. That's when John moved. His pulse thudded rapidly in his ear as adrenaline pumped through his body. Anita didn't see him until it was too late. John snarled as he lifted the gun and squeezed the trigger until her body fell.

Clap, clap, clap, clap, clap, clap, clap, clap.

CHAPTER 6

Junior sat in the recliner smoking a blunt of OG, watching the projection screen. He was sitting in the entertainment room at Six's house watching Scarface for the second time in a row, comparing his own life to that of the legendary movie gangster. Like Scarface, Junior came from the gutter, did time in prison, and didn't believe in breaking his word or balls for nobody. He had also elevated his status quickly and it was now in jeopardy because of a couple bad decisions on his way to the top. Namely, Fredo and Terrance. He didn't regret killing either one of them, but he did regret not playing it smarter. If he would've moved smarter, Quitta wouldn't be in jail, and he wouldn't be running in fear of losing his freedom. Damn hindsight was 20/20.

"You still watching this movie?"

He looked towards the door as Santana sauntered in the room wearing a small white robe.

"Yeah. Me and Scarface got a lot in common."

She sat next to him and raised an eyebrow. "Like what? You must be smoking that good shit."

"Ha-ha! Real funny, Ms. Comedian. But I'm talking about our upbringing. The hood. Prison. How he is his own worst enemy."

She nodded while reaching for his blunt. "Okay. Now, I see what you talking about. At first I thought you was too high but now I get it. You have been fucking up lately. So, what you gon' do about it?"

"That's what I'm tryna figure out, sis. I know that plugging in with The Family is a blessing. This kind of opportunity don't just drop in a nigga's lap. I know that. But it seem like I can't shake this street shit. Bullshit just pop up out of nowhere and I don't know how I'ma get out this shit."

She took a puff on the blunt and blew out a big cloud of smoke. "Heavy is the head that holds the crown."

"Church."

"Believe it or not, your brother struggles with some of the same things. He has so much on his shoulders that you don't even know about. Your family, The Family, his business. I'ma tell you the same thing I told him. It's true that crowns are heavy, but they are never too heavy for a King. James has one of the strongest minds and wills I've ever seen. And since you're his brother, I know that some of what he is made of is also in you. Remember who you are. You're a King. Fights and struggles ain't meant to kill you. They come so you can see what you made of."

Junior gave Santana a nod of respect. "That was some real shit, sis."

"What, you thought you and James was the only ones that drop jewels?" She laughed. "I'm going back to bed. Don't stay up too late because we have a big day tomorrow."

After she disappeared, Junior sat and thought about her words. She spat the truth. The troubles he faced weren't meant to kill him. They were there to reveal what he was made of.

***

Simi Valley is a small city on the outskirts of Los Angeles, California known for its rich neighborhoods. The kind of place where the people that made upwards of two hundred and fifty dollars escaped when they want to get away from the LA drama. A place no one would suspect a criminal enterprise to meet behind the gates of a $5.5-million mansion. Junior felt out of his element in the big ass mansion surrounded by some of the wealthiest criminals in the United States. A million dollars was chump change to the top members of The Family and their rivals, The Aceros. Junior knew that he didn't belong in the presence of these real bosses. Six brought him along just to watch and listen. They were in a dining room with cathedral ceilings and windows so big that the cleaners needed a ladder to reach the top. The white granite table was thirty feet long. Seated on one side of the table were seven members of The Family, Junior and Six mixed among the members. On the opposite side were seven members of The Aceros. At ends of the table, were the leaders of each syndicate. Mr. Chow at one end. Carlos Vegara at the other. Six stood to address the bosses.

"I called this meeting because something needs to be done about Molnarova. He moved into your territory last year and he infringed upon ours a couple weeks ago. Boundaries aren't being respected and I think we need to send a message. If something isn't done, this could lead to all-out war. If that happens, we need to know who our allies are."

Carlos snorted. "So, do you have your employees think for you too, Mr. Chow?"

"Fuck you, Carlos," Mr. Chow retorted. "James is a respected advisor and a personal friend. He's also a great fighter. I think you could take lessons from him so that you can learn how to take a punch. Last I remember, you have a glass jaw."

Carlos's top lip twitched with anger. "That was a sucker punch, you son of a bitch! I'll throw hands with you anywhere and anytime."

"Gentlemen, you can save the dick measuring contest for later!" Juan, Carlo's second in command yelled, slapping the table. "What James is saying is right. We need to come together to rid ourselves of a mutual problem. Our organizations depend on it."

Carlos's face remained twisted in a snarl, unwilling to admit he needed The Family's help. "We don't need their help. It was a mistake setting up this meeting."

Mr. Chow shook his head. "You will always be a fool, Carlos. Why can't we let bygones be bygones? Our men are right. We need to become allies again. The Russians have overstepped. We need to be united."

Carlos continued to look salty. "I swore that I would never do business with you again. I cannot go back on my word."

Junior understood Carlos's position. A boss couldn't break his word or balls for nobody.

"You made an emotional decision. In this business, you should never make a decision based on emotions. You know that," Mr. Chow admonished.

Carol sneered. "And you also know not to break the code. Never fuck with your partners woman."

"She wasn't your woman. She was your sidepiece."

"MY sidepiece. Keyword, MY!" Carlos yelled.

Junior gave his brother a questioning look when realized that a woman had come between the bosses. Six responded with a shrug.

"Okay. If it will make you feel better, I will let you sleep with one of my sidepieces. How about Sandy?" Mr. Chow offered.

An evil smile spread slowly across Carlos's face. "No. I want Olivia, the Peruvian."

Mr. Chow paused, about to deny the request.

Six nodded to his boss.

"Fine," Mr. Chow reluctantly agreed. "I will arrange it soon. You are an asshole for that. I hope your dick falls off."

Carlos smiled like he won a billion dollar prize. Junior sat at the table looking back at forth to each of the bosses, surprised they allowed pussy to come between them. What was he supposed to learn from all of this? What not to do? The atmosphere turned festive after the bosses agreed to squash their beef and come to each other's aid. The double doors of the dining room opened and in came the drinks, drugs, and fine ass women. Junior grabbed a glass of Hennessey from one of the women before finding his brother.

"What the fuck was I supposed to learn from that?" He asked, not hiding the disappointment. "Them niggas suckas. They got all this money and power but they fighting over some side bitches. Where they do that at?"

"When you have everything you ever wanted, you start owning people. Those side bitches mean more than money, guns, and work. They invested emotionally into those relationships."

Junior waved off Six's explanation. "That's bullshit, brah, and you know it. Them niggas was willing to jeopardize they whole organization over some pussy. I don't respect that. Ain't no lesson in that."

"You sure about that?"

Junior locked eyes with his brother for a moment trying to guess what he was implying. "The only lesson I can see is to not be like them suckas."

Six smiled. "You're learning. Good job."

"That's the lesson for real? To not be like them."

"That's it, lil brah. Stick to what you believe in. Our principles grew from our environment. That's who we are at our core. Don't let the money change that. When I am the leader of The Family, I'ma allow the instincts that I learned from running around in Parklawn to guide me."

Junior smiled at his brother, liking the jewel. And then it dawned on him what Six said while explaining the lesson. "You about to be the leader of The Family?"

"You caught that, huh?" Six grinned. "That's why I couldn't get to Milwaukee after the house got shot up. I was in Japan with Mr. Chow talking about his successor. He chose me."

Junior stared at his brother in amazement. "On what? Are you serious?"

"Yeah, my nigga. I'm finna be the boss of all bosses. Keep that to yo' chest though. We haven't told the other members. We gon' talk more later. Right now, I need to go see what's up with my girl and her company. In a minute."

Junior watched his brother walk away, still shocked by the news. Six was about to be a real boss. Damn, that shit was amazing. "He's not a God, is he?"

Junior turned as a tall light skinned nigga approached. It was Brian Tammany, a member of the family that loved giving him a hard time. "What's up, Brian?"

"The way you're looking at your brother is what's up. We have all these fine ass women walking around here in thousand dollar dresses, but you can't take your eyes off James. You straight?"

Junior mugged Brian. "Yeah, I'm straight. Fuck kinda question is that?"

"No, I don't mean are you straight like are you okay. I mean are you straight as in do you want one of those girls that have a little something extra, if you know what I mean?"

Junior thought about busting Brian in his shit. "I don't play that gay shit, fam," he said aggressively.

When Brian seen how mad Junior got, he bust out laughing. "Relax, kid. I was just playing. Damn."

"I don't play that gay shit."

"Okay, okay. I'll remember that. So, what did you think about the bosses fighting over pussy? They can have their choice in millions of women, but they want to start a world war over a sidepiece. I mean, Sandy looks good but she ain't worth going to war over. I could see if she was J-Lo. Now, that's a piece of pussy worth dying for."

Junior looked at Brian like he was from another planet. "What? Man, you tripping. Ain't no pussy worth dying or going to war or jail over. Especially, not J-Lo. She fucked everybody."

Brian's face became serious. "Hey, you don't play that gay shit and I don't play about J-Lo. You better watch your mouth."

Junior paused, unsure how to respond.

Brian bust out laughing. "I'm just kidding, kid. Relax. I know she fucked everybody in the industry, but I still love her. Anyway, how's the takeover going? You're supposed to take over the projects, right?"

Junior knew he couldn't tell Brian the takeover was slowed down because he was running from the police for about a murder. So he lied. "Yeah, it's going good. Just a couple more moves, and it'll belong to me and my team."

"That's good. I like to see the younger members succeed. Let me know if you need anything. I don't care what it is, if I can help you out, I will. Okay?"

"Okay."

"Now, let's put the straight talk and my J-Lo confessions to rest and find some women to party with. You see any you like?" Junior surfed through the sea of women that were walking around the mansion. There had to be at least thirty of them. A short and stacked Latin woman with purple hair caught his eye. She wore a form fitting pantsuit that showed her curvy frame. "Yeah. Purple hair and white pantsuit."

"Oh, you like 'em thick, huh? Okay. Who else?"

"That's it. I think she the baddest one in here."

Brian looked disappointed. "Lesson number one, kid. When the women are paid for, you can have as many as you want. I'm having a foursome tonight. Three pussies and three mouths are better than one. Later kid."

Junior watched as Brian walked through the mansion grabbing women like he was shopping for shoes. After collecting three sexy ladies, he gave Junior a nod and smile before walking up the stairs with his arms around their necks. When Junior looked around, he noticed members of both families linking up with women. Even Six and Santana had a bad Asian woman smashed between them checking her mouth with their tongues. Taking his cue, Junior approached the woman with the purple hair.

"You look like you need some company."

She smiled. "I was hoping that you approached me. Old guys are not really my thing."

He took a page out of Brian's book and wrapped an arm around her neck. "Nothing old about me, baby. How about you pick a friend, and we all go have a good time."

"Good time are my two favorite words," she giggled before searching the crowd. Then, she pointed to a slim dark-skinned woman with big breasts. "I like dark meat and I've been thinking about sucking her titties all night."

***

Junior hadn't answered the phone all morning and Quitta didn't know if she should be pissed off or worried. He was supposed to be staying with his brother for a week to let the heat cool down. Ever since she got the phone, they talked all day long, but she couldn't reach him this morning. It was 1:00 pm Milwaukee time and 11:00 am on the west coast. Junior was an early riser, normally waking up around 8 or 9. And he always answered when she called. Except for this morning.

Quitta lay on the thin mattress rubbing her stomach and thinking about the baby inside. It was too early to tell the baby's sex, but she hoped it was a girl. She wanted a daughter to dress up in all the flyest clothes and take care of her hair so that it would be long and pretty. And she would be a better mother to her daughter than her mother was to her. Teach her what to do and what kind of woman to be. And the most important lesson she would teach her baby girl is to be her own woman.

"Miss Ware, you have a visit." The intercom buzzed.

Quitta flinched, instinctively grabbing her chest as she looked at the intercom near her cell door. She thought she was busted with the cellphone. "Scary ass," she giggled, laughing at herself.

After tucking the phone on her hip and putting the charger in her bra, she left the room. Her stomach fluttered as she thought about Detective Russo. She liked the big bearded white man and couldn't figure out why. She wasn't attracted to him nor did she like the beard. But she did like his eyes, personality, and the fact that he would do anything for her. Even risk his job by bringing her a cellphone. Which she used to keep in touch with him and Junior. He made it obvious that he wanted more than a friendship. At first, it felt weird because she had never fucked around with a white man. Let alone, a cop. But the more she talked to him and got to know him, the more she thought about what it would be like. Now, her curiosity was starting to get the best of her.

"Thank you, officer. I got it from here," Detective Russo dismissed the guard. "Wow. That pregnancy glow is real. You make that jumpsuit look like high fashion."

Quitta giggled as she sat down, liking the compliment. "Stop playing."

"I'm serious. Maternity jail wear could be the next big thing. And you would be the perfect model."

"You over doing it now. Maternity jail wear will never be a thing. Nobody wants to look like they just got out of jail."

"You must not have any white friends. We support all kinds of crazy shit. Last year, my brother and his wife dressed up as inmates for Halloween."

"Y'all do do crazy shit." Quitta giggled. "I never understood why y'all jump out of airplanes or swim with sharks. That shit seem stupid to me."

"It's stupid to me, too. Some things just can't be explained. I never understood why y'all wear socks with sandals or why black men always grab their crotch. Is it because of the penis myth?"

"Socks with sandals is easy. Sandals are shoes. You wear socks with your shoes. Plus, some people got ugly feet and they need to hide them muthafuckas. The crotch thing and dick myth, I don't know. Maybe it's just a culture thing."

"Yeah. It's probably a cultural thing because the penis myth doesn't ring true with all the guys. I've seen some pinkies out there." He laughed.

Quitta bust out laughing. "Why are you looking at dicks?"

He lifted his palms in defense. "It's part of the job, Quitta. But believe me, I don't enjoy looking at other men's cocks. I'm straight. You don't have to worry about that. And how about we talk about something other than me having to look at another man's junk. So, how are you doing?"

"I'm okay. Kind of worried about Junior. He didn't answer the phone this morning. I've been a little worried ever since I found out Detective Johnson was looking for him."

"I can make some calls when I get back. I know some people that work at the 7th District Station in Milwaukee."

Quitta's eyes lit up. "Really? You would do that?"

"I would do anything for you to look at me like that again."

She didn't know how to respond and gave an awkward, "Oh."

Silence filled the room until the awkward moment passed.

"I'm sorry. I didn't mean to make you uncomfortable."

"It's okay," Quitta recovered. "It's just that nobody ever said that to me, so I didn't know how to react. Nobody talks to me the way you do."

"That's because nobody knows how special you are. You're a smart and loyal woman who deserves more out of the men you give yourself to. You can do a hell of a lot better than what you have."

The words made Quitta's insides melt. "Thank you. I really mean that. I feel like you really know me. It's crazy."

"You know why you feel that way? It's because I listen and pay attention. Most men don't know how to do that because they are so concerned with their own problems."

Quitta thought about the conversations she had been having with Junior. They were mostly about him and his problems. The realization pissed her off a little. "Damn. You're right. I'm the one in jail but damn near every time I talk to Junior, we talk about his problems."

"What if it's time for something different? Something new."

Quitta stared into the cop's eyes, reading the desire. The way he looked at her told that he would give her anything she wanted and worship the ground she walked on. "I don't even know what to say."

Detective Russo got up and closed the distance between them. Before Quitta knew what was happening, he leaned down and kissed her. She froze, shocked by the bold move. His thin lips and bushy beard felt foreign.

"I had to do that," he whispered with their faces a few inches apart.

Quitta stared into those eyes that had become familiar and yet still a little strange. They reflected that she was unsure about the kiss and hopefulness of more. And surprisingly, Quitta found herself wanting more. Without giving herself time to sort out thoughts or feelings, she grabbed two handfuls of his beard and pulled him close.

Sparks flew when their lips were touched again, mouths parted, and tongues danced. An involuntary moan escaped from Quitta's throat and for a moment she felt like Whitney Houston in The Bodyguard. Detective Russo became engulfed by desire and reached down to wrap one arm around Quitta's lower back and the other around her thigh, lifting her from the chair and into his arms. Quitta yelped, surprised, and turned on by his strength and passion, wrapping her arms around his neck and legs around his waist as they made out passionately. She didn't know where this was going, but she wasn't going to stop. Her pussy was dripping wet and if he wanted it, she was going to give it up.

"Damn. We can't do this here," he moaned, breaking the kiss.

Quitta continued holding onto her night in shining armor, wanting more. "Why not?"

He nodded towards the door. "Because of the windows."

Quitta turned to look out the small window on the door. When she realized what happened and what was at stake, she hurried from his arms and sat back down. "Shit. I forgot where I was."

"Shit. So did I," the detective said, wiping his forehead and adjusting the bulge in the crotch of his jeans. "If we would've been caught..." He didn't finish the sentence. There wasn't a need. They both knew what would've happened if a guard walked by and seen a detective making out with an inmate. "I have to get you back to your unit. I need to get out of here."

Quitta could hear the anger and frustration in his voice. "I'm sorry, Nate.

He shook his head and let out an irritated breath. "You didn't do anything. It was me. I kissed you. I don't even know what the fuck I'm doing. I could get fired and arrested for this shit. Give me the phone back. I have to stop this before I lose my job and my freedom."

Quitta wore the confusion on her face. She didn't understand how they had gone from almost fucking to him taking the phone. It had become her lifeline and she didn't want to give it up. "Wait, Nate. Why? What's going on?"

His eyes turned dark as storm clouds, and he became serious. "Give me the goddam phone, Quitta!"

The flash of anger scared and confused her even more. She pulled the phone off her hip and charger from her bra and gave it to him. They locked eyes while he shoved the contraband in his pocket. He looked like he wanted to say something, but he didn't. Then, he walked out the door.

"I'm done with her," he told the guard.

***

Quitta paced the small cell, moving ten steps to the door and another ten before she was back at the window. She had been walking for fifteen minutes, mind on overdrive, thinking about Nate. She didn't understand the abrupt change. He pursued her and broke the rules to get close to her. She had finally let her guard down and now that they were closer than they'd ever been, he flipped this script. It

93

didn't making sense. Did he really panic and overreact or was there something bigger at play? Was it about getting the phone back because they had gotten enough to convict her? She couldn't figure it out and the uncertainty made her want to move. So, she paced. And then there was Junior. Where the fuck was he and why wasn't he answering the phone? Did he get locked up? Damn, she needed the phone back. When she couldn't take the uncertainty any more, she left the cell and went to the phone bank. She dialed Junior's number and prayed that he answered. When he didn't, she called again and again. After the fifth try, he answered.

"Quitta?" He questioned.

"Yeah, this me. Where yo' ass been? I been tryna call you all morning."

"Man, I was out all night with Six. We had to go through California and didn't get back until four this morning. What's up with you? Where the slapper?"

"Some bullshit. He got mad and took it."

"He took it? For what? What he get mad about?"

"I can't say right now. It's some bullshit ass emotional shit."

"You didn't have nothing about me in it, did you? You know these muthafuckas tryna get me."

Quitta got mad. "Nigga, everything ain't about you, Junior! I'm the one in jail, nigga. You out in Vegas and California fucking all kinds of bitches and I'm in here pregnant with yo' baby fighting for my life. Fuck you! You talking about them tryna get you when they already got me and all you care about is what they tryna do to you. What kind of shit is that? Why is it always about you? I'm facing forty years in prison and they won't even give me a bail because of yo' ass. Fuck you, nigga."

Junior let out a long stressed breath. "What the fuck is you talking about, nigga? I'm tryna get yo' ass out. If yo' ass wouldn't have been fucking with Steph bitch ass, yo' ass wouldn't be in there. Don't try to blame me, nigga. I'm doing what I can to get you out. Fuck is you talking 'bout?"

His response sent Quitta over the edge. "Oh, that's what we on now? All this is my fault, nigga? You the one that wanted to go to that muthafuckin club, nigga. I told you I didn't want to be a part of none of that shit. That was you and—"

"Shut the fuck up, Quitta! This shit being recorded. What the fuck is wrong with you?" He snapped.

"You what's wrong with me, nigga! You got me in here and now you talking about this shit is my fault! You did that shit, not me. I'm tryna be a real bitch and take the case but you tryna treat me like a weak ass bitch. I got yo' baby in my stomach, nigga. Fuck you talking about?"

"Quitta, stop saying that extra shit, okay. If you wanna talk, we can talk. But you got to quit that extra shit or I'm hanging up. This shit is recorded, and they can use this shit in court. Control yo' emotions, nigga."

She didn't want him to hang up nor say anything that could be used against them, so she calmed down a little. "Well stop tryna make it seem like it's me. I'm doing what I'm supposed to do. I just want you to listen to me and my problems. I want to feel like a priority. It's always about you."

"Okay, Quitta. Tell me about your problems. What's on your mind?"

Now that she had his full attention, she didn't even want it. It actually irritated her. "Why you gotta say it like that? Like I'm some kind of charity case or you doing me a favor?"

"What is you talking about? You just said I don't listen to you and then when I ask you, you won't tell me. What am I supposed this do?"

The tears came quick. "I don't know, Junior. I don't know what to do or what to think. I think this damn baby making me crazy. I just want to come home," she cried.

"I'm tryna get you out, baby mama. You just gotta stay strong. They don't got nothing on you. Henrik said the same thing. You good. Just stay strong. You a souljah. You got this; you hear me? You got it."

"Yeah, I hear you." She sniffled and wiped away tears. "What are we going to do when I come home?"

"What you mean?"

"I'm talking about us? What's gon' happen? Is we gon' be together and raise our kids in a two parent house? Do you still love me? What's going to happen?"

"C'mon, Quitta. We already talked about this. Let's just focus on getting you out. We can figure the rest out later."

"I don't want to talk about it later. I want to talk about it now. This is what's on my mind. This is what I think about every day. I want you to tell me what we doing? Are we gon' be together when I get out?"

"Man, Quitta," he breathed. "We wasn't together before you got locked up."

The truth hurt. It felt like she got punched in the chest. "I'm going through this for you and this how you gon' do me?"

"But you fucked my cousin. You crossed the line."

"And you fucked Nyla, nigga. What you mean?"

"It's different, Quitta. Lo-Dog is my blood. That shit cut and I can't get past it. I'm being real and telling you how I feel. I can't let that go."

The tears came back stronger when she realized it was really over. "So, me going through this don't mean nothing? This don't show you that I love you and I'm loyal to you? This don't show you that I would do anything for you?"

Junior stayed quiet. There was nothing he could say to take away her pain, so he let her cry.

"So you can fuck who you want to fuck, and you just expect me to get over it but the shit I do last forever? That's some bullshit and you know it. I hate you for making me go through this. I'm still staying real to you and doing this time for you so our kids can have they daddy around, but you don't even give a fuck. You ain't shit, Junior. Matter of fact, I don't even want to talk to you no more. Bye."

CHAPTER 7

Dazè stepped onto to front porch of his Gail's house and sat on the steps. He looked towards his grandmother's project apartment across the street to see if anyone was awake. It was 8:00 in the morning so the apartment, as well as the rest of projects, were quiet. Squirrels ran across the grass with mouths filled with food and birds chirped and flew up from tree to tree. Cars passed by every few minutes and people with important business walked quickly towards their destination. Dazè relished in the early morning project serenity. This was freedom and it felt damn good.

"I'm ready," Renae said, popping up at his side.

"About time, girl. Damn. I thought you was in there making yo' clothes as long as it took you," he joked.

"Fuck you, nigga. When you this duggy, you gotta take yo' time, baby."

Dazè looked her from head to toe. She wore a lime green long sleeved Nike shirt, Rockstar jeans, and a pair of lime green and white Air Max. She wasn't one of those over made females who needed to dress sexy and show skin. She dressed for comfort, and he liked that.

"It took thirty minutes to put on some jeans, a T-shirt, and Air Max? We wearing damn near the same thing, and it only took me five minutes."

"But you don't make it look as good as I do." She smiled, squatting down and pecking his lips.

"You got a point there. Now, let's go before we piss my P.O. off and she lock me up."

They jumped in Renae's car and took the ten minute drive to the Probation and Parole Building. Renae waited in the car while Dazè went inside for the 8:30 meeting. While in the waiting room, Dazè surfed Facebook, taking a moment to study Jason's page. The snitch had no idea he was being stalked from a fake page or that his days were numbered. Visions of sticking a knife in the bitch ass nigga's face made Dazè smile.

"Mr. Crawford?"

Dazè snapped out of the murderous thoughts and looked up from the phone. Janice Dickens stood at the door wearing a smile. She was a fortyish white woman with maroon hair, lots of tattoos, and a bullring in her nose. "Good morning, Miss Dickens. How you doing?"

"I have the best job in the world. How could I be doing anything other than great?" She said sarcastically. "C'mon, let's get this meeting over with."

Daze followed her down a hallway filled with small offices and into her compact space.

"Have a seat, Dazè. How are you doing?"

"I'm good. Enjoying my freedom. Taking it one day at a time."

"That's good. You know that we have to meet twice a month for six months. After that, we'll go to Zoom visits once a month and then once every three months. You okay with that?"

"I don't really got a choice, do I?"

"Not really." she smiled. "So, did anything change since the last time we met? Buy a car, get a job, police contact?"

"No, to all or those. I enrolled in school, though. I'ma do it online. Associate Degree in Liberal Arts at MATC. I'm still looking for a job, too."

"That's good. Keep me posted on your progress. What about drugs? You staying clean?"

"I smoke weed here and there. It helps me relax. I be feeling kinda weird after doing all that time in the hole while I was locked up. I think that shit be messing with me a little bit. I'm thinking about seeing a doctor," he said, passing her the rehearsed lines.

"Yeah, you might need to do that. Spending thirteen years in a maximum security prison and almost half of that time in the hole can't be good for you. I would encourage you to see someone about that. You may be suffering from PTSD and not know it. I won't trip about the weed. We all need to let our hair down. But don't let it become a problem or get into anything harder."

"I won't. I don't like pills or having habits."

"Okay. If you don't have anything, our meeting is over. See you at this same time in two weeks."

After leaving the Probation and Parole Office, they headed back to the projects. Dazè was climbing from the car when John's Denali turned onto the block and parked in front of Gail's house.

"Sis, what's good? Daze, how you doing?" John asked as he climbed from the SUV.

"Cooling. Just came back from seeing the P.O."

"How that go? She on yo' ass to get a job, huh?"

"Not really. My P.O cool. She know I smoke and don't trip. I ran a script on her about PTSD from being in the hole for six years, so she let me do me."

"Damn, nigga! You did six years in the hole?"

"All together, yeah. Not six years straight. It was spread out. Three months here and six months there. They had a nigga on AC for two years for kicking off a riot in 2015."

John was amazed by Dazè's stories. "Damn, my nigga. You been through some shit."

"I know. But I'm good. Real gangsters don't fold. But how you doing? You out here kinda early. You aight?"

"I'm good. I'm finna slide over by RIP and drop off some work. Walk with me. I wanted to holla at you about something."

"Okay. What's good?"

"I wanted to ask you about catching a body. I saw that bitch in my dream last night. I went to the bitch apartment, and she answered the door wearing lingerie with bullet holes in her face. Shit had me tripping, my nigga. I couldn't even go back to sleep. Did that shit happen to you when you caught to first body?"

"Nah, it didn't happen like that for me. First time I put in work we stomped a nigga to death, and it wasn't just me. It was five of us. I'm the only one that got locked up though. I didn't dream about that shit, but I thought about it a lot. But I heard of shit like what happened to you happening before. I think that shit affect er'body different. Plus, you knew her so that shit probably hit different."

"Yeah, it do. But I know that bitch had to go. I still can't believe the bitch tried to do me like that. Punk ass bitch. Now er'body in the apartment building tryna be detectives and find out who did it.

That's why I'm glad I grabbed that bitch phone. You got rid of them mu'fuckas, right?"

"Hell yeah. Burned them Sim cards too."

"Bet. Good looking on helping me with the whole move. I don't know what I would a did without you, nigga. If Junior get knocked and I get the top slot, I'm definitely making you my right hand."

Dazè smiled at the comment, choosing to remain silent.

***

Darkness reveals truth.

Dazè played the phrase over in his mind as he hid in the bushes and watched for movement in the white house. Carolyn's house. He wore a black jogging suit, a black N95 mask over his face, and a pair of black gloves. On his waist was a 9mm Glock. In his pocket, was a hunting knife with a six inch blade. It was after midnight and heavy clouds blocked out the moon making the streets pitch black. It was the perfect night for a kill.

When he was certain the coast was clear, Dazè left the bushes, walked upon the porch, and began checking the windows until he found one that was unlocked. He opened it as quietly as he could before climbing inside. The living room was dark, so he paused to listen for movement. A TV was on in a room down the hallway. He was about to head towards the TV noise when he heard movement. Slippers were sliding across the floor, heading in his direction. Dazè moved against the wall, blending in with the dark and holding the pistol ready. Carolyn walked right by him and into the kitchen. She was short, fat, and black as tar. She wore a dark colored nightgown and slippers. He followed her into the kitchen and crept upon her.

"Oh, my God! What are you doing in my house!" Carolyn screamed.

Dazè lifted an index finger to his mask while pointing the gun at her. "Shut the fuck up," he whispered. "Where is Jason?"

"Ma, you good?" Jason called from a room down the hall.

"Tell him you good," Dazè instructed.

"I'm- I'm good. I thought I heard something," she called, staring at Dazè with wide terrified eyes.

"How many people in the house?"

"Just me and my son. Please don't hurt us. We don't have nothing here," she begged.

Her pleas had no effect on him. If anything they pissed him off even more. She didn't tell her son not to hurt him when he gave the police a statement. "Take me to Jason."

She moved slowly, walking down a short hall and into a bedroom. Jason lay in bed shirtless watching Power.

"What the fuck!" He cursed, shooting up in bed.

"You bet not move, nigga!" Dazè demanded, pointing the gun at him.

"What you want? I ain't got nothing here."

Dazè ignored him and flipped on the light while addressing Carolyn. "Find something to tie him up with."

Jason panicked. "Tie me up for what?"

"Shut the fuck up, nigga," Dazè said, keeping an eye on Carolyn. She searched the drawer and held up a two belts.

"Tie his feet together and his hands behind his back."

Carolyn did as she was told. Dazè inspected her work. When he was satisfied that Jason couldn't get free, he took off the N95 mask. The smile spreading across his lips and the horrified looks on the victims faces said more than words.

"Daze?" Jason questioned, wondering if his eyes were playing tricks on him.

"Please, Dazè. Don't hurt him. That happened a long time ago. He's sorry," Carolyn cried.

Dazè lifted the gun to Jason's face while looking Carolyn in the eyes. "What you gon' do to save him?"

She got on her knees and bowed at his feet. "I'll do anything, Dazè. Please don't kill my son. He's my only child."

"Suck my dick."

The request surprised the mother and son. Jason's face scrunched into a frown and Carolyn looked up at him with confusion in her eyes.

"What?" She questioned.

"You heard me. If you don't pull out my dick and start sucking, I'm blowing this snitch ass nigga brains out!" Dazè threatened, pointing the gun closer to Jason's face.

"Okay, okay! I'll do it!"

"C'mon, fam. What you on?" Jason asked in a whiney voice, not wanting to see his mother suck a dick.

"I'm humiliating yo' bitch ass, nigga. Let's go, Carolyn. Pull out my dick and put it in yo' mouth. This is yo' son's fault. He the reason why you doing this."

Carolyn's hands trembled as she reached up and unbuttoned Dazè's jeans. She dug inside his boxers for his semi hard dick and sucked it into her mouth. Jason closed his eyes and turned his head. Dazè swung the pistol and slapped him in the head.

"Nah, nigga. Look and see what yo' pussy ass got yo' mama doing."

Carolyn sucked Dazè weakly, barely putting more than the head in her mouth.

"C'mon, Carolyn. You almost fifty years old. I know you can suck dick better than that. You betta suck my dick like yo' son life depending on it."

The reminder of what was on the line was the extra motivation she needed to go to work. She began sucking him harder and faster, taking more of him down her throat.

"Damn, Jason. Yo' moms really know how to suck dick," Dazè moaned. When he was on the verge of busting, he stopped her. "Okay. That's enough. Stand up and take off that gown."

Carolyn shook her head as more tears formed in her eyes. "Please, Dazè. I did what you asked. Let him go."

"C'mon, fam. You proved yo' point," Jason added. "I'm sorry for giving that statement, my nigga. You ain't gotta do nothing else. I'll pay you whatever you want. Just leave my mama alone."

Dazè shook his head. "Nah, nigga. I ain't letting you off that easy. I want you to see what it look like for yo' mama to get fucked. Take off that muthafuckin gown, Carolyn."

Tears rolled down the older woman's face as she dropped the robe, revealing her sloppy body.

"Kneel on the bed."

When she assumed the position, Dazè spread her cheeks apart and spit on her asshole. Without warming her ass up, he shoved his dick inside, ripping her rectum. Carolyn's painful screams were music to his ears. He rammed her ass as hard as he could while Jason watched. Getting revenge in such a way excited Dazè, causing him to bust quickly. He thrust his hips one last time, emptying his balls in Carolyn's ass. And before she could move a muscle, he lay the pistol on the bed and pulled the hunting knife from his pocket. Then, he grabbed a head full of her hair, yanking her head back and exposing her throat. The knife cut deep into the flesh of her neck, slicing her carotid artery. She made a gurgling noise as she grabbed her neck and fell on the bed.

"MAMA!" Jason screamed.

Dazè stood at the foot of the bed and watched Carolyn flail around, shit dripping from her ass and blood pouring from her neck. Jason continued screaming for his mother until her movements slowed and she eventually ceased moving.

"Dazè, C'mon, brah! Please, my nigga! Don't kill me," Jason cried.

The killer smiled as he approached his victim, the knife dripping blood as it hung at his side. When Jason seen that he couldn't escape the judgement, he jumped up from the bed and hopped out of the room. Dazè caught up quickly and dug the knife deep into the middle of his back. Jason stumbled and fell on the floor. Dazè climbed on his back and reached an arm around to grab him by the chin, lifting his head and exposing his neck. Then, he sliced from one side of his neck to the other. Jason choked and gurgled on blood until his body began twitching.

After watching the life drain from Jason's body, Dazè went to grab his gun from the room and find something to start a fire. There was a bottle of alcohol in the bathroom cabinet. He poured half of it on Carolyn and the bed before setting it on fire. Then, he grabbed some clothes from the drawer and threw them on top of Jason's body on the hallway floor. He poured the rest of the alcohol on the clothes, the floor, and walls before lighting the hallway on fire. When the house began catching fire, he disappeared into the night.

***

"Girl, this bitch was tryna turn my ass out. I'm sitting on the damn bed scared to move while my baby daddy in the corner pulling on his dick and telling me to relax. I never messed around with a girl before, so I don't know what to do. I only agreed to the shit because he kept sweating me about it but now that the girl was in the hotel room, I was too scared to move," Tiffany explained.

Quitta's eyes were wide with excitement as she sat at the table listening to her friend's sexual escapade. "So what happened? Did you let her eat yo' pussy?"

Tiffany closed her eyes and shook her head from side to side like she was reliving the moment. "Did I! Girl, not only did this bitch eat my pussy but she damn near turned my ass gay!" Tiffany laughed.

"Hell nah!" Quitta yelled.

"Yes, girl! When she seen that I was new to threesomes and girls, she started doing shit to help me relax. Took off my socks and started sucking my toes and shit while looking me in my eyes. And she was a sexy bitch, too. Kissed her way up my thighs all the way to my pussy and started sucking my pussy like she had a vacuum in her mouth. And she did it all. Licked my pussy, fucked me with her tongue, and licked ass. Had me cumming like I was a water faucet. I never met a nigga that ate my pussy or made me cum like that bitch did."

"Damn, bitch. It sound like you got turned out. You sure you ain't gay?"

"Hell nah. I love dick too much to be gay. But if a bitch wanna suck my juices, I ain't gon' deny her the taste or myself the pleasure. I'm telling you, Quitta. You ain't never had yo' pussy ate until you let another bitch do it. Bitches know what other bitches want."

Quitta had a quick fantasy of Tiffany's snagged tooth ass between her legs. "I don't know if I need all that. I can cum from penetration. Shit, Junior never ate my pussy and I been fucking with this nigga since I was a teenager, and we got a baby together."

Tiffany's eye's bucked. "Yo baby daddy never ate yo' pussy?"

"Nope. He said he ain't eating nothing that bleed." Quitta laughed.

Tiffany shook her head. "I don't see how you could do it. Ain't no nigga I'm fucking with sticking his dick in me if he ain't licking me. Now if I'm turning a trick or some shit, I just want to fuck and get it over with. But my nigga got to get his face wet."

"Ware, you got a professional visit!" The guard called.

Quitta's heart skipped a beat when she heard the guard. It was Russo. "Okay. Here I come."

"Damn, girl. Yo ass get a visit once a week," Tiffany commented.

"It's probably my lawyer. He damn near the best lawyer in the state and he keep me in the loop about what's going on with my case," Quitta lied. She hadn't told anybody about Russo or the phone and planned on keeping it that way. Loose lips sink ships. When the escorting guard came for Quitta, they walked past the conference rooms she was used to meeting the detective in. "Where we going?" She asked.

"Oh, the conference rooms are being worked on, so you have to use the old ones," the guard explained nonchalantly. "They should be ready in a few days."

The rooms looked fine to her, and she didn't see any workers or equipment. Something was up. "Who am I seeing in it?" She asked, hoping they weren't playing a trick or setting her up.

"A cop, I think. Guy with a big, big beard."

She was nervous about seeing Detective Russo again. It had been a week since the last visit, and she didn't know what to expect. Would he still be mad? Was he about to flip the script and get on some police shit? And why the hell were they switching rooms? When they got to the room, Detective Russo was waiting.

"Thank you, officer. I'll call you when I need you."

Quitta looked around the room as she stepped inside. It was smaller than the old rooms and it didn't have windows.

"Have a seat," Russo said, gesturing towards the small table and two chairs in the middle of the room.

Quitta eyeballed the cop as she sat, trying to gauge his demeanor and attitude.

He noticed the look. "What?"

"I'm tryna see what you on, man. The last time that I saw you, you went from kissing me to snapping on me. I don't know what kind of games you playing and I want to know what you on."

Russo sat down across from her wearing a regretful look. "I'm sorry, Quitta, but I got scared and took it out on you. I panicked. After we kissed, I got so caught up in what would've happened if we got caught that I got scared. I didn't plan on meeting you and catching feelings for you. I never thought I would be sneaking cellphones into a jail for a woman being charged with murder that I barely know. I'm a thirty two year old detective that's been on the force for fourteen years. I've busted drug dealers, murderers, and rapists. I'm a cop. My friends and peers want you and your kids' father convicted for murder. I'm in a fucked up spot and when I thought about it all, I panicked. Can you blame me?"

Quitta listened to Russo's explanation, paying close attention to his body language as he spoke. He looked sincere. Like he was really conflicted about the choices he made and ones he would make in the future. "No, I can't blame you now that you put it like that. That's why I was scared to trust you. You the police. It was hard to believe that you would just risk everything for me. I'm pregnant with another man's baby and I'm being charged with murder and you coming in here telling me I'm special. I thought you was tryna set me up."

"I'm not trying to set you up. This is real. I could really lose my job and be charged with real crimes for what is happening."

They had a stare off, reading each other's eyes and the things they weren't saying with words.

"So, why are you here now? What's going on?" Quitta asked.

The detective reached across the table and grabbed her hand. "Because I want my friend back. I wanted to apologize to you and ask you to still be my friend. I thought about you a lot during this past week and realized you're somebody that I want in my life. I really meant it when I said you were special."

Quitta still hadn't decided if she could fully trust him. She wasn't sure if he was really catching feelings or just being a good detective and doing whatever necessary to get incriminating evidence on Junior. "I don't even know what to say, man. I have so many questions still. Why me? How do I know you not just being a good detective?"

He chuckled. "I mean, I'm a good detective but I'm not so good that I could make up feelings or kiss someone I'm trying to stick a murder on. And I can't really explain why you. I've never met anyone like you and your loyalty intrigued the hell out of me. And then I got to know you and discovered that you're a good woman. So, I guess that's why you. My question to you is, why not you?"

Quitta was lost for words. He sounded so convincing.

"I also brought you this," he said, pulling out the phone and charger. "I'm sorry that I took it. Plus, I missed hanging out with you. Now, we can talk whenever we want."

Quitta was happy as hell to see the phone but hesitant to take it.

He noticed the hesitation. "Go ahead. Take it. I won't take it back."

"It's not that. It's just... I don't know if I can trust you."

Disappointment flashed in his gray eyes. "Okay. Tell me what else that I could do to make you trust me. You name it and I'll do it. Anything."

Quitta thought for a moment. What could he do to show her that he wasn't setting her up. Only one thing came to mind. "Shit, break me out."

He bust out laughing. "C'mon, Quitta. You have to be reasonable. It's damn near impossible to break out of jail. Too many doors, too many guards, and we'll probably get killed. Think of something else. Reasonable."

Quitta thought for a moment. Suddenly, Tiffany's face jumped in her head along with the story about getting her pussy ate by a woman. There were no windows in the room, and she knew for sure that the police couldn't have sex with the people they were investigating. There was no way they could explain that to a jury.

"Eat my pussy," she blurted.

His eyes grew wide. And wider. And wider. "What?"

She doubled down. "I would believe you if you ate my pussy."

He laughed, running a hand through his beard, face turning red. "You serious?"

Quitta nodded. "I am."

He sat back in the chair to stare at her for a moment. Then, something flashed in his eyes. "Okay. If I do this, there is something that you have to do for me?"

Quitta cocked her head to the side. "You want me to suck your dick?"

"No. I mean, you can if you want to," he stumbled. "But that's not what I want. What I want is for you to set up a meeting with me and Junior. I've been thinking about an insurance policy. If I get fired or charged with anything for messing with you, I'm going to need some financial stability. I want to work for him in Lacrosse."

Quitta knew Junior wouldn't agree to the meet. "I don't know if he'll do that."

"That's why I need you to convince him that I'll be an asset. I'm not trying to set you guys up. I'm serious. I want to sell drugs for him in Lacrosse. Who better than me? I can do whatever I want. I'm the police. And a detective at that. On my mother's life, I'm not trying to trick you."

Quitta studied him for a long moment. "I could talk to him, but I can't promise you that he'll talk to you."

"I believe you can," he challenged. "You have more power than you know."

They stared at each other for a long moment. Quitta's mind raced with uncertainties. Could she convince Junior to meet with him? Should she let him eat her pussy? What would it feel like to get her pussy ate by a white man? Could they do it without being caught? Would he want more?

Detective Russo got up, grabbing Quitta's hand and pulling her to her feet. He stared into her eyes for a moment before leaning down to kiss her. Then, he hooked his thumbs into the waistband of her pants and panties, pulling them down while dropping to his knees. Lust danced in his gray eyes as he moved forward and kissed her hairless V. Quitta's body shivered when his lips touched her pelvic area, her pussy dripping wet with anticipation. He removed one of her pants legs before pushing her onto the table and spreading her legs. He flicked his tongue up and down her slit a few times making Quitta suck in deep breaths to keep from moaning. Then, he used his fingers to spread her lips, exposing her swollen pearl. When his mouth clamped on her pleasure button, Quitta felt like she was about to lose it. It took all her will power not to moan as Russo sucked and licked her. It had been so long since she got her pussy ate that the orgasm came quick.

"Mmmmmm!" She let out a muffled moan, biting her bottom lip while grabbing his head and grinding her juices all over his beard.

"Damn, you're wet as hell," Russo smiled as he stood and tried to wipe her juices from his beard.

"It's been a minute," Quitta breathed, checking out the bulge in his pants. She wanted to know what he was working with.

Russo seen where she was looking. "Can I get mine?"

Quitta thought of Junior and his baby inside of her womb. A part of her felt wrong for fucking around while she was pregnant with his baby. But then, she thought of the last conversation about their relationship. It was over. Plus, she knew he didn't feel guilty about fucking other women while she was locked up. "Let me see what you working with."

Russo moved quickly, unbuckling his pants, and unleashing the meat. Quitta was pleasantly surprised by the package. He wasn't packing, but he wasn't short either. The head was reddish purple and looked like he was about to bust if he didn't hurry inside her. So, she didn't make him wait any longer.

"Holy shit!" He whispered as he slid into the wettest and warmest pussy he ever felt in his life.

"Oh, yeah," Quitta whispered.

The cop moved his hips quickly, fucking her with short fast strokes. Two minutes later, he plunged deep inside her and bust a nut. "Holy shit! I can't believe we just did that," Russo said as they pulled up their clothes.

"I can't believe I just fucked a white man," Quitta giggled, shaking her head from side to side in disbelief. "And in jail, too. Oh my God."

"Once you go white, you'll always be alright," he cracked.

Quitta laughed. "What that mean?"

"It means that I got you. Forever," he said before leaning down to kiss her.

Quitta accepted the kiss hungrily, wishing they could spend more time together. "Damn, Nate. You keep on surprising me."

"I know. That's how I do. And when you beat this stupid ass case and get released, I'm going to have so many more surprises." Quitta stared at him for a moment trying to figure out how she would explain to everyone in her world that she was friends with a detective. If he planned on surprising her when she got out, that meant he wanted more.

"Why you looking at me like that?" He asked.

"I don't know what to do with you. I never expected this and now I'm trying to figure it out. You are one of the craziest things that has ever happened to me, and I don't know what to do or how to explain it."

"I was thinking the same thing a few days ago. I just decided to go with the flow and see where we end up. Kind of like white water rafting. You can't fight the current. You have to go with it."

Quitta frowned. "What the hell you talking about?"

"White water rafting. Its where you get in a little kayak and go with strong river currents," he explained, watching Quitta's face to see if she was catching on.

"Oh. Okay."

"You have no idea what I'm talking about, do you?" he laughed.

She shook her head. "No. Sounds like some white people shit because we definitely don't do that in the hood."

"Yeah. It's definitely white people shit. Shit that you will learn about. Eventually."

She picked up on the hidden message. "Yeah. Eventually."

"Good." He smiled at the confirmation, happy that she was feeling the same way.

"I think we've been in here too long and you probably need a shower, huh?"

"Yeah. Yo' nut is dripping down my leg."

J-Blunt

CHAPTER 8

It was a little after ten in the morning when Junior pulled up in front of his mother's house and parked. He had just come from the airport and hadn't been in Parklawn for ten days. It felt good to be back home. He missed the sights and sounds of the projects. And the smell. A combination of grass, gasoline, and creek water from the creek that ran down Congress Street. He walked in the house and was quickly greeted by Assassin and Mooka.

"Daddy!" Mooka yelled, running beside the German Shepard and into his father's arms.

"What's up, Young Money! What you up to?"

"Nothing. Playing with Assassin. You not leaving no more, right? We gotta play my new game that Uncle John bought me."

"What? You got a new game! Let me see."

Mooka climbed from his father's arms and turned on the thirty two inch TV on the wall and the PlayStation 5. "It's called Final Fantasy. It's cold, dad."

Junior had just settled on the couch to play the game when his mom walked in the living room talking on the phone. "Hey, son."

"What up, moms. Who you talking to?"

"Yo sister. Here. She want to talk to you."

"Lil white girl, what's up?" Junior cracked.

"What's up, ugly? What you doing?"

"Shit. I just got back from Vegas. Sitting here playing this game with Mooka."

"What you was doing in Vegas?"

"I needed to get away for a minute. Dude that booked you tryna get me too. I gotta get up with my lawyer later on and go in."

"Damn, brother. His bitch ass tryna take down our whole family."

"I know. But he don't got shit. He fishing. What's up with you? How you doing?"

"I'm good. Tryna keep my head up and tryna stop from beating these girls ass. I don't know how I'ma do this five years without killing one of these bitches. They all talk jazzy like I don't got these hands. Like I ain't with the shit."

"Man, you might have to make a couple examples and then once they see you don't fuck around, they gon' leave you alone."

"Don't tell her that, Junior!" Gail yelled. "You supposed to be telling her to calm down so she can come home."

"It don't work like that, ma. They prey on the weak in there. If she acting like she won't go, they gon' keep trying her and eventually start tryna take her stuff," Junior explained. "You gotta get yo hands dirty early so you can chill later. That's the way it work in the joint. If they see that you sweet, its gon' be worse."

"And ain't nothing sweet about me, nigga," Nicole said matter of factly. "You gon' come visit the next time mommy nem come? You missed the last visit, nigga."

"I just told you I was out of town. But don't trip. I'ma be at the next one. That's my word."

Junior kicked it with his sister until the call ended and then played the game with Mooka. Dazè came downstairs about thirty minutes later.

"Junior, what's good, family? When you get back in town?"

"I just came from the airport. What's up with you? How the hustle going?"

"I'm good. Nigga line slapping harder than Will Smith when he slapped Chris Rock," Dazè cracked.

"I'm 'bout to make some rounds in a minute. Check on RIP nem. How John do filling my shoes while I was gone?"

Dazè paused, causing Junior to shoot him a glance.

"Did something happen?"

"He did aight. Had a minor situation that we took care of."

Junior dropped the joystick, forgetting about the game. "A minor situation? What that mean?"

"Lil bro had to put in some work."

Junior's mouth dropped open and eyes bucked. He talked to John almost every day while he was out of town, and this was the first he heard about John putting in work. "John laid something down?"

Dazè nodded. "He had to. It was a setup."

"Daddy, you gotta play the game with me!" Mooka whined.

Junior wanted to spend time with his son but the news about John demanded his attention. "I'ma play with you later, Young Money. I need to holla at Dazè."

The men stepped onto the front porch and Dazè explained Anita trying to set John up and how they got back. Junior was blown away by the news. "Damn. I can't believe that lil nigga didn't tell me about this."

"I don't know why he didn't tell you. Maybe he was ashamed to tell you that he fucked up. He probably didn't want you to be mad."

Dazè's explanation of John's decision not to tell him about the setup and bodies didn't make him feel better. "I hear you, Dazè, but that nigga was still supposed to tell me. That's too important to leave out. Y'all almost got robbed and killed. I needed to know about that. He made two bad decisions. Not trusting his gut and fucking with Anita nigga and not telling me about it. If he would keep that from me, I don't know what else he would try to hide."

"Yeah, that make sense," Dazè nodded. "If you ever need somebody to run shit while you gone, I can do it. I told you I ran Green Bay, right? I got experience with leadership. That's why I told John to trust his gut. That was his instincts telling him that something was wrong."

"You right, my nigga. I'ma definitely keep you in mind the next time I need somebody to step in."

"You ever thought about giving nigga's slots? Treating the Parklawn Grinders like a real organization with structure? That way niggas will know the roles and what's expected."

Junior thought for a moment. "Nah, I never really thought about that. I was just focused on getting to the bag. But that don't sound like a bad idea."

"I think it's a good idea. You gotta study nigga's strengths and weakness. Might have to even let some niggas go or reevaluate they slot. We only gon' be as strong as the weakest niggas in the crew.

You gotta be careful about who you got around you. Betrayal ain't as far as you might think."

Junior gave Dazè a look. "Betrayal?"

"I ain't saying that nobody finna betray you, but that don't mean that some niggas don't got larceny in their heart. Niggas tried that shit on me when I first got my slot in The Bay. Niggas be envious. Tried to snake me. Shit, look at Rich and Alpo. Them niggas was like brothers, but you see how that ended. That's why it's important to pick the right people for certain slots. And you also got to find balance establishing trust and discipline. If you find the right mix, the sky is the limit. I can help you put this shit together, my nigga. We fuck around and make Parklawn Grinders some national shit. Turn it into a movement."

Junior smiled at the jewels Dazè dropped on him. "You a beast, my nigga. And you definitely gave me something to think about. I'ma holla at you about this some more later. Right now, I need to go holla at John."

Junior jumped in the Lexus truck and drove straight to John and Nikki's apartment. During the drive, he thought about John not telling him about the move and killing his side bitch. Why didn't he tell him? It didn't make sense. Now, he understood what Six went through when he did dumb shit. After he parked in front of the building, he sent a text to John to open the door.

"What's good, brah? When you get back?" John asked after letting Junior in the apartment.

"About an hour ago. What's up with you? Where Nikki?" he asked, flopping down on the couch.

"At work. I just got up a lil while ago. I was finna get dressed and go to the hood."

"We can ride together. It was something I wanted to holla at you about anyway. How did it go with everybody? Was you able to handle leading this shit?"

"Yeah. Shit was light, brah. All I really had they do was pick up money and give niggas work. Wasn't really shit," he said confidently.

"So, you didn't have no situations?" Junior pried, giving John the opportunity to open up. "Didn't nothing happen?" John's voice raised a pitch higher. "Nah. Ain't nothing happen." Junior stared at him for a moment. "What happened with Anita?" John lowered his head. "Damn. Dazè told you, huh?"

"Yeah. Why didn't you tell me? That was something that I needed to know."

John shrugged. "I don't know. I guess I didn't want you to feel like I couldn't handle the spot. I would've eventually told you but I just didn't want to tell you right away."

"Brah, that was a bad decision not to trust yo' gut and then you made it worse by not telling me. Everything you do affects PLG. Especially if you leading and you gotta lay something down."

"I know I fucked up, brah, but I fixed it. You see I made a good choice by taking Dazè with me. That nigga a beast."

"Yeah. He told me about that. He was also saying some shit about starting structure with PLG and giving nigga spots. It don't sound like a bad idea. He wanna be second in command."

John didn't like the idea. "Hell nah, brah. We fuck with Dazè, but we don't know that nigga like that. Not to be second. That's me. Right? Me you, RIP, and T-Murda started this shit. If anybody be second, it's gotta be one of us."

Junior stared at John, evaluating him. He could see the desire to be second reflecting in his little brother's eyes. "I didn't make no decision yet. But when I do, I'ma do what's best for us as a team. I ain't gon' make the decision based on emotions. Emotions can get a nigga killed."

John wasn't hearing it. "Fuck that shit, brah. You gotta give me that slot. Give me a shot. Six didn't stop fucking with you when you was on yo' bullshit. Now, look at you. Niggas about to take over the projects. Gimmie that same opportunity."

The brothers had another staring contest. "We gon' see what happen, my nigga. But let me ask you this. How did it feel to finally whack something?"

John let out a breath and shook his head like he was reliving the shooting. "That shit fucked me up a little bit, my nigga. I was dreaming about the bitch and everything. I don't even know if I can call it a dream because it felt like a nightmare. Did that happen to you?"

"I dreamed about it but not no nightmare shit. That might be because you knew her. I think that shit affect you differently."

"I don't know. I had to do what I had to do. I can't believe that bitch set me up like that. I thought she fucked with me."

"Now you know these hoes ain't shit. And you shouldn't a put that shit past her anyway because she was letting you fuck when she had a whole nigga. That bitch was scandalous, for real."

"I know. That shit just let a nigga know how real it is out here. Betta believe I learned my lesson. I ain't fucking with no more hoes that got a nigga. Fuck that."

"That's good. I'm glad you learned something. Now, get dressed and let's go check on this money."

The brothers left the apartment and drove back to Parklawn to get up with their crew and check on the hustle. They were walking down 46th and Congress when Diamond walked out of her apartment looking like a snack. She wore pink spandex with a matching sports bra, flexing her killer curves.

"Hey, Mr. President. Welcome back," she waved.

He blocked her path, invading her personal space. "What's good? So, this where you live, huh?"

"For now, yeah. I'm not with this project shit, though. I'm just passing through."

"You know I got a spot for you in the Black House, right? I'm looking for a First Lady. Whenever you ready, we can do it."

"Stop playing, Junior." She laughed. "The last time you was supposed to come through, you stood me up. Had a bitch thinking you was finna show me a good time and I ended up canceling my plans for nothing."

"Hold on, shorty. I didn't stand you up. I told you I had to leave town. I got real shit going on in my life that demand me to change plans on short notice. I'm not one of these regular niggas that hustle to buy clothes and cars and shit and be in the way. I'm really tryna start Black Wall Street in the projects. I'm on another level with the moves I make. I don't fly commercial airlines when I fly. Me and my niggas rent jets and go private."

She gave him a skeptical look. "You really expect me to believe that you flying in private jets?"

Junior looked towards John. "She think I'm lying about flying private, brah."

John gave Diamond a serious look. "No cap, baby. All facts."

Diamond gave Junior a nod of respect. "I never met a nigga that flew on private jets. Do your thang, baby."

"So, now that you know I'm on a different level than them niggas you used to, how about you cancel whatever plans you got tonight and make plans to be with me."

She gave his words some thought. "I ain't gon' lie. You flying private jets definitely elevated how I see you. You on another level and I believe that you going places. But just because you got money, don't mean I'ma drop everything I'm doing, again, and fuck with you. It's your turn to show me something. Tonight, I got a feature show at Silk Exotic in Madison. Show me how bad you want to know how wet my pussy get."

After saying her piece, she walked away, putting an extra switch in her hips as she strutted to the sky blue Camaro parked at the curb. Junior smiled while watching her ass bounce away.

"She did that, brah," John grinned. "That's a bad bitch."

After taking care of things in Parklawn, Junior made the dreaded call to his lawyer and had the meeting set up with Detective Johnson. The questioning would happen in the conference room at Henrik's Law Firm. An hour later, Junior was sitting on one side of the table next to his lawyer. On the other side was Detective Johnson. He wore a big smile, acting genuinely happy to see Junior.

"So, how was the trip?" The detective began.

"C'mon, man. Beat it with the small talk. What do you want? What we here for?"

"You not concerned about how I knew you was out of town? That don't bother you?"

It did bother Junior that the detective knew he was out of town, but he didn't want to give the cop the satisfaction of thinking he was worried. "Man, I don't care nothing about that. That's why I posted pictures on Facebook. Why you looking for me?"

"Look at you, all serious and shit. Okay. Let's do the damn thing," the detective said, adjusting in his seat and putting on a serious face. "That was you in the club with Quitta the night Fredo died, right?"

"You know that was me. You saw the video and she already told you."

"Yeah, I seen that video. And it look like you and Fredo had some words. Did y'all have an argument? What was that about?"

"It wasn't an argument. We had a few words and I left."

"Nah, I'm pretty sure that was an argument. When you left the table, he tried to holla at your girl. You come back with drinks and start arguing. Quitta had to get in the middle. Looked like Fredo might've even reached for a gun. That's when you left. Is that a good description of what happened that night or don't you remember? Cause I can get the video if you want."

"Nah, you don't need to get no video. That's what happened. We had some words and that was it."

"So, you killed him because he tried to holla at your girl?"

Junior looked to his lawyer.

"C'mon, detective," Henrik said, raising his arms.

"It's a valid question. He's seen on camera arguing with the victim over Quitta right before he died. That's motive," he told the lawyer before turning back to Junior. "So, did you do it?"

Junior shook his head and gave a one word answer. "Nah."

"I think you did," the detective sang.

Junior didn't respond. "So, where did you go after you left the club?"

"I took my ass home."

"Did you go right home? Did you make some stops along the way?"

"Nah. I left the bar, jumped in the car, and went right home."

"Can anybody vouch for you being at home?"

"Yeah. My girl's mother and step daddy."

Detective Johnson gave a smirk. "You got it all figured out, don't you? Think you got away with it, don't you?"

Junior returned the smirk with his own. "I don't know what you talking about. I went home. And you don't got shit on me so why you bring me all the way down here to waste my time?"

"Because I know that you killed Fredo. And I'ma prove it and bust yo' ass wide open."

The gay reference got under Junior's skin a little. "Man, what's up with you and my ass? You gotta crush on me or something, nigga? You gay?"

"C'mon, Junior. Calm down," Henrik said.

Detective Johnson smiled, happy to have gotten under his skin. "Yeah, I got a crush on you, Junior. I can't wait to strip you ass naked and make you lift your nuts and bend over and cough. And I really can't wait to see a judge sentence your ass for murder."

"Is we done, man?" Junior asked, ready to leave. "I got shit to do."

"Nah, man. Just a couple more questions. Have you heard of BGM?"

Junior shrugged. "Nah."

The detective gave him a leer. "You sure you never heard of Bread Gang Mafia?"

"I just said no."

The detective took his time responding. "Fredo was BGM, Junior. But I'm sure you already knew that. And over the last month, there have been five BGM deaths. All of this happened right around the time your mother's house got shot up. You see where I'm going with this?"

Junior was shaking in his red bottoms but refused to let the cop see him sweat. "I don't know no BGM niggas. My mama house didn't get shot up, and I didn't kill nobody."

The detective slapped his knee and bust out laughing. "That grip getting tight on them balls, ain't it? It's just a matter of time, Junior. You going down, son. I promise you that."

The Parklawn Grinder refused to acknowledge the detectives antics and comments.

"Got any more questions, detective?" Henrik asked.

Johnson continued to eye Junior while speaking to the lawyer. "Nah, that's all I got for now. I'll be sure to be in contact if I have any more questions. Have a nice day, counselor. And Junior, keep doing your thang because your days are numbered. I'll find my way out."

When the cop left, Henrik turned to Junior. "Do you know what he's talking about? Do you know about any of the homicides?" Junior looked to his lawyer, wondering if he should tell the truth. "I heard of BGM. And I might know something about the bodies he talked about."

Henrik's eyes grew wide. "Can you be connected?"

"I don't think so. But it seem like he got some snitches because he know a lot of shit. We never called the police about my mama house getting shot up and I don't know how he found out about that."

"Shit." Henrik rubbed a hand through his hair. "Okay. I'll do some digging to see if I can find out where he's getting his information. As long as he doesn't have a smoking gun, like an eyewitness or fingerprints, or someone with personal knowledge of the murders that could tie you in, you should be okay. Does any of that stuff exist?"

Junior thought for a moment. "Not that I could think of."

"Okay. I'll be in touch. It wouldn't hurt if you kept your head down. We don't need to give Johnson any more ammunition against us."

Junior left the lawyer's office and hopped in the Lexus truck. During to drive back to Parklawn, he got a call from Quitta.

"What up, baby mama?"

"Nothing. Just woke up from a nap. What you doing?"

"Just came from talking to Johnson bitch ass. This fag ass nigga really tryna get me. I think he got some CI's too because he knew about me going out of town and my mama house getting shot up. A couple BGM niggas got whacked and he tryna put them bodies on me too."

"Damn, baby daddy. I'm scared for you. He really tryna get you. You don't think that you should take Mooka and just leave?"

"I can't do that right now. I'm still on a mission to take over my projects. I'm getting close. Plus, he don't got shit. If he did, he wouldn't be meeting me with Henrik. He would just take my ass to jail."

"I think you too cocky. He tryna build a case against you and you just gon' sit there and let him do it. Leave, Junior. Or at least get some people on your team that can help you."

Junior laughed. "I know you ain't talking about yo' boyfriend."

"Fuck you, nigga. He ain't my boyfriend," she snapped.

"I'm still tryna figure out what he doing. He brought you a phone, took it, and then gave it back. That shit don't make no sense. You telling me that he brought you a phone while you in jail because he like you and want to help you out? What's in it for him? You ever ask yo'self that? That nigga recording this, that's why. He tryna bust our ass and you fell right into his trap."

"No, he not, Junior. How many times I gotta tell you that. He want to fuck with us. He want more money. I know what I'm talking about. You think I would be stupid enough to try to introduce you to somebody that's tryna cook us?"

Junior thought for a moment. "Actually, I do think you would do that because he tricked you. You believe one of the police that interrogated you is now tryna help you. You tripping."

"Oh my God, Junior!" She yelled in frustration. "The nigga ate my pussy, okay. Wouldn't no police go that far. He can't go that far. It's unethical. He not tryna—"

Junior cut her off. "He ate yo' pussy?" He asked, making sure he heard what he thought he heard.

Quitta's voice raised an octave as she prepared for his response. "Yeah. He did."

Junior was quiet for a moment, trying to process what she just said. If he ate her pussy, what else had they done? Were they fucking? What did she tell him? Was she telling him everything? "You let the police eat you out?" He asked again in disbelief.

"Yes," she answered, getting a little frustrated by his tone. "Why do that matter to you? You not my man."

"Bitch, that ain't the muthafuckin point!" He exploded. "How the fuck you gon' start fucking with the muthafucka that's tryna get us knocked? Is you stupid, nigga? Have you lost yo' rabbit ass mind?"

"I know what the fuck I'm doing, Junior. I ain't no stupid ass bitch. If you could've fucked a C.O. bitch while you was locked up, you telling me you wouldn't have done it? I got a real police nigga all up in my pussy letting me know what's going on and tryna help me. You should be applauding me instead of thinking I'm stupid. I know what the fuck I'm doing."

"No you don't. You can't know what you doing if you letting the police eat yo' pussy. Did you suck his dick? Favor for a favor? Did you give him some pussy, too? You let him fuck while you pregnant with my shorty?"

"You know what, Junior? I ain't finna argue with you, nigga. You out there sticking yo' dick in damn near every bitch you walk by and now you tryna make it seem like I'm bogus. I'm tryna get us some help but you can't see because you think you know everything. That's gon' be yo' downfall. Thinking you know everything. Detective Johnson is coming, nigga. Keep being stupid if you want to. Bye."

Junior threw the phone on the passenger seat in frustration. He couldn't believe that she was fucking the police. The same police that was trying to pop they ass for murder. Shit sounded stupid as hell. He wanted to pick the phone up and call her back to curse her out but that wouldn't do nothing but piss him off even more and maybe push her closer to the cop. He needed to sit back and think of a way to protect himself in case Russo was using Quitta to get to him. Then, he began to think about what it would be like to have a cop on his side. What if Quitta was right about Detective Russo and he really wanted to join the team? What if he could have a real inside man? What if she had created an opportunity for him?

"Damn," he mumbled, unsure of what to do next.

CHAPTER 9

Despite all the bullshit going on in his life, Junior still made time to have fun. And tonight's fun came with the added benefit of being entertained by Diamond. He rented two Sprinter vans and took all of his PLG niggas with him to Silk Exotic in Madison, Wisconsin. John, T-Murda, RIP, Willow, Shamar, Dazè, Kanesha, and Ebony were all dressed in high end fashion, looking like a clique of rich niggas. They drank top shelf and had bricks of money sitting on their VIP tables. They had already made it rain so much that their section had to be swept up twice. And they still had two thousand singles in plastic, waiting for the main event.

"C'mon, baby. Put yo' back into that shit!" Willow cheered, getting his eighth lap dance from a bad ass thick dancer named Snow Bunny.

"She gon' break yo' ass, fool ass nigga!" Kanesha laughed.

"You might as well just give her all yo' money and tell her to sit on yo' lap for the rest of the night," Ebony added.

"Nigga, I just did two years. That shit taught me that you can't put a price on having a good time," Willow said, dropping a bank roll on the stripper's lap. "Keep my lap warm for the rest of the night, aight?"

Her hazel brown eyes lit up when she seen that there were twenties, fifties, and hundreds in the wad of cash. "Baby, I'ma do you one better and cook you breakfast in the morning."

"It ain't tricking if you got it!" Junior laughed, holding up a bottle of Ace Of Spade.

The lights in the club turned down for a moment before the MC began speaking. "Okay, okay, okay! How is everybody doing tonight?"

There were applauds and cheers from this crowd.

"Y'all ready for another sexy performance?"

There was more applauding and cheering.

"Okay. Get ready for a real treat. Let's welcome to the stage one of the baddest chicks that you will ever see in your life. I know they say diamonds are a girl's best friend but after today, you fellas gon' wanna be friends with this jewel. Coming from Milwaukee, give it up for Diamond!"

The main lights flickered again and ground lights near the stage lit up. Diamond strutted up the stairs and onto the stage like she was a runway model. She looked good and knew it. Bad and boujee. She wore an emerald blue shoulder length wig, a white body suit that hugged her tight and toned body, and heels. She walked to the edge of the stage and did a pose while looking over the crowd. Then, her eyes found Junior's. They exchanged smiles before she walked to the pole in the middle of the stage.

"She on you, my nigga!" Dazè grinned, wishing he could swap places with his nigga for the night.

Junior responded with a nod, grabbing a brick of money, and walking to the stage, never taking his eyes off of Diamond. She climbed the pole and did some tricks, twirling and spinning to the ground. Then, she began crawling around the stage, hiking her ass high in the air and allowing a few people to spank her as she crawled by. When she got to Junior, she paused, keeping seductive eye contact with him while lowering her face on the floor, keeping her ass in the air, and making it jiggle.

"Spank me, nigga." Her gray eyes sparkled.

He reached a hand back and slapped her cheeks, making them ripple.

Diamond closed her eyes, biting her bottom lip. "Do it again. Harder."

He slapped her on the ass again, making her moan.

"Now rip my clothes off."

"What?" The request surprised him.

"You heard me, nigga. Rip my clothes off."

"Okay," he shrugged before grabbing a fist full of fabric near her thigh and ripping.

Diamond continued to shake her ass while he ripped at her clothes. Then, she stood, dancing around the stage and letting others rip her clothes off. When she was in panties and a bra she went back to the pole to do more tricks. Junior began throwing money, making it rain while she twirled on the pole. Then, she broke out the baby oil and let people rub on her body while she danced. When it was over, she left the stage with a shopping bag of money and went to clean up. She came out of the dressing room fifteen minutes later dressed in a Fendi track suit.

"You a beast, baby," Junior grinned when she walked over to his section.

"You really liked it?" She squirmed.

"I ain't never ripped nobody clothes off before. That was good shit."

"A plus, plus." John gave her two thumbs up.

"Thanks." she smiled before turning back to Junior. "You ready?"

He looked surprised. "That's it? We only been here a couple hours. It ain't even midnight."

She lifted the bag of money. "I got what I came for. I really don't do the club like that."

"Say less." Junior stood and began shaking hands with his niggas. "I'ma fuck with y'all later."

"Love, cuzzo," T-Murda smiled. "And make sure you tear that shit up!"

"Fool ass nigga!" Junior laughed before escorting Diamond from the club. "So, what we doing? Where you want to go?"

She stopped in the middle of the parking lot, spinning to face him, giving erotic eye contact. "Are you a good kisser?"

Her eyes told him that words would ruin the moment, so he leaned in and tongued her ass down. When they broke the kiss, her face was flushed red with desire.

"Okay, Mr. President. You passed the test with flying—"

She didn't get to finish before Junior was all in her grill again. They groped each other and made sounds of pleasure while kissing. When they came up for air, they agreed to skip the two hour drive back to Milwaukee and spend the night in Madison. A ten minute ride in her Camaro took them to the Sheraton. They pawed at each other all the way to the room.

As soon as the door closed, clothes came off. Junior lay back on the bed and Diamond kneeled between his legs, grabbing hold of his dick, and stroking while looking into his eyes. Then, she took the head into her mouth slowly, bobbing a couple of times, making sure to keep eye contact. Junior tried to keep his eyes open but the more that she sucked into her mouth, the heavier his eyelids got. It felt like he was riding a Percocet high as he fought to keep his eyes open. She sucked just enough to get him turned on before rolling onto her back.

"I'm ready to get fucked now."

Junior was disappointed that the head ended so soon because she was good at it, and she looked good sucking his dick. But he was also eager to see what that pussy was like and how wet she got. He rolled between her legs, holding his piece like it was a weapon as he prepared to dig in her guts. Her pussy looked as good as she did. Shaved bald, juicy pink lips, and no hair bumps or razor bumps. He rubbed the tip of his dick around her juicy outer lips, teasing her. She reached down and held herself open. "Stop playing and fuck me, nigga."

He pushed halfway inside her slippery tunnel, letting her get used to him. Then, he pulled out of her and pushed again, going deeper.

"Hell yeah nigga! Oh shit," Diamond moaned, closing her eyes.

Junior continued working himself inside her until he was balls deep. He kept a steady pace, loving the way her titties bounced while he dug her guts.

"Twist my nipples," she said. "Be rough with them. I like that."

He pinched and twisted her nipples while fucking her. Diamond moaned in pleasure while rubbing her clit as he drilled her. When he felt her legs scissor against him, he knew she was close to cumming.

"Oh shit! Oh yeah!" She came, her pussy gripping his dick as she climaxed. "Damn, Junior! Oh shit!"

Junior watched her face as she got her rocks off, loving the looks of pleasure she made. Wanting to keep her pleased, he lifted her legs onto his shoulders and started hitting it fast and deep. Diamond sucked in sharp breaths, screaming like crazy as he tore that pussy up. When he couldn't hold back any more, he pulled out and bust on her stomach.

"Damn, baby. You got that bomb," Junior breathed.

"I hope you don't think we done," Diamond said in between breaths.

"Is you crazy? I just blew five racks in the strip club. We fucking all night."

After some marathon sex that took them from the bed, to the floor, to the shower, and back to the bed again, Junior and Diamond lay in the bed to smoke a blunt and bask in the afterglow of good sex.

"You surprised me with them dancing skills. How long you been doing it?"

"I only been dancing for about six months. At first, I didn't want to do it because I didn't want that reputation as a hoe, so I just did lil bullshit online. Fucking with Onlyfans and shit like that. But I didn't have that buzz, you know? Its plenty of bad bitches out there. Some of 'em get money and some of 'em still living in the projects. Like me. I knew I needed to do something to get my followers up, so I started following dancers and checking out they videos. I saw some of them bitches making twenty grand a night and their Onlyfans was popping like crazy. That's when I said fuck that and jumped in the game. I want to buy my first house and get the fuck out the projects by the end of the year."

Junior smiled at her response. "That's what I'm talking about. Ownership. I need to buy me something because I don't own shit."

She looked surprised. "With all the money you got? You don't own nothing?"

He shook his head.

"Well, you need to think about doing something with your money because you can't be hustling forever. What if something happens to you? You need to be in a position to take care of yourself and your family."

"Look at you giving good advice and shit."

"You a good nigga and I want to see you win. You need to be prepared for anything. Life is crazy. Be smart with your money. And if you need my help, let me know."

***

"You still mad at me?" Quitta asked.

Junior took his eyes off the road to glance at the phone screen. "What you think?"

"I don't think you should be mad. I think you should trust me. If you was in my position, you would've done the same thing. If a female C.O. or police was bringing you shit while you was locked up, you would be fucking with them too."

"But this is different, baby mama. This nigga is investigating you."

"He not investigating me. He help if they need it. But he not the main one. He good. Why can't you just trust me? Can't you see that I'm tryna help you?"

Junior was quiet for a moment. Thinking. He didn't want to meet with the cop. Not only because he was the police, but because he was fucking his baby mama. He didn't want nobody fucking or eating Quitta's pussy but him. But if Russo could be an asset, it would be foolish to deny the opportunity. "What do this nigga want?"

Quitta smiled. "He want to meet with you and talk business. He want to get some real money."

"Aight. Gimme the nigga number. I'ma meet with him only because you been sweating me about it but that don't mean I'm fucking with him. I'm bringing Mooka to Lacrosse in a day or two so we can visit you and I'ma meet him while I'm there. Don't tell him that I'm coming. I want it to be a surprise. Just tell him that I got his number and I'ma call."

***

Junior parked the Lexus in the grocery store parking lot and waited for Detective Russo. He had gone back and forth about whether or not to keep the meeting, finally deciding to meet with the cop. Five minutes later, a beige unmarked sedan pulled into the lot. Junior flashed the high beams so the cop could find him. When the Crown Victoria pulled alongside the Lexus, both men got out to meet. Junior laughed to himself when he seen the cop. Nate Russo was a big white boy with a big beard. He wore a camouflage T-shirt, jeans, and some kind of hiking boots. Looked like of one of the people that ran in the Capitol building on January 6th.

"Junior, how's it going?" He asked, extending a hand.

Junior remained cool. "Chilling. What's up?"

"I'm good. I didn't know you were coming to town."

"Yeah, I brought my son to see his mother and thought I'd kill two birds with one bullet. Why you want to meet with me? What do you want?"

"I want what everybody wants, man. More money. But I don't want you to put me on a payroll or nothing. I want to work for it." Junior studied the cop as he spoke, looking for signs that he was on some bullshit. "Man, why should I trust the police? How I don't know that you tryna book me and my baby mama?"

He laughed. "Trust me, man. I'm not trying to book anybody. Quitta has way too much on me for me to do anything to her."

"You talking about you eating her pussy?"

Detective Russo looked surprised that he knew. "Yeah. That and a few other things."

Junior wanted as much dirt as he could get. "Like what?"

The cop thought for a moment. "Like she knows where I live. She knows my birthday. Not to mention, I bought her the phone and a few other things."

"Okay," Junior nodded. "So, how do you want to get money? Tell me what you got in mind?"

"Well, I heard that you were a mover and shaker. I want to move and shake for you in Lacrosse. It's an open market and I could take advantage of that. I could also be your eyes and ears around here. Might even be able to help you with that Terrance case and Quitta with the OD."

"I hear you, Russo. And I like everything you saying. But I still got a problem trusting you. You the police, man, and for all I know you might be deep cover right now."

Russo nodded. "I get it. This is a first for me, too. Tell me what I can do to get you to trust me. Something reasonable because I ain't killing nobody."

Junior already knew what he wanted. "Take me to meet yo' mother."

Russo was surprised by the request. "C'mon, man. My mother? Seriously?"

"Yeah, man. Right now. I need some insurance. If you on some bullshit, I don't even got to tell you what's gon' happen. If you valid, we gon' do business. It's up to you."

Russo studied Junior for a moment. "Man, you're making this hard. I don't want to put my mom in danger."

Junior moved to walk away. "Then, I guess we ain't got nothing else to talk about."

The detective let out a huff. "Okay, man. Get in the car. She lives a town over. Hope you don't mind farms."

Nate Russo's family lived on the fifty acre farm in Lacrescent, Wisconsin. When the sedan pulled into the rocky driveway, three Border Collies came running up to the car.

"Hey, Rocky! Hey, Aladdin! Hey, Zack!" Nate greeted the dogs, bending down so they could lick his face.

"Look like they missed you," Junior cracked.

"These are my best friends, man. Never gotta worry about being betrayed by your dogs."

"Nathaniel, is that you," a woman called as the farm house's screen door opened. A short plump woman with gray hair stepped onto the porch a moment later. She wore a yellow and white sundress, her big fake breasts spilling out the top.

"Hey, mama bear!" Nate grinned as he walked upon the porch a wrapped her in a hug.

"Hey, grizzly bear. Why didn't you tell me you were coming by? And who's your friend?" She asked, giving Junior a long look.

"I was just passing through and thought I'd stop by to see you. This is my buddy, Junior. He's a detective too. He's new to these parts and I was showing him around."

Junior waved. "Hey, ma'am."

"Oh no, Junior. Don't you ma'am me. I'm not an old lady. My name is Pam. Nice to meet you," she said, walking over to give him a warm hug.

"Nice to meet you, too."

"Mmm. You smell good and you're handsome. Bet you get all the girls, don't you?" She flirted, batting big blue eyes.

"Mom, knock it off!" Russo yelled.

"I'm just kidding." she giggled. "C'mon in and let me get you guys something to drink before you leave."

"Sorry, man," Nate apologized as they followed Pam into the house. "She always does that to my friends but she's harmless."

"It's cool." Junior nodded.

"What do you want to drink?" Pam asked as they walked in the kitchen. "Coffee, water, juice, beer? My husband makes a really good special brew."

"Dad is back brewing?" Nate perked up. "Gimmie one."

"I'll have what he's having." Junior nodded.

"Okay. Have a seat. Two Russo's coming right up," she said opening the fridge and bending over to dig inside.

Junior was looking around the kitchen when he noticed the dress digging into Pam's ass. The older woman had a nice body and the curves had him stuck for a moment. Pam looked over her shoulder and caught him checking her out. They made brief eye contact and she smiled.

"Where is papa bear?" Nate asked, flopping down in a chair.

"Out in the barn messing with the cows. Thinking about selling some of them. Cost of feed is getting expensive," Pam said, giving the men beers and letting her fingers linger on Junior's a little longer than necessary.

Nate cracked the top and took a sip form the bottle. "Daddy did really good with this one. I'ma go down to the barn and speak. You wanna see the rest of the farm?" He asked Junior.

"I don't—"

"Nope. I need his help getting the trunk from the attic," Pam interrupted. "Go speak to your dad. I'll bring him over when we get it down."

Nate stood and looked to Junior. "You good?"

Junior looked to Pam and seen mischief lighting her eyes. She wasn't his type but considering that Nate had fucked his baby mama, he was down for anything. "Yeah, man. I'll help real quick."

"Okay. Come out to the barn when you're done."

"Damn, that kid." Pam laughed, grabbing Junior's arm. "Come to the attic and give me some help."

Junior grabbed the beer and followed, watching the sway of the older woman's hips. He knew what was about to happen and couldn't wait to fuck Russo's mom. Nobody would believe him when he told this story.

"So, Mr. Junior. Are you a breast or ass man?" Pam asked, looking back over her shoulder. "Most of the black men that I've met are ass men."

"I'm an ass man. But I like breasts, too. Can't have one without the other, right?"

She stopped in front of him and poked out her chest. "What do you think of mine?"

Junior looked at the tanned cleavage spilling from the top of her dress. "They look nice."

"My husband bought them for my fortieth birthday. Ten years old and still look like they did when I left the operating room. Best ten grand ever." She smiled, grabbing the bottom of her breasts, and lifting them.

Junior decided to speed up the process. "Can I see?"

She smiled proudly while pulling down the top of her dress, exposing her 34DD and pink nipples.

Junior lowered his head and started sucking.

"Oh, yeah! That feels so good!" Pam moaned, rubbing the back of his head.

After sucking one nipple, he moved to the other.

"Okay, okay." Pam stopped him. "Come to the attic. I need some right now."

Junior followed her swaying hips up to the fully furnished attic and over to a window that overlooked the farm.

"The barn is over there. Let me know if they come out. We don't have that much time," she said while slipping the spaghetti straps from her shoulders and letting the dress fall to the floor. She wasn't wearing panties. Junior checked out her fleshy body as she dropped to her knees and went for his zipper. Russo's mom was strapped!

"You sure about this?" He asked, glancing towards the barn.

Pam didn't miss a beat as she dug in his pants, unleashing the meat. "I've slept with almost every boy Nate brought home since he was in high school. My older son, too. I love sex. My husband is sixty five years old and has had erectile dysfunction since I met him. When he can't get it up, I find me another one. You're the second black man. And you're much bigger. This is going to be fun."

After licking the head, she tried to swallow his dick, gagging when he touched her tonsils. Then, she used her hand to jack off what she couldn't get in her mouth. She moaned while sucking him, looking into his eyes as spit dripped from the sides of her mouth.

"Damn!" Junior groaned, surprised at the older woman's skills.

She took him from her mouth, continuing to give him a hand job while sucking and licking his balls. Then, she went back to sucking, using one hand to stroke him and the other to massage his balls. A few moments later, he was busting down her throat.

"Awe, shit! Damn!" Junior groaned as she continued sucking, swallowing every drop.

"Damn, that was hot." Pam smiled, continuing to give him a hand job. "Now I'm ready to take this big thing in my pussy. I'm dripping wet."

She got up and bent over. Junior spread her cheeks apart about to stick his dick in when he seen movement near the barn. Nate walked out with an older white man wearing overalls.

"Damn. They leaving the barn." He panicked.

Pam stood with her eyes wide in surprise. She looked out the window and yelped. "Oh shit!" Then, she quickly slid back into her dress. "Dammit, Bill! Always ruining my good times. C'mon, Junior. The chest is in the other room. The next time you come around I'm getting some of that big black thing."

After meeting Nate's father and finishing the beer, Junior hopped in the Crown Victoria with Nate.

"Do you trust me now?"

"I don't know if I trust you, yet, but we can definitely do business. Tell me what you had in mind."

"I think I should start off small. Maybe a couple of ounces until things start rolling."

"Okay. Let me think about it. I'll let you know something in a couple of days."

Nate smiled. "Sounds good to me."

CHAPTER 10
3 WEEKS LATER

Dazè turned the royal blue Challenger Scat Pack onto 37th and Townsend, looking for the address that matched the one on his phone screen. Today was a special day. His nigga Cee-Cee got released this morning and he was picking him up from his grandmother's house. When Dazè found the address, he sent a text. A few moments later, a tall dark skinned nigga with brushed waves stepped onto the porch of a brown two story house in the middle of the block. He wore a fitted Gucci T-shirt that showed a physique sculpted by mandatory workouts in The Bay, dark Gucci jeans, and Gucci runners.

"My nigga, Cee-Cee!" Dazè yelled, jumping out of the Challenger, and wrapping his nigga in a hug.

"What's good, G? I'm here, my nigga! I'm here! They done released the demon!" Cee-Cee yelled, excited that his five year stretch in Green Bay Correctional Institution was finally over.

"Get in the car, nigga. You with me for the rest of the day. I gotta take you shopping and get you some pussy, nigga."

Cee-Cee paused to check out the ride. "Damn, this bitch is bussin, my nigga! This you?"

Dazè smiled proudly at the sports car. "I told you I was having my way out here, nigga. Get in. We finna kick it like real bosses. This that shit we was daydreaming about when we was listening to Meek Mill and Rick Ross while we was locked up, nigga." When Cee-Cee climbed in the passenger seat, Dazè jumped in the driver's seat and made the tires squeal as he sped away playing *'Do U Wanna Ride' by Jay-Z and John Legend.*

"You strapped?" Cee-Cee asked.

Dazè pulled a Glock with a twenty-one shot clip in it from under the seat. "This you. I'ma grab another one when we get to the hood." Cee-Cee kissed the gun. "This bitch beautiful!"

"You a fool, my nigga," Dazè laughed, pulling a blunt from the ashtray. "Welcome home, folks."

Cee-Cee lit the blunt and took a couple big puffs, letting out a moan. "Damn, I missed this shit, my nigga."

"I felt the same way. So, what you wanna do? Shopping or get some pussy?"

Cee-Cee gave Dazè a crazy look. "What kinda question is that, my nigga? I ain't had no pussy in five years."

"I got you, G. And I know just who to call. Shorty is a beast."

Dazè pulled out his phone and called Lisa.

"What's up, nigga? You want some more of this poonany?" She answered.

"Not me this time. I'm tryna get my nigga right. He just got out this morning. Where you at?"

"I'm at home. Who is yo' nigga?"

"He right here. This my lil bro, Cee-Cee."

"What up, baby?" Cee-Cee said.

"Hey, baby. You sound sexy. You know ain't nothing free, right?"

"Don't say nothing to us about no money," Dazè cut in. "We Parklawn Grinders. That shit light."

"Talk that shit to me then, baby. You know where I live. Come over."

"Say less," Dazè said before ending the call.

"So, you really serious about this Parklawn Grinders shit, huh?"

Dollar signs lit Dazè's eyes. "We eating for real, nigga. And I'm finna put you right in. I'm tryna get these niggas to organize and get some structure. My nigga Junior created the team, and he got the plug. Nigga getting bricks from some Mafia type niggas. But the nigga got a couple bodies hanging over his head and might finna get cooked. I should be second in line because ain't none of the niggas in the clique really capable of running this shit if he go down. I think everything I went through in The Bay prepared me for this shit. If the cards fall in my favor, I might have an entire projects and bricks of dope handed to me on a platter."

Cee-Cee's eyes were wide in astonishment. "On what, fam?"

"Facts, my nigga. Facts."

"Damn, I didn't know niggas was getting to it like that. Put me in, nigga."

"I got you. I already told niggas who you was so you good. Soon as you finish fucking this bitch, walk around the corner and I'ma be outside with these niggas waiting. Here go five hunnit. You probably gon' need all of it 'cause shorty got that fiya."

After dropping Cee-Cee off by Lisa's house, Dazè spun around to 47th Street to post up. The projects were alive with activity. Everybody and they mama outside enjoying the summer weather. Dazè hopped out and joined the crowd gathering in front of Junior's mother's house. About thirty minutes later, Cee-Cee rounded the corner.

"There go my nigga right there," Dazè said, pointing to Cee-Cee as he walked over.

"That nigga walking like he bowlegged!" Fifty cracked. "Lisa got that WAP!"

"How long you say that nigga do?" Black asked.

"My nigga did a nickel," Dazè answered.

"I bet she got all the money he had in his pocket," Junior said.

Dazè laughed. "That ain't too hard to believe cause she damn near broke me on my first day out."

Cee-Cee wiped the sweat from his brow as he approached the large crowd in front of Gail's house.

"She get you right, my nigga?" Dazè asked.

Cee-Cee's eyes grew wide as he smiled. "I didn't know I could buss that many times, my nigga."

The crowd bust out laughing.

"Lisa the truth, on what? What she hit you for?" Junior asked.

Cee-Cee laughed. "She took it all, my nigga."

The crowd bust out laughing even harder.

"Ay y'all, this my nigga Cee-Cee that I was telling y'all about. Cee-Cee, these all my Parklawn niggas," Dazè introduced. Everyone was in the middle of welcoming Cee-Cee home when Renae walked out of the house with Patricia and joined the crowd. When the newly freed man seen Patricia, he couldn't take his eyes off her. She had a dark chocolate complexion, long hair, dimples in both cheeks, and a body shaped like the number 8. Her style of dress was simple. Black Gucci glasses, a T-shirt, jeans, and sandals. To Cee-Cee, she was perfect.

"What's up, nigga? It's good to finally see you in person," Renae greeted. "Welcome back to the free world."

"Appreciate it." Cee-Cee nodded, eyeing the dark skinned beauty.

"Who is you?"

"I'm Patricia. Welcome home."

"That's my cousin, nigga. Watch out," Renae teased.

"My bad," he laughed giving Patricia one more look.

"You ready to fuck up this mall, nigga?" Dazè asked.

"Hell yeah, nigga! Get me fresh."

"Aye, we gon' fuck with y'all later, fam. I'm finna get my nigga together," Dazè said, heading for the Scat Pack.

"We coming, too baby," Renae said, interjecting herself and Patricia into the mix. "You ain't going shopping without me, nigga." They hopped in the Challenger. Renae in the front with Dazè and Patricia in the back with Cee-Cee.

"I like yo' glasses. What kinda frames is them?" Cee-Cee asked.

"Just some plain Gucci," she said nonchalantly. "I'm blind as a bat."

"They fit you, though. They look good on you."

"Thank you," she blushed. "What you was locked up for?"

"A punk ass robbery. Took a nigga sack and shit and he called the police on me and got me out the way."

"Damn, that's messed up when a nigga call the police and tell 'em you took his dope," Patricia laughed. "He sound like he was scared of you."

"You not?"

She twisted up her face. "Don't let the glasses and college degree fool you, nigga. I used to be in Parklawn with them demons, too."

Cee-Cee bust out laughing. "In Parklawn with them demons, huh? Okay, Gangsta P. I respect yo' slot. What you go to college for?"

"I got a Bachelor's Degree in Sports Medicine."

"That's cool," he nodded. Then, he gave a thoughtful look. "What the fuck you gon' do with a degree in Sports Medicine?"

"I want to work with professional athletes. Help them rehab when they get injured. Right now, I'm doing physical therapy at a small clinic downtown, but I want to eventually link up with the Milwaukee Bucks"

Cee-Cee nodded in approval. "That's good shit. Get you one of them million dollar niggas to support you, huh?"

Patricia's face twisted. "Did you just call me a gold digger?"

He was surprised by her reaction. "I thought that's what all females wanted. Get a nigga with a bag to take care of them? They call that security, right?"

"Not me. I don't want to be dependent on a man. I went to college so I can have my own career and depend on me. I want to open my own clinic. You won't see me fucked up because a nigga cut me off. I want my own."

Cee-Cee stared at her for a moment, loving what she said and how she said it.

"What?" She asked.

"I think I just fell in love with you."

Patricia bust out laughing. "You crazy, nigga."

He continued to stare at her, his gaze serious and unblinking. "You know you gon' be mine, right?"

Patricia laughed again, feeling something grow warm in her stomach. "You crazy."

Dazè took his squad to the mall and blew ten bands fucking it up before going to a strip club. Later that night, he got a text from Junior about a PLG meeting. After leaving the club they headed back to Parklawn. Dazè, Cee-Cee, Willow, Shamar, T-Murda, RIP, Kanesha, Ebony, and Junior were seated around Jeff's living room. There were also a few extra people present; Fifty, Black, and Toe Tagga. When everybody was settled in, Junior began speaking.

"Man, a few months ago I never thought I would be in this position to be one of the creators of a real life money getting family of hustlers. But here we is. And when I say family, I mean that. We all brothers and sisters. That's how we got to move. If somebody fuck with one of us, they fucking with all of us. And when I say I'm one of the creators, I say that because we all playing a part in building this. It ain't no big I's and little yous. We all family. It's niggas that's not in this room that's screaming PLG and getting money with us. That means we growing. We expanding. The dream of creating a Black Wall Street is starting to become a reality. And because we growing, I need to talk to y'all about different slots and responsibilities. I had a conversation with Dazè, and he put me up on some game. We only as strong as our weakest member. I want to treat the Parklawn Grinders like a real organization with structure. That's how corporations move. Analytics do what they do, accountants do what they do, security do what they do and so on and so forth. Niggas gotta know they roles and what's expected. Y'all know that we got the plug on more shit now. When I went to re-up, I told them our plans and they like what we doing in Parklawn and opened up the store. Now, we can get any pills from Percs to Xans. Molly to Adderall. We got dog food and loud too. So this how I wanna do. Murda, you got the pills. RIP, you on the dog food. John, you got the loud pack. Willow, you got the girl. Dazè and Fifty, ain't nobody fucking with y'all when it comes to putting that murder game down so I want y'all on security and in charge of them shooters. I'ma be the President and in charge of distribution and collection. Second in command is John. If y'all can't reach me, holla at him and he'll either get at me or help you figure out whatever your issue is. I know I didn't say some of y'all names but that don't mean I view y'all lesser than the others. It's only so many spots but we still family and we still getting money. Do anybody got anything to say about how it's playing out?"

Dazè felt some type of way about not being second in command but kept the thoughts to himself.

"You telling me that you finna pay me to shoot niggas?" Fifty asked. "Best job in the world!"

"I got something to say," Cee-Cee spoke up. "I wanna know if I can be part of the team. Dazè told me y'all some real niggas and I wanna get money with y'all."

Junior looked to Dazè. "That's yo' man. You gon' vouch for him."

"My nigga super valid," Dazè said confidently. "I'ma keep him on security with me. He a certified shooter."

"Well, I guess that's it then. You on security. Welcome home and welcome to the Parklawn Grinders. If don't nobody got nothing else, we can get up out of here. I gotta get up with my new first lady. Her son is by her mama house, and I plan on fucking all night."

"Is Mercedes over there?" John asked, wanting to see the thick temptress again.

"I think so. It's a couple hoes over there. We can turn they spot into our spot."

"I need to see that muthafucka twerk again. I'm going," T-Murda said.

"So am I," RIP added.

After ending the meeting, the Parklawn Grinders dispersed. Dazè and Cee-Cee trailed the Junior, John, RIP, and T-Murda towards Diamond's apartment.

"How you feeling about him putting you on?" Cee-Cee asked, keeping his voice down so the others couldn't hear.

Dazè let out a breath. "I feel some type of way about that shit, low key. Even though I know this ain't the mob, I know I'm capable of running this shit, not managing shooters. His lil brother ain't ready for that slot. Nigga gon' fuck around and run shit into the ground if Junior get knocked."

"We can just get them niggas out the way and take over."

Dazè shot his nigga a look. "Nah, we can't do that. That shit would fuck up our money because Junior the only one that can get to the plug."

"What about knocking off John first and then seeing if you can get that slot. If you do, then when you get info on the plug, we knock Junior."

Dazè shook his head and laughed. "Nah, nigga. We not offin' nobody. These my niggas. We good where we at."

"You sure?"

"Yeah I'm sure, nigga. We locked in. Let's just focus on getting this paper. We good."

***

"That nigga give bad vibes," John said, keeping his voice down so no one could hear him.

"What you talking about, man?" Junior asked, more focused on fucking Diamond again than hearing about John's vibes.

John snuck a look around to make sure no one was in ear shot. "I'm talking about that nigga, Cee-Cee. That nigga shiesty, fam. I can feel it. And he a jackboy. You should've took a look at that nigga before we brought him in. He just got out this morning. We don't know this nigga."

"I used to be a jackboy too. And so did Fifty. But now this a better opportunity. And we brought Dazè on deck as soon as he got out. Why you didn't say nothing about him?"

"Because we know his family. We don't know shit about this new nigga."

Junior thought for a moment. He couldn't turn around and kick Cee-Cee out of the clique after he gave him a slot on security and Dazè vouched for him. But he also didn't want to ignore his second in command's bad vibe. "I hear you, brah. Dazè vouched for him and that's our nigga so we can't go back on that. But what we do is keep our eyes on that nigga. Let me know if you see or hear any bullshit out of this nigga. Then, I'ma deal with it."

"You already know," John said, shooting a glance over his shoulder.

When they got to Diamond's apartment, the Parklawn niggas turned it into their spot. They broke out drinks, weed, pills, and turned up the music. Diamond's sister, Mercedes, and two of her cousins, Tiffany and Breezy, kept them company. An hour later, Junior was sitting on the couch with Diamond, rubbing all over her body and trying to convince her to go upstairs and bust it wide open. Then, the doorbell rang.

"Who is it?" Diamond asked, getting up.

"Goldie."

She looked through the peephole and mumbled a curse under her breath while shooting Junior a panicked glance.

"You good?"

"It's my baby daddy," she breathed while unlocking the door. "What you want, Goldie?"

"I want you to open the door, nigga," he said, forcing his way into the house.

Junior eyed the chubby light skinned nigga wearing a track suit.

"Oh, that's why you ain't wanna let me in. Y'all in here being hoes," Goldie said, looking around at the women kicking it with the Parklawn Grinders.

"Who that nigga?" Cee-Cee mugged.

The newcomer strolled boldly into the middle of the living room. "My name is Goldie, player. Who is you?"

"Nigga, I'm about—"

"I'm Junior and these my niggas." Junior cut in. "We Parklawn Grinders."

Goldie and Junior shared a long look.

"Parklawn Grinders, huh?" Goldie chuckled.

"Yeah, nigga. This our shit," Dazè added.

Hostilities filled the air as tensions rose.

Diamond could sense something about to go wrong and spoke up. "What do you want, Goldie?"

He mugged her. "First of all, I want you to talk to me like you got some sense. You know how I get down. Second, I need to talk to you. Let's go upstairs."

Diamond rolled her eyes and let out a frustrated breath as she lead the way upstairs. "We not together no more, man. You can't keep on doing this."

"You always gon' be mine. How many times I gotta tell you that?" Goldie laughed in amusement as he followed her.

"Fuck up with that nigga?" Junior asked Mercedes.

She looked a little nervous. "He always be doing this shit. He be tryna control her life."

"I know that nigga betta quit acting like he want this shit before I give it to him," Cee-Cee spat.

"He finna leave. He just tryna fuck up her night," Breezy added.
"Nigga gon' get fuck around and get fucked up," Dazè mugged.
"Please, y'all. Don't do nothing. Just let him leave," Mercedes begged.

"Yeah, let that nigga leave," T-Murda added. "Don't let that fuck nigga fuck up our night."

Five tense minutes later, Goldie walked down the stairs and out the door. Diamond came down the stairs a few moments later looking frustrated.

"You good?" Junior asked.

She shook her head. "I hate when that nigga do that shit. Just be popping up to see what I'm doing. Don't even be wanting shit."

"I think niggas only do what you let 'em. Y'all son ain't even here. He with yo' mama so what that nigga coming through here for?"

"I know. I'ma figure it out. But I don't even want to think about that nigga no more. I want to enjoy your company. What you wanna do?"

Junior pushed the baby daddy from his mind and leaned closer. "You know what I wanna do. What you wanna do?"

She leaned in for a kiss. "I wanna feel yo' lips on my body."

"So, why we still sitting here?"

Diamond led the way upstairs and Junior followed, slapping her perfect ass every time she took a step. Clothes started flying off as soon as the door closed. He pinned her to the bed, climbing on top and kissing her lips, neck, and breasts.

"Mmm, yeah!" Diamond moaned, thrusting her hips, wanting him inside.

After getting her hot, he slipped his dick inside her walls and began stroking. Then, the doorbell rang. Diamond's body went stiff, but Junior was in too deep to stop.

"Goldie here!" Mercedes yelled up the stairs.

"Wait, Junior! Stop!" Diamond panicked, pushing him up and opening the door to scream at her sister. "Don't open that door!"

"What you doing?" He asked angrily.

Diamond dressed quickly, forgetting to put her panties back on. "Goldie came back. I'm sorry."

"What he got to do with us? That ain't yo' nigga, right?"

She checked her appearance in the mirror before heading towards the door. "Wait right here. I'll be back."

"Ain't this bout a..." Junior mumbled as he got dressed. No way he was about to hide and be somebody's little secret. He put on everything except his shirt and left the room. Diamond and Goldie were on their way up the stairs when he stepped into the hallway.

"What the fuck do you want, nigga? Why you keep doing this?" Diamond yelled.

Goldie was about to respond when he noticed Junior wasn't wearing a shirt. The men locked eyes and Junior could see the baby daddy processing the information. When he realized Diamond was getting fucked, he exploded.

"Bitch, you was up there fucking this nigga?"

Diamond looked up the stairs at Junior and then back at Goldie. She looked like a deer caught in the headlights. Instead of facing the music, she ran in the bathroom and locked the door.

"Bitch, open this muthafuckin' door!" Goldie screamed while banging on the door.

Not wanting to be in a domestic situation, Junior headed downstairs. Most of his Parklawn niggas were still in the living room except Dazè. They looked amused while Diamond's girls looked worried.

"What that nigga on?" John laughed, listening to Goldie beat in the bathroom door and yell threats.

"Man, I don't even know, but I ain't with this shit. Y'all ready to mob?"

T-Murda headed for the door. "Yeah because it sound like that nigga finna kill that bitch and I ain't tryna be no witness to no bodies."

"And she bad too," RIP added, following his brother. "Nigga fuck around and try to kill er'body."

"Where Dazè at?" Junior asked as they stepped onto the porch.

"He drove Breezy to the store," Cee-Cee answered. "He should be back in a minute."

"Aight. Let's wait for fam and then we gon' vamp," Junior said before sitting on the porch.

Loud noises and women screaming could be heard coming from this house.

"Damn, that nigga ain't playing." John laughed.

"He bout to kill that bitch," Cee-Cee chuckled.

"She must got that WAP, Junior. On what?"

Junior looked towards the closed curtains in the windows upstairs to see if he could see something. "She got a shot but that shit ain't worth dying or going to jail for."

The front door being snatched open got the Grinders attention. Goldie stepped onto the porch breathing heavily. A stream of blood trickling from a scratch on his face, and shirt wrinkled. He addressed Junior.

"Ay, brah. You just fucked my baby mama?"

Junior laughed. "C'mon, my nigga. What me and her do ain't got nothing to do with you."

"Brah, you came down the stairs with no shirt on and she ain't got no panties on. I know you fucked."

Junior shook his head and laughed.

"Yeah, my nigga fucking yo' bitch," Cee-Cee jumped in. "Fuck you gon' do about it, nigga?"

Goldie looked to the shooter, seeing the venom in his eyes. He was outnumbered and outgunned, but he didn't want to look like a coward. He nodded, the promise of vengeance in his eyes. "Okay. You got that. But y'all gotta move around. Party over."

"Nigga, you know where the fuck you at? This our shit. You the one that betta move around, nigga," Junior mugged.

Goldie continued to get deeper in the dangerous water. "I don't care about that shit. This my bitch house and y'all gotta move around."

Cee-Cee pulled the pistol, about the body the jealous fool. "I'm tired of this bitch ass nigga!"

Junior grabbed his arm. Six's words about foolish killings popping into his head. "Nah, brah. Not right now. This ain't the right time. Them hoes gon' be witnesses."

Goldie lifted his arms, palms up and moved towards the door. "It's like that? Okay. You got it, boss," he said before ducking into the house.

Junior looked at Cee-Cee and shook his head. "Damn, my nigga. I see Dazè wasn't lying. You a goon."

"I just hate bitch ass niggas."

Dazè pulled up a few moments later and the Grinders filled him in on everything as they left.

J-Blunt

CHAPTER 11

Quitta sat up in bed and stretched, making sure to keep the phone tucked away in the corner of her bunk and out of view. She had been cramped up on the thin mattress for half an hour, trying to keep the phone hidden from anyone that walked by her room while talking to Russo.

"Do you think he'll ever trust me enough to make me a member of the Parklawn Grinders?" Russo asked. "So far he's given me nine ounces and I've shown that I can get money."

"I don't know. Maybe. He don't really tell me what he thinks no more. I think he's still mad that I fucked you, but he won't say anything or talk about it. But something is putting distance between us."

"I hope he doesn't let our relationship come between this money because I think I can be a real asset."

Quitta climbed back in bed and grabbed the phone. "Nah. He won't let nothing come between him and his money. That's for sure."

"You want to hear some the crazy?"

"What?"

"My mom keeps asking me about him. Actually, asked me for his phone number or Facebook name."

Quitta was surprised. "Really?"

"Yeah. It's kinda weird, to be honest. My mom is cool with all my friends, and she still talks to some of them online, but those are guys I went to high school with or people I've known for a long time. She meets Junior one time and she's all asking about him and wanting me to bring him over again."

Quitta wondered if Junior fucked his mother but didn't know how to ask. "Do you think your mom is crushing on him?"

Russo eyes got big. "What? Hell no! My mom loves my dad and wouldn't cheat on him." Then he thought for a moment. "I don't think she would. I mean, we left them alone for a little while, but it wasn't long enough for them to... Or was it?" Then, he got mad. "If I find out he touched my mother..."

"Calm down, Nate," Quitta giggled, amused by his anger. She knew that Junior fucked his mother, but she didn't want to create any problems between them, so she tried to clean it up. "It was probably nothing. Plus, I don't think Junior would mess with an old white lady. I've seen some of the females he cheated on me with, and they are pretty."

"Are you calling my mom ugly?"

"What? No! I was just saying that he likes younger girls. Like around our age."

"Now you're calling her old?"

"C'mon, Nate."

He bust out laughing. "I'm just kidding. I had you going for a minute though."

"You know what Nate? Fuck you."

He gave a wicked smile. "Now you're talking my language."

Seeing the look in his eyes gave her a flashback of having sex in the conference room. They had done it three times.

"You want to eat my pussy again?"

"Do you want me to eat your pussy again?"

"Hell yeah."

"Say it. Tell me that you want me to eat your pussy."

"I want you to come eat my pussy right now, Nate."

"Damn, that was so fucking hot. My cock is so goddamn hard right now. I can't wait to be inside you. I'm on my way right now. I'll see you in a minute."

Quitta giggled as she ended the call and allowed thoughts of Russo digging in her guts fill her head. She really liked him. She wasn't sure if she could be in a relationship with him, but she was going this keep him around. He would do anything for her, and she couldn't let a man like that get away. And he really liked eating her pussy. Having the furry face between her legs was a different feeling. It tickled and felt good at the same time. And when he sucked her pearl... Just thinking about it made her hands slide into her panties and begin stroking her clit. She was fantasizing about cumming on his beard when a voice crackled through the room's intercom, startling her.

"Ware, you have a professional visit."

"Damn," she flinched. "That was fast."

After washing her hands in the sink, she cuffed the phone and left the cell. The escorting officer showed up a few moments later to take her to the conference room. When he stopped outside of one of the rooms with a window on the door, Quitta paused to look inside. There was a white man sitting in the room that looked like the District Attorney that was trying to convict her of murder.

"This is the wrong room, officer. I'm visiting somebody else."

He gave her a questioning look. "You're Marquitta Ware, right?"

"Yeah, but I was expecting somebody else."

"Sorry, but this is your visitor," he said before opening the door.

Quitta eyed the District Attorney warily as she stepped into the room.

Steven Milan sat at the table, a phone in front of him. A serious look on his face. "Please, Miss Ware. Have a seat. I'll take it from here, officer."

Quitta sat down slowly trying to figure out what the fuck was going on. Did Russo really set her up? Was Junior right?

"You look like you were expecting to see someone else."

"I don't want to talk to you without my lawyer."

He lifted a hand in a defensive gesture. "Normally I wouldn't talk to someone I was prosecuting without their lawyer or at least one of my colleagues present, but I needed to keep this meeting between me and you. The less people that know about this, the better. I just wanted to run some things by you. It's up to you if you want to talk. You don't have to if you don't want to. But I think you should at least listen to what I have to say. It's important."

Quitta studied him for a moment, considering the offer. All he wanted was for her to listen. "Okay. I'll listen."

"I'm going to make this simple, Quitta. Is Detective Russo dirty?"

Quitta flinched a little, unable to hide the surprise at being asked the question. "What?"

"I told you I wasn't going to bullshit you so don't bullshit me. I've seen your visitor records and Detective Russo has visited you seventeen times. Something is going on and I want to know what. If you cooperate with me and I find out that Russo is a dirty cop, I will drop the murder charges against you and let you go. I will not have a dirty cop in my city. That can comprise every case where he was an investigating or arresting officer. This is very serious, Quitta. More serious than the overdose death. This could be federal. If you're involved with his activities in any way, you will be charged with even more charges. This is your opportunity to guarantee that you get to raise that kid at home as well as give birth to the one you're pregnant with in a real hospital."

Quitta didn't know what to say, think, or do. Beads of sweat popped up on her forehead, her underarms perspired, and palms turned clammy. The District Attorney served her some serious shit and she could face more charges. Federal charges. Just thinking the words *federal charges* scared the shit out of her.

"I-I don't know if he's dirty."

Steven looked down at the table and shook his head. When he looked up again, he was smiling. "Just listen." He unlocked the phone and began playing a recording.

"Quitta?"

"Yeah, this me. Where yo' ass been? I been tryna call you all morning?"

When Quitta heard the beginning of the argument she had with Junior, she knew it was all bad.

"Man, I was out all night with Six. We had to go through California and didn't get back until four this morning. What's up with you? Where the slapper?"

"Some bullshit. He got mad and took it."

"He took it? For what? What he get mad about?"

"I can't say right now. It's some bullshit ass emotional shit."

"You didn't have nothing about me in it, did you? You know these muthafuckas tryna get me."

"Nigga, everything ain't about you, Junior! I'm the one in jail, nigga. You out in Vegas and California fucking all kinds of bitches and I'm in here pregnant with yo' baby and fighting for my life. Fuck you. You talking about them tryna get you when they already got me and all you care about is what they tryna do to you. What kind of shit is that? Why is it always about you? I'm facing forty years in prison, and they won't even give me a bail because of yo' ass. Fuck you, nigga."

"What the fuck is you talking about, nigga? I'm tryna get yo' ass out. If yo' ass wouldn't have been fucking with Steph bitch ass, you ass wouldn't be in there. Don't try to blame me nigga. I'm doing what I can to get you out. Fuck is you talking 'bout?"

"Oh, that's what we on now? All this is my fault, nigga? You the one that wanted to go to that muthafuckin club, nigga. I told you I didn't want to be a part of none—"

"Shut the fuck up, Quitta! This shit being recorded. What the fuck is wrong with you?"

"You what's wrong with me, nigga! You got me in here and now you talking about this shit is my fault. You did that shit, not me. I'm tryna be a real bitch and take the case but you tryna treat me like a weak ass bitch. I got yo' baby in my stomach, nigga. Fuck you talking about?"

"Quitta, stop saying that extra shit, okay. If you wanna talk, we can talk. But you gotta quit that extra shit or I'm hanging up. This shit is recorded, and they can use this shit in court. Control yo' emotions, nigga."

"Well stop tryna make it seem like it's me. I'm doing what I'm supposed to do. I just want you to listen to me and my problems. I want to feel like a priority. It's always about you."

"Okay, Quitta. Tell me about your problems. What's on your mind?"

"Why you gotta say it like that? Like I'm some kind of charity case or you doing me a favor?"

"What is you talking about? You just said I don't listen to you and then when I ask you, you won't tell me. What am I supposed this do?"

"I don't know, Junior. I don't know what to do or what to think. I think this damn baby making me crazy. I just want to come home."

"I'm tryna get you out, baby mama. You just gotta stay strong. They don't got nothing on you. Henrik said the same thing. You

155

good. Just stay strong. You a souljah. You got this; you hear me? You got it."

Steven stopped the recording and stared at her for a moment. "Junior and your lawyer were right. The case against you was weak and we didn't have much. I would've probably tried to get you to cop to a lesser charge just to get the conviction. But that argument you had gave us and the Milwaukee Police Department everything we need to convict you. I know that a slapper is a cell phone. I can get you and your cell searched and find that phone just like that," he snapped a finger. "I'm guessing there is a mountain of evidence on that phone that we could use against you. Oh, and that club that you said Junior wanted to go to is the club where you met Fredo, right? According to you, it was all Junior's plan. Don't try to play hardball with me on this, Quitta, because you'll lose. Fortunately for you, a dirty cop is more important than a drug addict killing herself on some bad Heroin that I know you didn't sell her. If you help me get Russo, I will drop the charges and let you keep the phone until you are released. But you can't delete anything from the phone. I need that to get a conviction. So, what do you want to do?"

Quitta was stuck. She was in way too far over her head and didn't trust herself to decide. She needed help but didn't know who to confide in. The shit was too serious. Then, she began to panic. "Oh, my God! I don't know what to do. Oh, my God! Oh, my God!"

Steven reached across the table and grabbed her hand. "Calm down, Quitta. Don't fall apart. I know this is a lot but I'm giving you the opportunity to free yourself. As a matter of fact, you don't have to make the decision right now. No one knows about this conversation except me and you. We can keep it that way if you want. Or you can get advice from your lawyer. But whatever you do, don't talk to Russo or anyone else about this. Okay?"

Quitta felt numb inside. She wanted to go home and be with her family. She missed her son. She didn't want to be in jail fighting for her life and freedom. Every time she turned around, there was another twist. The shit was stressing her out, threatening to ruin her sanity.

"I need you to keep this between us, Quitta. Can you do that?"

She nodded.

"Good. You can go back to your unit now. I'll be in touch."

Quitta's head was so fucked up after leaving the conference room that she didn't remember the walk back to her cell. The next thing she knew is she was lying in bed crying her eyes out with life with her family and friends flashing before her eyes. The thought of federal charges were terrifying. She was raised not to snitch. If you got knocked, you took your own weight. But she didn't know if she was built to spend the rest of her life in prison following a code that was dying. And how much loyalty did she owe a cop? She understood protecting family and friends, but the police? She needed advice from someone that wouldn't judge. The only person she could think of was her mom, but she didn't want to tell her everything she was going through. Her mom would start preaching and talking about God and blah, blah, blah. Quitta wasn't ready to have that conversation. She also needed to tell Junior that they recorded their conversation and were threatening to use it against him. That was the most important call. Keeping her children's father free meant everything. As soon as she powered on the phone, it vibrated. Nate was calling. She didn't want to answer but her finger pressed the green button.

"Hey, I was trying to warn you that Steven Milan was coming to see you. Are you good?"

Quitta closed her eyes and exhaled. "Yeah. He's coming for me. He played a recording of me and Junior arguing where I said it was his plan to go to the club and that I'm in here because of him. He said they can use that for the Milwaukee case and wants me to turn on Junior to save myself."

"What did you say?"

"I told him no. What did you think I would say?"

"I didn't mean it like that, but I had to ask. Did you talk to your lawyer yet or Junior?"

"No. I just stepped in the room and when I turned on the phone, it was you."

"Oh, okay. Do you need me to do anything? How can I help?"

"I don't know. I just got all of this, and I need some time to think and call my lawyer. I'll call you later."

"Okay. I'm going to do some digging around and see what I can find. I'll text you if I find anything."

"Okay, thanks. Bye."

Quitta let out a stressed breath. She wasn't sure why she didn't tell Russo that Steven was investigating him. For some reason, she wanted to keep the information to herself. At least until she made up her mind about what to do. She wanted to tell Junior about the DA's offer so bad, but she didn't want to hear his speech on how snitching wasn't an option. He would definitely pressure her to keep it G and she didn't want to let anyone make a final decision about her freedom. The decision had to be her own because she had the most to lose. Damn. After a few more moments of going back and forth, she called her baby daddy on Facebook. He answered with a smile.

"What's good, baby mama?" When he noticed the swelling and redness of her eyes, he became concerned. "What's up, girl? You good?"

She didn't want to cry but the tears came anyway. "No. The DA just came to see me, and I'm scared. He played the recording of us arguing when I said that I'm in here because of you and that it was yo' plan to go to the bar."

"Shit," Junior cursed. "Damn, baby mama. That shit is fucked up. What did Henrik say?"

"He wasn't there. It was just me."

"Henrik wasn't there?" Junior screamed. "What you mean? Why the fuck you talking to the DA without a lawyer?"

"I didn't know it was him. I thought it was Nate but when I got to the room, it was the DA. He said he just wanted to talk to me, and I didn't have to say nothing. I just listened."

"What did he say?"

"That he want me to tell on you and he will let me go."

"Goddam, Quitta! This why I told yo' ass not to talk on the muthafuckin phone. Shit!"

"I know I fucked up, nigga. Damn. I'm sorry. But you don't got to throw the I told you so in my face. I'm the one locked up, not you. That's not what I need to hear right now."

They went silent. Both of their minds were racing with possible outcomes.

"Okay, listen. You gotta call Henrik. Tell him what the DA said and see what he think. I'm in traffic making moves right now but tell him I'ma call him as soon as I'm done. I hope this shit didn't jam us up, baby mama. I'ma call you back later."

After ending the call Quitta didn't feel so bad about not telling Junior about that deal. She knew he wouldn't understand. Instead of trying this comfort her, he jumped to worrying about himself.

"I hate yo' ass, Junior," Quitta mumbled before calling her lawyer.

"Hey, Quitta. How you doing?"

"It's all bad, man. Steven Milan just came to visit me. He played a recording of me and Junior's argument and said he was gon' give it to the police in Milwaukee if I didn't cooperate with him."

Henrik became irate. "He did what? When?"

"About twenty minutes ago."

"That slimy sonofabitch! Okay. What else did he say?"

Quitta paused, wondering if she should tell him about the Russo deal. "He offered to let me out if I tell on Russo."

"Wait, what?"

"He knows that Russo has been coming to see me. He even knows about my phone. He thinks Russo is dirty and told me that he would drop all the charges against me and won't give the recording to Milwaukee if I turn on Russo."

"Damn, Quitta. That's a hell of a deal. How bad is the recording? What did you and Junior say?"

"We argued and I said going to the club was his idea and that I was locked up because of him."

"Okay. You incriminated yourself a little bit, but I need to hear more of the call. I'm going to contact the DA to listen to the tap. Have you talked to Junior about this?"

"I told him about the recording, but I didn't tell him about the Russo deal. They been doing business and he would've told Russo about it. I want to make the decision on my own. I want it to be my choice so I would appreciate if you didn't tell him either."

"Okay. I'm your lawyer so I have to do what you say. But I think you should at least tell him the truth about the offer. Just so he isn't blind in all of this, you know?"

"No. I'm not ready to tell him right now. I need more time to figure out what to do. Just tell him they want me to turn against him. That's what I want."

"Okay, I won't tell him. I'm going to call the DA to see if I can listen to the recording. So, Russo brought you the phone, huh? How serious is your relationship with him?"

Quitta thought about how much to reveal. Henrik was her lawyer and probably needed to know everything just in case it came out later. "We've had sex a couple times and he wants to be with me when I get out."

"Wow. I wasn't expecting to hear that. Sounds like he's serious. Where is your head at as far as a relationship is concerned? Are there feelings on your end?"

"I think he's cool, but I don't want to be with him. I think it's more of me liking what he can do for me."

"Sounds like you might be willing to cooperate if it can help you and Junior."

"I might."

CHAPTER 12

Cee-Cee reached out an arm and pulled Patricia close, loving the feel of the beautiful and soft skinned woman snuggled against him. He spent five years in a cell dreaming of this simple moment. He never imagined the first woman that he would link up with when he got home would be a therapist. He was a street nigga that had only dealt with thotties. For him to have a woman as pretty and smart as Patricia was like hitting the lottery. They were in her bedroom at her mother's house, laying in the bed, watching the old school classic movie, The Best Man. This was the second time he'd been invited over to Netflix and chill. The first time he was a gentleman and the night ended with an innocent peck on the lips. But based on the way she was cuddled up next to him, her left leg resting between his, arm around his waist, and head on his shoulder, he knew that tonight would be the night.

"You think you could forgive someone for cheating on you?" Patricia asked.

"I don't think so. Once that trust is broken, it's over. I'm out."

"But what if it was a mistake? What if she really loves you but fucked up that one time?"

"Fuck that. One time is too many. I think that if you forgive somebody for fucking you over, you gave them permission to do it again. Cause keep it real; how many peoples cheat one time? I used to watch Cheaters marathons while I was locked up and I saw how niggas and females be moving. Ain't nobody finna have me looking stupid."

"I think people can change. Plus, you know that show was fake, right?"

Cee-Cee looked stunned. "Yeah, right. I saw Joey get stabbed and when the white boy knocked out his girl. That shit way real."

"Sorry to tell you that it's all staged. It was a thing online a little while ago. All fake."

Cee-Cee pinched her thigh. "Don't say that shit no more. Cheaters is real!"

"Ouch, nigga! Don't pinch me," she said, biting his shoulder.

"Ahhh! I know you just didn't bite me, nigga." He rubbed the spot. "And I think you left a mark."

Patricia giggled. "Let me see."

When he lifted the shirt, Patricia took a look and slapped him on the chest. "It ain't even no mark right there, crybaby."

Cee-Cee rubbed the place where she slapped and bit him. "Yes, it is. I can feel teeth marks."

"You mean to tell me that you rob and shoot people but start whining about a little bite?"

"I'm showing you my sensitive side, girl. You betta appreciate this shit before I turn into Ike Turner. Eat the cake, Anna Mae!"

Patricia bust out laughing. "You crazy, dude."

"Now what you gon' do to make my pain go away?"

"Oh, my God! You such a baby. You want me to kiss it and make it better?"

"I do. But kiss my lips."

"What yo' lips got to do with a bite on your chest?"

"Thigh bone is connected to my knee bone. Chest bone connected to my lip bone."

"Do you even know biology? I'm pretty sure you don't have a lip bone." She laughed while lowering her head.

Cee-Cee met her lips, parting them with his tongue and tasting the Pepsi that she had been drinking. Sexy moans escaped from her throat as the kiss became increasingly passionate. Then, he flipped her onto her back, climbing between her legs, grinding his pelvis against hers as they continued to make out. When his hands tugged at the bottom of her shirt, she sat up so that he could remove it. The bra came off next and he didn't waste time sucking and teasing her breasts.

"Damn, that feels so good," she moaned.

When she was hot, he kissed his way down her stomach, unbuckling her jeans and kissing the top of her pussy.

"Let me take them off," she groaned, wanting to see what he was about to do with his mouth.

He got up to undress while she lifted her butt off the bed and shimmied out of the rest of her clothes. When he was naked, Patricia reached out a hand to stroke his hard tool.

"Damn." She shivered with anticipation.

"You the one that got me like this," he said, staring down at her naked body like she was a doe and he a hungry wolf.

He climbed back into bed and grabbed her leg, bringing her foot to his mouth and sucking her toes. Then, he kissed and licked his way past her ankle, knee, thigh, and in between her legs. He licked circles around her outer lips before spreading her pussy and sucking her clit. He continued going back and forth from licking her slit to sucking her clit. Patricia's excitement and orgasm built with each flick of Cee-Cee's tongue until she exploded on his face. Then, he climbed between her legs and gave her the meat, entering her slowly until they were pelvis to pelvis. He kissed her some more while letting her walls adjust to him being inside. When she began moving her hips, he gave her what she wanted, working his way into long, fast, and hard strokes. Patricia dug her nails into the skin of his back, crying out from the pleasure and pain. The sound of her moans were music to Cee-Cee's ears, keeping him energized and hard. Patricia had another orgasm. The second one was bigger than the first, making her pussy dripping wet and finally pushing Cee-Cee over the edge. After shooting inside of her, he lay between her legs and kissed her some more while staring in her eyes.

"Do you believe in love at first sight?"

Patricia was still a little speechless from the good sex and had to find her voice. "I don't know. Why?"

"Because I think I loved you from to first moment that I saw you."

She had no words to describe how the great loving and beautiful words made her feel. So she let her heart do the talking. "I think I love you, too."

***

"She love me, nigga. I made her say it last night." Cee-Cee grinned while climbing in the passenger seat of the Scat Pack.

"Fuck is you talking 'bout, nigga?" Dazè asked.

"I'm talking about Patricia. I got her, my nigga. I fucked her so good that she told me she love me, nigga."

Dazè shot him a skeptical look. "Stop capping, nigga. You only knew her for a week."

"All facts, no jacks. She love me, my nigga. I bagged a mutha-fuckin doctor, nigga!" Cee-Cee celebrated.

"You did good," Dazè chuckled, giving his nigga props. "Bet you never seen shit happening like this when we was locked in them cages. Now, we out here eating good and fucking bad bitches. We bosses."

"We bosses." Cee-Cee nodded in approval. "I never thought we was gon' get to the bag this fast. I knew niggas was gon' eventually get what they wanted because we talked about having it and wanted it too much. But to have it all drop in our laps like this is a blessing."

"Preach."

"Now, all we gotta do is get one of them top spots and we really gon' be eating."

Dazè shot his nigga a glance. "You still on that, huh?"

"I been around these niggas for a week, and I see all they weak-nesses. You need to be in one of this top spots. I feel like you was made for that. All the shit we went through in The Bay prepared you for this. Tell me that shit don't cross yo' mind."

"You already know it do. Everything that I been through made me everything that I am. I'm ready to lead, no doubt. But I also fuck with these niggas. They put us right in, no questions asked. Without the Grinders, we wouldn't be in the position that we in. We can't burn that bridge because of our egos. Sometimes you got to accept what happens and make the right moved when the opportunity pre-sents itself."

Cee-Cee pretended to agree. "Yeah, I hear you."

"But you don't agree?"

"You already know I don't. But you made a valid point about them niggas putting us in positions to win. Without them niggas, we wouldn't be shit. So, we do owe them some loyalty. But when the opportunity presents itself, I think we should take it."

Dazè shook his head and laughed.

When the newest members of the Parklawn Grinders pulled up to the hood, they spotted a pretty light skinned female standing on Diamond's porch. It was Diamond's friend, Breezy. Dazè made eye contact with her as he drove by. A few moments later, his phone rang. It was Breezy.

"What's good, shorty?"

"That's how it is, nigga? You don't know how to speak?" Breezy asked with a little attitude.

"Stop flexing, baby girl. You know I got a girl."

"So, what that mean? I bet her pussy don't get wet as mine."

Dazè laughed. "Stop playing with me, Breezy before I break yo' back."

"That's what I'm talking about, nigga. Talk that nasty shit to me. I like it gangsta."

"Man, you gon' fuck around and make me come see you. What you doing tonight?"

"I'm doing you, nigga. Tell yo' bitch to fall back because you mine tonight. Put this pussy on you and make you forget her name."

"Keep that same energy. I'ma call you when I finish taking care of my business."

"Pop a roller and a Viagra before you come because I ain't with that one and done. I need my pussy beat up; you hear me?" "Keep talking shit and I'ma make you tap out." Dazè chuckled while pulling up to Gail's house. "But let me take care of this business. I'ma fuck with you later."

"Damn, my nigga. She was jacking good." Cee-Cee laughed.

"That was Diamond friend, Breezy. I'ma slide through there later and break her back for talking to me like that."

After a full day of hustling and running through the projects, Dazè and Cee-Cee made their way over to Diamond's house later that night and found Breezy home alone.

"Where er'body at?" Dazè asked as they had seats in the living room.

"Ever since Goldie bitch ass put Diamond in the hospital, ain't nobody been over here. Tiffany and Mercedes come through every now and then, but they don't want to stay here without Diamond. They scared of Goldie."

"Dude is a bitch ass nigga," Dazè laughed.

"If I see that nigga, I'ma lay his ass down," Cee-Cee promised.

"Somebody need to fuck that nigga up. He won't fight a nigga, but he would beat a bitch up quick. I hate that bitch ass nigga."

A key being inserted into the lock on the front door grabbed everyone's attention. Goldie walked in a moment later. Breezy looked disgusted by the sight of him. Dazè and Cee-Cee looked ready to kill. Goldie noticed the men's hostile looks and chose to focus on Breezy.

"What's good?"

"What you want, Goldie?"

"Fuck you mean what I want?" He mugged." This my bitch house. Matter of fact, you and yo' niggas can ride up out of here."

"I ain't going nowhere, nigga. I live here too. You ain't gon' do me like you did Diamond. I ain't scared of you."

"It's time for you to leave, nigga," Dazè stood up.

"You can't be in Parklawn no more, nigga, or we green lighting yo' ass," Cee-Cee added.

Goldie looked in the eyes of the Parklawn Grinders. He could read the animosity on their faces, hostilities hanging in the air like a thick fog. But he wasn't about to let them put him out of his baby mama's house. So, he went for the gun on his waist.

Dazè read the fight or flight decision playing in Goldie's eyes. And as soon as he reached, Dazè started throwing punches. Cee-Cee knew that Goldie was about to pull it and as soon as he reached, Cee-Cee went for his gun too. Goldie caught two punches to the face, stumbling backwards, arms flailing as he clutched the black 9mm. Before he could catch his balance, Cee-Cee started shooting.

Pop, pop, pop

Goldie fell to the floor as bullets entered his face, never getting the chance to fire a shot.

"Ahhhhh! Oh my God!" Breezy screamed, jumping on the couch, hand covering her mouth.

When Dazè seen the terrified look in her eyes, he turned to Cee-Cee. "She gotta—"

Cee-Cee started gunning before he could get all of the words out.

Pop, pop, pop

After making sure Goldie and Breezy were dead, the killers wiped their prints from around the living room as best as they could before leaving.

***

Junior whipped the Subaru Ascent SUV through traffic, watching the mirrors for signs of being followed as he drove down Capitol, headings for Parklawn. Ever since Quitta told him the DA threatened her with the recording, he'd been extremely cautious. He put away the Corvette and Lexus truck and bought the Subaru. Whenever he was out, he checked his surroundings constantly. He knew that Detective Johnson and a squad could pop up at any time. He thought about leaving town, but Henrik told him it was unnecessary because the hadn't submitted the recording as evidence. He was holding it and wouldn't say why. Wouldn't even let Henrik listen. So, all Junior could do was wait.

"I can't do life, my nigga."

Junior looked over at Fifty. "What you talking about?"

"I been thinking about yo' situation, fam, and I can't do a life bid. I be surprised when I hear about niggas that kill a bunch of mu'fuckas go without a shootout when the police come. Them niggas be knowing that they ain't never getting out the bing but they still go in. Fuck dying slow. I'm going out on my terms."

"What if they holding on to the hope that one day they can get out again. Some niggas be getting back on appeal."

"But that shit be rare. Especially, if you offed more than one person. Look at that lil bitch ass nigga that shot all of them kids at that school in Texas. The nigga should've made them kill him or did it his self because they gon' execute him. That's the kind of shit I'm talking about. Fuck going to jail. I'm going out like a gangsta and I'm taking a couple police with me."

Junior thought about his situation. He talked to Henrik about the amount of time he would be facing if they came with charges. Sixty years. Doing that much time seemed impossible. "Henrik told me that I could be facing sixty years if they come with charges."

Fifty shook his head, giving Junior a serious look. "Ain't no way, brah. Don't let them punks put you in a cell for the rest of yo' life. Go out on yo' terms."

The friends were interrupted by Junior's phone ringing. It was Dazè on Facetime. "What's good family?"

"Don't go to the hood, my nigga. It's hot."

Junior's heart started racing. Johnson must've rolled through. "What happened?"

"We had to knock off Goldie and Breezy. They probably finna lock the projects down."

Junior wasn't expecting to hear that. "You did what!"

"Yeah, fam. The nigga got out of his body and Cee-Cee banged both of them."

"That nigga knocked off both they ass!" Fifty asked, excited by the murders.

Junior's mind raced with possible outcomes. More police, less money, and Johnson asking more questions. "Damn, fam. I don't like that shit. Where you at?"

"I'm driving up Capitol. We gon' duck off for that night."

"I'm coming up Capitol too. Meet me at the gas station on 60th so we can holla."

Junior pulled into the gas station and parked behind Dazè's Challenger. They all got out to greet each other.

"Why y'all off the nigga? Where it happen at?" Junior asked.

"In the living room at Diamond house," Dazè answered. "Bitch called me on some smashing shit, and I slid. This nigga shows up talking reckless and got fucked up."

"We told that nigga to leave and he reached. I bodied his ass. Had to bag the bitch too because I ain't leaving no witnesses." Cee-Cee added.

Junior shook his head. "Damn, my nigga. Wasn't no other way? Y'all had to off 'em?"

Dazè gave Junior a searching look. "That nigga had a Glizzy, my nigga. What you think we was supposed to do? You know how we move. Niggas don't ask questions."

"Plus, you seen how that soft ass nigga was tryna act like he wanted to get active the night you was fucking Diamond. He already got a pass. I wasn't giving out no more," Cee-Cee added.

Junior didn't like the bravado Cee-Cee displayed and attempted to put him in his place. "You ain't the one that decide who get passes in my hood, my nigga. If the police swarming, that slow down er'body money. Y'all know Johnson on my ass and y'all just gave him a reason to get closer. We getting real money, my nigga. The whole projects is ours. We can't be burning down our own shit over some pussy whipped ass nigga. Y'all could've followed the nigga and did it somewhere else. Y'all had options."

Anger flashed in Dazè and Cee-Cee's eyes.

"We security, fam. What you mean we can't decide who get a pass? You saying' we gotta get permission to put a nigga down?" Dazè asked.

The situation changed quickly, and Junior was suddenly at odds with his niggas. But he couldn't fold. He created the Parklawn Grinders, and everybody needed to respect his slot. "I don't know where this is going, fam, but this is the reason I created positions. Everybody got a role to play and it's my decision as to who does what. I make the final decisions. If I say something, that's law, regardless of who like it or not. Y'all decided that's about to affect er'body. Twelve finna start asking questions. People finna talk. And all this shit could fall back on me. So yeah, my nigga, if y'all putting niggas down on Black Wall Street, I need to know about it before it happens."

Fifty watched the exchange, paying close attention to Cee-Cee's body language. The untamed shooter sucked the back of his teeth while mugging Junior. Envy, betrayal, and violence showed in his eyes. The Grinders let in a snake, and he was about to bite.

"Okay, Mr. President. You calling the shots. We made a bad move." Dazè nodded, throwing up his hands, defiance in his eyes.

Junior could feel the energy shift when he put the shooters in their places. John's warning about Cee-Cee played through his head as he looked back and forth from the members of his security. "Ain't nothing we can do about it now. Just fall back and see what tomorrow bring. I'ma fuck with you niggas later."

"You got it, boss. Y'all stay safe." Cee-Cee nodded as he walked backwards to the Challenger.

Junior maintained eye contact with him, trying to decide if he was just threatened. "You, too."

"I'ma get up with y'all later then," Dazè said before hopping in the Scat Pack and driving away.

Fifty and Junior stood side by side, watching the shooters leave. "That nigga threatened me, Fif."

"It's a snake in the grass, my nigga. We got to cut that bitch head off."

***

Junior was awakened by his phone vibrating on the bedside table. When he seen Diamond's name on the screen, he thought about not answering. Her baby daddy and friend died last night. For all he knew, she could be working with them people trying to book him. But another part of him was sympathetic towards her pain. She wasn't a fly by night female that he fucked and forgot about the next day. He put in effort and connected with her. At one point, he considered making her the first lady. He felt like he owed her some answers.

"Hey."

"Did you really have to kill him," Diamond cried. "And what did Breezy do?"

"That wasn't me. I wasn't even in the hood when it happened."

"But that don't mean you don't know what happened. Why, Junior? Why you do this to me?"

He let out a frustrated breath, wishing he would've let the phone go to voicemail. "It wasn't me, Diamond. I didn't do nothing. That's my word as a man."

"What am I supposed to tell my son? What about Breezy's family? I could understand killing Goldie, but Breezy didn't do shit to nobody. Why her?"

"Listen, I don't want to talk on this phone. Tell me where you at and I'ma come to you."

"You think I'ma snitch?" She scoffed. "You think I'm working with the police to get you now? They showed me a picture of you and asked if I knew you, but I didn't tell them nothing. I ain't no punk ass bitch."

Alarms, bells, and whistles went off in Junior's head. "They showed you my picture? Who?"

"Yeah, Detective Johnson questioned me about who could've did it and showed me your picture and asked if I knew you."

"What did you say?" Junior asked, his heart thudding so hard that he thought it was going to jump out of his chest.

"I lied. I told him I've never seen you. I could've fucked you up, but I didn't. I'm not built like that. So, can you at least tell me why? I want to know what happened. I need to know. Please."

"Tell me where you at."

"I'm by my mother's house on the Southside. 6th and Pierce."

"Alright, I'm on my way."

After waking Mooka and getting dressed, Junior jumped in the Subaru with his son and headed to Diamond's mother's house. The whole way he was hoping that she wasn't setting him up. When he turned onto the block, he did a drive by, looking for anything that didn't look right. After circling back around, he parked at the corner and sent a text, letting her know he was pulling up. She stepped outside a few moments later, searching up and down the block. He watched her for a moment to see if she would try to signal anybody or do something suspicious. When he was satisfied that she wasn't on any bullshit, he drove towards her. She climbed in the passenger seat with swollen red eyes. There was also a healed scar on the left side of her neck.

"I'm sorry about what happened to yo' people, but that wasn't me."

"Just tell me what happened. That's yo' hood. I know you know."

"Breezy called my nigga to come through. When they get there, yo' baby daddy pop up talking shit. They told him to leave the hood. They had some more words and he reached. Breezy was a witness. They did 'em both."

Diamond shook her head in disbelief as tears rolled down her face.

"Why she crying, daddy?" Mooka asked.

"Somebody she know died, man."

"Awe, I'm sorry. You want me to give her a hug?"

"My son want to hug you."

Diamond reached in the backseat to hug the toddler. "Thanks, lil man."

"You welcome. Don't cry. Whoever died is in Heaven with God."

Diamond wiped away tears, trying to keep it together. "He is too cute and too smart. Don't you think you should leave the streets alone for him? You a good nigga, Junior, and I don't wanna see you end up like my baby daddy."

"I think about it a lot. I keep telling myself that I'ma leave it alone once I get enough money, but I don't know how much is enough. I got so much shit going on in my life that I'm not sure if I'ma make it to next week. My whole life could be turned upside down at any moment. That's why I was pissed off about what them niggas did. I didn't condone that shit, Diamond. They did that shit on they own, and I probably just got into it with them niggas about it. They can't see that everything that happens in the projects is gon' fall back on me. That's why Detective Johnson showed you my picture. He been tryna book my ass and the shit that happened last night only made my situation worse. Even though I wasn't even in the hood when it went down, I'll still get the blame."

"Damn, Junior. I didn't know you was going through all of that. But if you know that he coming for you, why don't you move or do something else?"

Junior shook his head. "I can't give you a good answer. All I know is that I can't walk away right now."

She stared at him for a moment. "Well, just know that I didn't tell Johnson nothing."

"I appreciate you keeping my name out of that. Thank you."

"I know my baby daddy wasn't shit and he was probably gon' get killed one day or end up in jail. I even wished he was dead while I was in the hospital, but I didn't think it was actually going to happen. I guess that was God answering my prayer, huh?"

"Be careful what you pray for because it just might come true."

"It just hurts, man. And I'm really hurting for my son and Breezy's family. But we gon' be okay. Thanks for coming to talk to me. I need to get back in the house."

"Before you go, let me give you this." He dug into the console and pulled out twenty five thousand dollars. "This so you won't have to go back to that house in Parklawn. Buy all new stuff and start over somewhere else. And if you need anything, don't hesitate to call me."

She gave him a peck on the lips before taking the money. "Thanks, baby. I appreciate everything. Take care."

Junior pulled away from Diamond's mother's house thanking his lucky stars that she didn't tell Johnson about him. He'd dodged a bullet. But he didn't get too cocky. Detective Johnson was a bloodhound and now that he had a reason to be in the projects, there was no doubt in Junior's mind that he would be seeing him soon. He would have to be careful and keep his eyes open. Thoughts about the detective were interrupted by a call from another cop.

"Russo, what's good?"

"You got it, man. How you doing?"

Junior let out a breath. "I'm still alive and free. What more can I ask for?"

"Damn. It's been that kind of a day already?"

"Man, you don't even know. Detective Johnson is probably about to make life hard for me. Some shit happened last night, and my name came up."

"That's fucked up, man. You need me to do anything?"

Junior thought for a moment. "I don't know. I can't think of anything right now, but I'll let you know. What's up with you?"

"I just wanted to let you know that I would be in town later. I need another one."

"Okay. Just hit me when you get here."

"All right. Will do. Oh, I meant to tell you that my mom keeps asking about you. You left a good impression."

Junior smiled as thoughts of Pam on her knees with his dick in her mouth popped into his head. "Tell mama bear I said hi the next time you talk to her."

"Will do. See you soon."

Junior drove to his mother's house with plans to spend the rest of the day inside, only moving when necessary. Knowing that Johnson was lurking and could strike at any moment, kept him on his toes. He drove past Diamond's apartment to check out the activity. There was a squad car parked out front and yellow tape on the front door but no sign of Johnson. When he walked in his mother's house, Renae was sitting in the couch watching TV.

"What's up, bro? Hey, Mooka," Renae greeted.

"What up?" Junior said before going to look out the window.

"Hey, Tee-Tee! Can I play my game?" Mooka asked, already turning on the PlayStation before she could agree.

"I guess you gon' do it any way." She laughed. "What you looking out of windows for, nigga?"

"Johnson bitch ass out there lurking. He been asking about me."

"Is that because of that shit that happened last night? They said two people got killed on 46th."

Junior nodded. "I wasn't even in the hood and my name is in that shit."

"Damn, bro. That's fucked up. Do you know who did it?"

Junior looked into his sister's eyes for a moment, wondering if he should tell her. "Dazè and Cee-Cee."

Her eyes grew wide in surprise. "On what?"

"For real. Where he at?"

"He said they was staying by Cee-Cee sister house. So, that's why."

"When the last time you talked to him?"

"Last night. He said he was supposed to come get me this morning. We want to go look for a house."

Junior frowned. "Y'all looking for a house?"

"Yeah. I need some privacy. We need our own shit."

"I guess so." Junior nodded. "When you talked to him last night, did he say anything about me?"

"Nah. Why?"

"I checked them niggas about killing Breezy and Goldie. All the shit that happens out here fall back on me. They got mad and Cee-Cee sent me a subliminal threat."

Her eyes grew even wider. "On what, bro? He really threatened you?"

"Real shit. I think shit finna go bad. I need you to let me know if them niggas say or do anything that don't look right. I need you to keep yo' eyes and ears open."

"I don't think Dazè on that, brah. He love us. The whole family. He really fuck with you. I think it might be just a misunderstanding."

Junior knew that his sister's point of view was clouded by her love for Dazè and that anything contrary to what she believed would be hard for her to comprehend. "I hope you right, my nigga. But I know what I seen and heard. I need you to be my eyes and ears. If you see or hear anything, I need you to let me know."

"Say less, bro. I got you."

J-Blunt

CHAPTER 13

Dazè was awakened by the warmth and wetness of Jenny's mouth slurping on his dick like she was having breakfast. He opened his eyes and seen her smiling at him like she was having the time of her life.

"You don't get tired, do you?" He asked, palming the back of her head.

"Mmmh mmmm," she mumbled, taking more of him into her mouth. She sucked him until he was hard and climbed on top. "You guys made my fantasy come true last night and I don't want it to be over yet."

After getting Dazè inside, Jenny leaned over and began playing with Cee-Cee's dick while he slept. When she leaned over and started giving him head, he came to life.

"Damn, girl," he groaned, reaching for the back of her head.

When he was fully awake and turned on, she stopped sucking him and sat up to focus on riding Dazè.

"Hold on, girl. Where you going?" Cee-Cee asked, wanting to be in her mouth some more.

"Get up and give it to me." She smiled, loving the sexual freedom she felt from having two men in her bed.

Cee-Cee stood up in bed and Jenny inhaled his meat while she rode Dazè. The threesome changed positions a few moments later. Jenny was on her hands and knees, Cee-Cee was fucking her from behind, and Dazè had two handfuls of her hair fucking her throat like it was a pussy. Jenny gagged and spit ran down her chin as her mouth took a pounding. A few minutes later, they switched positions again, Dazè went to fuck her in the ass while Cee-Cee enjoyed her mouth again. When they couldn't hold back any more, the men emptied their loads into Jenny's mouth and ass and fell onto the bed.

"Damn, girl. You don't fuck around, do you?" Cee-Cee breathed, reaching for his pants, and pulling out a sack of loud and a blunt.

"I've never felt this good before. You guys make breaking up with my boyfriend not seem so bad."

"You could record it and send him a clip. Really piss him off." Dazè laughed.

Jenny looked thoughtful. "That's actually not a bad idea. Motherfucker cheated on me with my sister. I want him to feel how I felt when I found out he was cheating."

"We here if you need us."

"Thanks, guys. You hungry? You want me to make you something to eat?"

"Hell yeah." Cee-Cee rubbed his stomach. "I'm hungry as a muthafucka."

"Me too. What up with some breakfast?"

"Okay. I'll make you guys some sausage and eggs. That okay?" She asked while grabbing a shirt.

"Yeah, that's cool. But that's not," Dazè said, pointing to her shirt.

She stopped putting on the shirt and looked at it. "What's wrong with my shirt?"

"You covering up them titties. Don't do that. I want you naked until we leave."

Jenny dropped the shirt, giving a sexy smile while poking her chest out. "You like my breasts."

"I love 'em. And after we finish breakfast, I'ma fuck them titties while you suck my dick."

"Well, let me hurry up and make this food." She giggled before switching out of the room.

"Shorty a fool." Cee-Cee laughed, handing Dazè the blunt. "White hoes treat niggas like kings. All she want is some dick."

"That's my baby. She would do anything for me. If I wasn't fucking with Renae, I would've kept Jenny. But I'ma keep her in the cut. She gon' be my duck off."

Hearing about Renae made Cee-Cee think of Junior. "I wanna fuck up her brother, my nigga. That shit he pulled last night wasn't a hunnit. He tried to treat us like some workers."

"I know. That was some hoe ass shit. I fucked with that nigga until he pulled that. Now, I want his slot. I'ma be the President of

Parklawn. That nigga got so many muthafuckas gunning for his ass that they won't know who knocked him off."

Cee-Cee reached for the blunt. "How you wanna do it? I'll do that shit tonight if you want me to."

"Nah, we gon' play it smart. If we move too fast, we might fuck it up. Plus, that nigga Fifty could be a problem too. He looked like he was ready to get on that last night at the gas station and folks is a fool. Ain't nothing about fam sweet and I respect his guns. We gon' holla at Junior and make that shit from last night seem like water under the bridge. I'ma start fucking wit 'em real tough and see if I can figure out how to get in contact with the plug. Once we get that, we gon' put that nigga down."

Cee-Cee nodded in agreement, murder in his eyes. "I like the way you think, my nigga."

***

Junior stood on his mother's front porch smoking a blunt while watching late evening's sun cast shadows over the projects. People moved about, minding their own business, seemingly unconcerned and unaffected by the murders that happened last night. Shootings, drugs, and violence were an everyday part of hood life. Nobody questioned why bad things were happening to the people around them because they were too busy thanking God that it didn't happen to them. No one asked why more people didn't work harder to leave the hood. Why did so many people accept their fate being tied to a place filled with crime and hopelessness? Why didn't more people leave? Those were Junior's thoughts as he stood on the porch playing back the conversation with Diamond.

She didn't understand why he wouldn't leave or stop doing what he was doing if the police were looking for him. And neither did he. He was the unstoppable car with no brakes headed towards the busy intersection. If he was truly the captain of his fate, why did he willingly choose a route that would fuck him up in the long run? Why didn't he leave the projects?

Dazè's Challenger parking in front of his grandmother's house pulled Junior from the reflective thoughts and back to last night at the gas station. He remembered the betrayal brewing in Dazè and Cee-Cee's eyes when he checked them about the killings. The veiled threat from Cee-Cee played in his mind along with Fifty's warning to cut the head off the snake. His hand itched to pull the gun from his waist and lay them down in front of the entire hood.

"Bitch ass niggas," he mumbled.

The snakes climbed from the Scat Pack and strolled up Gail's walkway, smiles on their faces and caution in their eyes.

"What's good, my nigga?" Dazè asked.

"Shit. Just out here posted. What you niggas on?" He asked, keeping his tone even, showing no signs of hostility.

"Shit. Came to see what's going on in the hood," Cee-Cee spoke, also hiding his true feelings and intentions behind calm words and a smile.

"It's been quiet. They got Diamond shit taped off. Ain't really seen too many police. They probably did most of the investigating over on 46th. But Detective Johnson involved so he probably gon' be coming through here soon."

Dazè's eyes grew wide with concern. "Detective Johnson? On what? How you know?"

"I talked this Diamond this morning. She said he asked her about me last night, but she didn't say shit. Told him she don't know me."

"You believe her?" Cee-Cee asked.

"I do."

"You can't trust that bitch, fam."

"On the G," Dazè added. "Her baby daddy and friend got killed. I don't think that bitch just gon' let that shit go like that. She know too much. We need to get that bitch."

Junior shook his head. "I took care of it already. But this is why I said what I said last night. We got to move smarter. We can't just pop off because a nigga talking shit. We got too much to lose. Everything that happens in Parklawn gon' fall back on me or the Grinders. We got an opportunity to get some real money, but we need to move smarter."

Dazè nodded in agreement. "I talked to folks last night and we was saying the same shit. At the time and in the heat of the moment, niggas was charged and couldn't see past that nigga talking shit. We never really had shit, so niggas didn't know we had so much to lose. But after cooling off and thinking about it, we was bogus, fam. We moved without thinking and put the whole team in jeopardy. That's on us, my nigga. We fucked that up."

Junior was surprised by the admission of their mistake, but also not entirely convinced that they were sincere. He still believed they were snakes. "We just gotta learn from this shit, you know. I fucked up so many times, my nigga. Six was ready to choke me out. But I'm finally seeing what that nigga been tryna tell me all along. Took me a minute, but I see it now. I think that's gon' be the same lesson for all the Grinders. We still learning, my nigga. Everybody gon' fuck up at least once."

"That's real shit." Cee-Cee nodded. "I just wanted to let you know that I really fuck with y'all. I'm a hot headed nigga and sometimes I move before I think shit all the way out. But one thing about me is I'm loyal. If I fuck with you, then I really fuck with you. Dazè been telling me about you niggas ever since he got out and I was in The Bay dreaming about riding foreign and fucking bad bitches. I want to be a part of something real and I'm really locked in with you, fam."

Junior extended a hand to both men, and they shook. "We all the way locked in, for real. Y'all my niggas. Like I said, er'body fuck up. It's all about that bounce back." After the thug love fest, Junior's phone began ringing. It was a text from Russo. "Aye, y'all. I gotta slide. I'ma fuck with y'all a little later."

Junior drove to T-Murda's spot to get a half brick before going to meet the cop. He had been meeting Russo a couple blocks from the hood at the Midtown Mall. He didn't want to bring him to Parklawn and fully involve him in his dealings because even though they got money together, he was still a cop. So, just to be safe, they met in the mall parking lot.

Junior was driving up 53rd Street when a blue unmarked car with tinted windows turned onto the block, driving in his direction.

A prickly feeling ran up his spine when he seen the cop car. Then, the damnedest thought crossed his mind. *What if that's Detective Johnson's car?* He unconsciously held his breath as the Subaru passed the unmarked car. A chill entered Junior's body when he locked eyes with his worst nightmare. Panic filled him as his eyes shot to the rearview mirror. The brake lights on the cop car lit up and Detective Johnson began making a U-turn. The pistol and half kilo in the passenger seat made Junior panic. If the detective found the work and gun, a trip to prison was certain. So, he did the only thing than made sense. Hit the gas!

He made a quick right into the traffic on Fond Du Lac, dipped into the far left lane and crossed the busy street, pulling into the mall's parking lot a block away from where he made eye contact with the cop. He looked around and spotted the unmarked car speeding across the busy intersection, almost crashing in pursuit of the Subaru. Junior knew he wouldn't be able to outrun the cop. Plus, Johnson knew who he was and where his mother lived. The best chance he stood was getting rid of the hot shit in the passenger seat. After spotting Russo's F-150, he whipped the Subaru into a parking space next the truck and jumped out with the shit in hand. Before Russo knew what was happening, Junior threw the merchandise through his half rolled down window. Russo jumped out looking confused.

"What the hell—"

"Johnson coming! Act like you getting on my ass!"

Russo looked up as the unmarked car's tires screeched a few feet away. Then, he quickly jumped in cop mode. "Hey! Hold it right there!" He yelled, grabbing Junior's arm.

"Get yo' muthafuckin hands off me!" Junior yelled, snatching away.

Russo grabbed him again, more forcefully this time. "Hey, knock it off, Junior. Where do you think you're going? We need to talk."

Johnson approached at the same time Russo was hemming Junior up. "That's okay, man. I got it from here."

Russo gave Detective Johnson a look. "Who the hell are you? This is my guy."

Johnson returned the look. "Who the fuck are you?"

"Man, both of you muthafuckas tripping! Let me go. I didn't do shit," Junior yelled.

"Shut up!" Both cops yelled at the same time.

"I'm Detective Johnson with the Milwaukee Police Department. Who are you?"

Recognition flashed in Russo's gray eyes. "I thought you looked familiar. I'm Detective Russo with the Lacrosse Police Department. You came to town a couple months ago and talked to Marquitta Ware, right?"

"That's right." Johnson nodded. "You working that case? An OD, right?"

"Yep. Came to Milwaukee because I needed a word with the baby daddy. Been tailing this guy for about an hour."

Detective Johnson smirked. "Is that right? You hear that, Junior. You so famous that you got double duty. You about to get DPed, boy!"

"C'mon with the gay shit," Junior mugged. "What the fuck y'all want?"

"I came to talk. And I'm hoping we can do this the easy way," Russo said.

Detective Johnson invaded Junior's personal space, looking in his eyes. "I want it the hard way. Long and hard."

Junior took a step back. "Man, you keep coming at me with that fag shit and I'ma buss you in yo' shit."

The cop smiled, an insane look in his eyes. "I dare you."

Junior let out a stressed breath and shook his head. "What the fuck do y'all want? If y'all finna arrest me, do it. I don't got shit to say and I want to call my lawyer."

"I don't want to arrest you, Junior," Detective Johnson said. "I was on my way to Parklawn to interview a few witnesses about the double homicide that happened last night when I saw you. I know that's your stomping grounds so you're high on my list of people to talk to."

"Ooh! Double homicide!" Russo perked up. "You guys get all the good shit in Milwaukee. I might need to transfer. What happened?"

"Guy and a girl shot multiple times in the head and face right around the corner from Junior's mother's house," he explained before turning to Junior. "You know anything about that?"

"I told you I don't got shit to say. If you want to talk, call my lawyer."

Detective Johnson got serious, pulling out a pair of handcuffs. "Okay, Junior. If you want to play tough street nigga, I can take yo' ass downtown and book you for Fleeing and make you sit for three days while I interrogate yo' ass about the murders that you probably didn't do. Or we can talk like men. Choice is yours."

"I think you should hear him out," Russo advised.

Junior crossed his arms over his chest, leaning against the back of Russo's truck. "What you want man? What?"

Detective Johnson pulled out a phone. "Mind if I record this? Just in case I need to do a follow up?"

Junior shrugged. "Whatever, man. What you want?"

"I want to start with where you were last night? Were you in Parklawn?"

"I was there earlier but I got up with one of my hoes and fucked her all night. Yeah, I like pussy, nigga."

Detective Johnson smiled at the dig. "Who is she and where does she live? Just in case I need to do a follow up."

Junior told the truth, thankful that he wasn't in Parklawn. "Porscha. I don't know her last name, but she live out by the Meadows. I can give you her number if you want."

"Yeah. Give it to me."

Junior searched his phone and gave him the number.

"If you would've cooperated this much during the other interviews, I could've already had your ass in The Bay fucking your hand." He laughed.

"That was good." Russo chuckled.

Junior let out an impatient breath. "Is that all? Can I go?"

"I'm almost done and I'll turn you over to Russo. Do you know anything about the people that were killed last night?" "Nope. I told you I was by my bitch house."

"So, you don't know Goldie or Breezy? Never spoke to them or seen them around? Nothing?"

"I might've seen them around because I be all over Parklawn. But I didn't know neither one of 'em."

The detective smirked like he knew something Junior didn't. "Tell me what you know about the Parklawn Grinders."

A chill ran down Junior's spine when the cop dropped the name of his clique. "The who?"

"You heard me. Answer the question."

Junior locked eyes with the cop for a moment, trying to get a read on what he knew. The cop's brown irises reflected a desire to bust him for the smallest lie. So, he told a half truth. "I heard of 'em."

"Are you a member?"

"What that got to do with anything?"

"Because I heard you were."

Diamond's face passed quickly through his mind. He wondered if she told him about the clique. "Somebody lied to you, man."

"Okay. We'll see about that one." Detective Johnson smirked. "You ever heard of a clique called BGM?"

"C'mon, man. We been through this already. Fredo was BGM. I didn't have nothing to do with that."

"I'm not talking about Fredo. I'm talking about the others. Do you know anything about them?"

"I never heard of them niggas before you brought it up the last time we talked."

"So, I'm guessing you don't know anything about the Parklawn Grinders beef with BGM either, huh?"

Junior shrugged. "Nope."

Johnson stopped recording and put the phone in his pocket. "I got your balls in a vice, Junior, can you feel that? And I'm about to squeeze them tighter. It's just a matter of time. Your arrogance is what's going to put you in a cell, man. And I'll be smiling like a tranny in a prison shower threesome when the judge gives your ass life."

The men shared a long hostile look before Johnson smiled and headed towards his car. "He's all yours, Russo. I warmed that ass up for you."

"Damn, Junior. He really has it out for your ass," Russo mumbled as they watched the unmarked car drive away.

"I hate that bitch ass nigga and all the fag shit that be coming out his mouth."

"You know that if he gets his hands on the recording of you and Quitta arguing, he's coming. That could be the smoking gun."

Junior looked thoughtful. "I know. That's why I need you to get rid of that muthafucka. Whoever you need to pay, ain't no amount too much. My freedom is on the line."

"Steven Milan is keeping that shit to his chest. He's holding it for some reason, and I don't know why."

"I need you to get rid to that shit, Russo. I don't care how you do it, just do it."

"Okay. I'll see what I can do. I got the money from the last flip in my truck. Hang on."

"Nah, you keep it. Use that to pay whoever you need to pay to get rid of that recording. Just gimmie my heat so I can get the fuck outta here."

Junior pulled out of the mall parking lot with a lot on his mind. There was way too much shit happening around him and to him. And on top of that, somebody was snitching. Somebody told Detective Johnson about the Grinders, but he didn't know who. It could've been anybody, even Diamond. That was the thing about snitches. You didn't know who it was until they bussed your head and you see it in black and white. Then, there was Dazè and Cee-Cee. Even though they *squashed* the little dust up they had, he still didn't trust them niggas. They were snakes. And snakes needed to be killed before they got the chance to bite.

CHAPTER 14

Dazè sat on the couch looking around the living room at the Parklawn Grinders. Soon, they would all be pieces on his chessboard. John, T-Murda, RIP, Fifty, Cee-Cee, Kanesha, Ebony, Willow, and Shamar were all sitting around the living room at Jeff's apartment. Junior called the meeting but hadn't shown up yet. No one knew why he called the meeting. Dazè wondered if it was about their altercation over Cee-Cee killing Goldie and Breezy. Was he about to put them on blast in front of the team? Or was Junior about to shut down operations until Detective Johnson stopped coming around? No one knew.

"Why you looking all serious?" Kanesha asked.

Dazè glanced at the brown skinned cutey with dimples and nice smile. "I'm thinking about this meeting. Don't nobody know nothing?"

"Nah. You know that nigga been keep shit to his chest lately. He think he a real President." She laughed. "He need to get some pussy and calm his ass down."

"I heard they was tryna put them bodies on him from the other night. Goldie and Breezy," Ebony spoke.

"Who told you that?" Cee-Cee asked.

"That's what the streets saying."

"Who is the streets?"

Ebony gave him a head to toe look. "You ain't my daddy, nigga. The streets said it."

"Yo' face too pretty to be mugging me. Calm down, lioness. I was just asking a question."

"Did you just call her a lion?" Kanesha giggled.

"Yeah. She look like a sexy female Lion when she get riled up." Cee-Cee grinned.

Ebony liked the comment. "So, don't piss me off if you don't want to hear me roar."

Cee-Cee laughed. "What if I want that kinda smoke? I like a challenge."

She eyed him for a moment, about to comment when the front door opened, and Junior walked in.

"About time, nigga," Fifty griped. "Got niggas in here sitting on crushed velvet couches. I didn't even know they still made crushed velvet couches."

"My bad. I was taking care of some shit and got caught up," Junior explained. "I'ma try not to keep y'all in here too long. I just wanted to run some shit by y'all, and I didn't wanna talk about this on the phone or send a text."

"Damn, nigga. You good?" Willow asked, a look concern spread across his face.

Junior shook his head. "Nah. Shit starting to get bad for me and I wanted to let y'all know what was going on just in case something happen. I got this bitch ass nigga, Detective Johnson, on my ass tryna cook me for bodying that BGM nigga, Fredo. And that shit that happened on 46th a couple days ago came back on me, too. Johnson bitch ass investigating them bodies and they must've questioned some muthafuckas that told them about the Parklawn Grinders. He pulled up on me yesterday and now he asking questions tryna find out who we is."

"The police know about us?" Shamar asked, the fear of prison in his eyes.

"I don't know if they know who we is individually, but they heard of the clique. He asked me if I was a member. Somebody talked to him. So, y'all be on point and watch y'all asses out here."

"You think we should fall back for a little while until the heat die down?" Ebony asked.

"That's a personal decision, my nigga. You gotta do what you gotta do. Right now, they tryna solve them homicides."

"What if they tryna connect the Grinders to them bodies?" Dazè spoke up. "Some of Diamond's neighbors know who we is. What if they planning to come snatch up all of us? They probably got muthafuckas out their recording us."

Junior nodded. "Yeah. You might be right. That's why I said it was a personal decision on whether or not y'all wanna fall back. I can't tell y'all not to get money. Shit, niggas gotta eat."

"I think I'ma fall back. This shit hot right now," Shamar said. Junior looked over the room. "Anybody else?"

Nobody spoke up.

"Aight. That's it, I guess. Y'all be safe out here and watch y'all asses. John, let me holla at you, brah."

When the meeting was over, everybody filed outside. Cee-Cee stopped Ebony before she could walk away.

"Lioness, let me get a word in with you before you leave."

Ebony spun around, showing every tooth in her mouth as she smiled. "What you want, Cee-Cee?"

"I wanna know if I can see you later. If we can kick it?"

She gave him a *nigga, what is you on?* look. "Don't you got a girlfriend?" She fished.

"I just got out the joint and I came home by myself. I'm married to the streets. Do you got a nigga?"

"Nah, baby. I'm married to the bag."

"So, how about yo' single and fine ass get up with me later so we can do us? I just did five years and it's some things I don't know nothing about that I'm hoping you could teach me."

"Ohh, you got some game, don't you?" She asked, looking him over, judging whether or not she was going to give him the pussy. "I tell you what. Show me a good time tonight and I might teach you a lil something."

Cee-Cee nodded, licking his lips, and giving her the *I'ma fuck the shit out of you* stare. "Say less. I'ma see you later, lioness."

After their conversation, Cee-Cee went to join Dazè.

"I see you tryna fuck Ebony bad and boujee ass."

"I need yo' help getting that pussy, my nigga. She wanna kick it tonight and I don't know where to take her."

"She getting money, so you know you gotta step yo' shit up. She ain't no four for four hoe."

"So, what you think? Club? Movies? Go eat?"

"Shit, knowing her, you probably have to do all three and probably buy her some shit."

Cee-Cee frowned. "What? Nigga, you tripping. I ain't no trick."

Dazè laughed. "You can't think about it like that, my nigga. She used to certain shit. She got her own bag. You gotta keep up with her to get that pussy. She looking for somebody equal."

Cee-Cee thought for a moment. "I ain't hustling, my nigga. I don't got paper like that. If that bitch don't want to smoke and fuck, then I'm good."

Dazè laughed again. "Don't trip, my nigga. I'ma help you out because I want to fuck Kanesha bad ass. I'ma rent a Sprinter Van and we gon' fuck up The City. Just be my wingman. I got it."

After spending the day hustling, Dazè rented a Sprinter Van, grabbed Kanesha and Ebony, and hit the highway for Chicago. They arrived in the Windy City a little after ten o'clock and went to King of Diamonds Strip Club. They were getting out of the van when Dazè noticed a group of niggas piling out of two vans. The chubby dark skinned nigga with dreads looked familiar.

"D'shon?" Dazè called.

The clique of niggas turned in Dazè's direction. After a brief stare off, D'shon smiled. "Is that my nigga, Dazè?"

"Yeah. What's good, family?"

The men closed the distance and shared an embrace. "What's good, G? Look like you doing good out here and I'm glad to see you still free," D'shon said, looking Dazè from head to toe.

"Hell yeah. I ain't finna let them white people put me in the trick bag no more. We having our way in the Mil. Let me introduce you to one of the folks, Cee-Cee. He was on count in The Bay. And these some female bosses, Kanesha, and Ebony. This big folks, D'shon."

D'shon nodded towards the women while exchanging a handshake with Cee-Cee. "Welcome to the city, folks. You welcome anytime," he said before turning back to Dazè. "How long y'all gon' be in the land?"

"We just came for the night to kick it with shorty nem. But I might be back soon. I got a power move in the works that's gon' elevate a nigga to top dog status."

D'shon looked very interested in the power move as he wrapped an arm around Dazè's shoulder. "C'mon, in the club with us and

I'ma introduce y'all to the rest of the guys. Y'all with the us tonight. VIP. Let's talk about that power move and how we can all benefit from it."

They got drunk, blew a bag, and kicked it like bosses before jumping back on the highway and heading back to Milwaukee. Kanesha sat up front with Dazè while Ebony sat in the back with Cee-Cee. She was sitting on his lap grinding and teasing him to Future's song, *For A Nut.*

"So, is we spending the night together or what?" Cee-Cee asked, gripping her thighs and ass.

She looked over her shoulder and smiled, loving how turned on he was. "I already told you I'm not fucking you tonight. You can touch but you can't fuck."

Cee-Cee was drunk, high, and tired of being teased. So, he tried to stick his hand down the front of her pants. "Aight, if you don't wanna fuck, at least let me stick my finger in it."

She grabbed his hand and closed her legs. "What did I say, nigga?"

He became aggressive. "C'mon, girl! You got my dick hard as a muthafucka. Let me rub that pussy."

"No, Cee-Cee! Stop!"

He didn't stop. Instead, he began wrestling his hands free, trying to force them down her pants. "Let me touch it. C'mon, girl!"

"Ay, nigga, chill!" Kanesha yelled from the front.

"Bitch ass nigga, I said stop!" Ebony screamed, punching him in the balls.

"Punk ass bitch!" He roared, punching her in the side of the head before doubling over in pain.

"Nigga, why the fuck you hitting my girl?" Kanesha snapped, pulling a 380 from her purse as she went towards the back of the van. "She said no!"

"Hey! What the fuck y'all doing?" Dazè yelled.

"That bitch hit me in my nuts," Cee-Cee groaned. "And you betta put that pistol down before I push yo' shit back, Kanesha!"

"Because you tried to stick yo' hand in my pussy, bitch ass nigga!" Ebony snapped.

Cee-Cee pulled his pistol. "Y'all hoes gon' quit disrespecting me. On my mama!"

"Er'body calm the fuck down!" Dazè yelled as he pulled the van to the side of the highway and went to the back. "Both of y'all put them bangers up. Fuck wrong with you niggas?"

"That nigga hit my bitch. We don't play that bitch ass shit!" Kanesha snapped ready to get it popping.

"That bitch shouldn't have hit me in my balls. Y'all lucky I ain't blazed y'all stanking pussy asses."

"Ayy! Ayy! Both of y'all chill!" Dazè yelled. "Kanesha, y'all go in the front and drive. Just take us back to the Mil. I'ma stay back here with my nigga. Damn, lil brah! What the fuck you on? You know she with the team and we don't condone no rape shit. You foul, family. You foul."

Cee-Cee lowered his head, unable to justify his actions.

"You ain't got nothing to say, nigga?" Dazè asked.

"Ain't shit I can say. I fucked up, G."

Dazè just shook his head.

***

Junior was awakened by a late morning call from Ebony. He listened as she explained how she was almost raped by Cee-Cee on the way back from Chicago. The news made his blood boil. Not only did this nigga bring heat on the team by killing Goldie and Breezy, now he was disrespecting other members of the team. Something had to be done about this nigga before he brought the team down or caused any more trouble. After ending the call with Ebony, he called Fifty and John to tell them the news. They agreed to meet in the hood. Thirty minutes later, they were all standing in front of Gail's house. It was a sunny late summer morning but by the end of the day, darkness would settle over Parklawn and the Grinders.

"Where that nigga at?" Fifty asked, ready to deal out vengeance.

Junior pulled out his phone. "I don't know. He didn't answer when I called him earlier but I'm calling Dazè right now."

After a couple rings, he answered. "What's good, fam?"

"Where you at, my nigga? I need to holla ASAP."

"I'm over here with Renae. Where you at?"

"I'm outside. Where Cee-Cee?"

"I don't know. I just got up just now."

"Aight. Come outside. We need to holla."

"Say less."

"He in there?" John asked.

"Yeah, but he ain't talked to Cee-Cee. I'ma holla at him first and have him call Cee-Cee. That nigga gotta go, fam. Nigga can't come back to Parklawn. If that nigga come back over here, anybody that see him got the green light."

"I told you that bitch ass nigga was cancer. He fucking up the team," John said. "What kinda nigga try to rape a bitch when pussy damn near free?"

"A pussy ass nigga," Fifty spat. "I think you should've just let me put something in his head and saved yo' words, my nigga. This talking shit is unnecessary."

"This shit really just a formality. Both of these niggas gotta go," Junior was saying when the front door opened.

Dazè stepped outside. "You talked to Ebony?"

"You already know I did. What's up with yo' boy, Dazè? You vouched for that nigga and all the nigga do is make shit worse."

"I talked to him just now and told him to ride down on us. I can't speak for my nigga's actions last night. He gon' have to speak for his self. That shit was foul, and I told him about it. We don't condone taking no pussy or none of that fuck shit."

"Well, I'ma tell you this before he get here so you know the level. After today, that nigga can't come back through the hood. Nigga can't step foot in Parklawn or he ain't gon' leave out. I'm giving er'body the green light."

Dazè looked taken aback by Junior's words. "You put a green light on my lil nigga?"

"Hell yeah! That nigga got the whole team hot when he clapped Goldie nem. Now, he try to rape one of our bitches. That nigga bogus. He lucky I'm giving him the opportunity to walk away. The shit he did put the whole operation in jeopardy. And then on top of that, he put his hands on one of my niggas. That shit is unacceptable, fam. I don't got no mercy for that shit."

Dazè glanced to Fifty and John, taking notice of their serious faces. His time with the Grinders was coming to an end as well. He could feel it in the air. "I don't agree with the green light on my nigga, fam. And I got too much love for lil bro to let anybody put a hand on him. I agree that he need to be disciplined, but if anybody pull it with my nigga, I'm getting involved. And I put that on everything I love."

Junior's lip curled into a mug. "You said what you had to say but that don't change nothing. After today, that nigga ain't allowed in the hood or he getting dropped. I'm standing on that."

Dazè returned the mug. "And I'm standing on what I said, too."

The energy on the porch remained tense and filled with animosity. Other niggas from Parklawn arrived in the hood and as soon as they approached, they noticed the tension.

"What's good?" Toe Tagga asked. "Why y'all niggas looking like it's finna go up?"

"Cause it might," Junior answered. "We waiting on that nigga Cee-Cee to pull up. Nigga did some fuck shit last night and can't come back to Parklawn no more."

Black's eyes bulged. "On what, fam? What happened?"

"Soon as that nigga pull up, you gon' find out," John jumped in.

Renae stepped outside and noticed the tension. "Damn, why er'body look so serious?"

"Niggas on some bullshit with lil bro," Dazè spat.

Renae looked to her brothers. "What happened?"

"Go in the house, nigga. This don't got shit to do with you," Junior said.

"Fuck you, nigga. I ain't going nowhere. I'm grown."

Junior was about to get on her ass when Cee-Cee pulled to the curb in Dazè's Challenger. Instead of getting at his sister, he left the porch followed by the crowd that had gathered. "You taking pussy now, my nigga?"

Cee-Cee stepped from the car mugging. "C'mon, my nigga. Don't try to put me out there in front of the whole hood. That's some bitch ass shit."

Junior closed the distance between them, staring into Cee-Cee's eyes, wearing a mug. "Nah, nigga. Bitch ass niggas do bitch ass shit. And what you tried to do the Ebony was some bitch ass shit. How you gon' try to rape one of the niggas on the team? Fuck you was on?"

"You tried to rape Ebony?" Renae asked, surprised by the accusation. "What the fuck?"

Cee-Cee was humiliated by the charge and tried to defend himself. "Man, ain't nobody try to rape that bitch. Fuck you talking 'bout? That bitch was dick teasing. She was the one grinding on my lap, nigga. Get yo' fucking facts right before you come at me with that bitch ass shit. Fuck that bitch. She lucky I ain't blow her shit out for hitting me in my balls."

Dazè could see the situation about to get out of hand and stepped between them. "Ay, y'all niggas getting too charged up. We gangstas, my nigga. Y'all chill with the subliminal disrespect. Keep it a hunnit."

Junior looked Dazè from head to toe like he was an op. "Fuck you talking 'bout keeping it a hunnit with a fuck nigga? Yo nigga foul. Nigga got the whole team hot. You brought this nigga in. This shit on you too, Dazè."

Cee-Cee tried to shove Dazè out of the way to get at Junior. "I ain't no fuck nigga, bitch ass nigga! On the G, I'll whoop yo' ass, hoe nigga!"

Dazè grabbed Cee-Cee before he could get by. "Chill, Folks!"

"What's up, nigga? Let's get active! I ain't Ebony, nigga!" Junior yelled, shoving Dazè aside.

Dazè stumbled, losing his grip cn Cee-Cee and Junior rushed him throwing a wild haymaker. Cee-Cee ducked just in time and lunged at Junior, tackling him to the ground. Before they could throw punches, Toe Tagga grabbed Junior and Dazè grabbed Cee-Cee, pulling them apart.

"Y'all niggas chill on that dumb ass shit!" Renae screamed.

"Chill, fam! Chill!" Toe Tagga said, trying to get through to Junior.

"Y'all can't be out here like this. This ain't how it go," Dazè told Cee-Cee.

"Fuck that nigga, Tagga! It's a greenlight on that nigga!" Junior yelled struggling to get free. "He ain't allowed in the hood no more. If y'all see this nigga in the projects, put him down where he stand. Fuck that nigga!"

"Fuck you and all yo' pussy ass Parklawn Grinders, nigga! I'll rob and kill every single one of you niggas. You niggas is bitches!" Cee-Cee yelled back.

The commotion, noise, and size of crowd caused people to start coming outside. A few moments later, 47th Street was filled with people watching Junior and Cee-Cee scream and wrestle with the people trying to hold them back.

"Junior, what the fuck is wrong with you, boy?" Gail yelled.

The sound of his mother's voice cut through Junior's rage. When he turned and seen his mother walking towards him, he stopped wrestling with Toe Tagga. "This don't got nothing to do with you, mama. I got it."

"It don't look like you got nothing. Why the fuck is you out here tryna fight everybody?"

Junior mugged Cee-Cee one last time before turning to his mother. "I'm good, ma. Just a misunderstanding. Ain't nothing," he said, walking towards the Subaru. Before he drove away, he gave Cee-Cee one final warning. "Don't come to my hood no more, nigga. This yo' only warning."

CHAPTER 15

It was almost three o'clock in the morning, but Quitta couldn't sleep. She had a strange feeling that something was wrong as she sat on her bunk watching the video of Junior and Cee-Cee's fight that one of the neighbors recorded yesterday and posted on Facebook. When she asked him about the incident, he downplayed it as nothing serious. He said the same thing about the double homicide that Russo told her about when Detective Johnson chased him into the Midtown Shopping Center's parking lot. But things weren't going as Junior was saying. To Quitta, it looked like he was being boxed in on all sides. He had the police behind him and enemies in front of him. If any one of them got to him, her unborn baby would meet him in a prison visiting room or have to spend time at his headstone. Quitta didn't want either. In her heart she believed that he needed her to be there with him, riding by his side and helping him figure it out. And freedom could be hers. It was literally at her fingertips. All it took was a phone call. She had everything she needed. Text messages from Russo talking about trying to get rid of the recording. Videos of him talking about selling drugs. Plus, they had sex and she had dick pictures and videos of him jacking off. But what would Junior say if she got one of his partners locked up? Or even worse, what if Russo flipped on Junior? She was stuck. Damned if she did and damned if she didn't. The phone ringing pulled her from thoughts of betrayal and freedom. It was Russo on Facetime.

"Hey, Nate. What you doing?" She smiled, acting like she wasn't just having thoughts of stabbing him in the back.

"Just thinking about you and I thought I'd call. I think I can still smell the scent of your cum in my beard."

Quitta laughed. "What? How? We haven't messed around in a while."

"That's what I was thinking. But I swear I just got a whiff of you. Or maybe I just miss seeing you."

"Awe, you miss me?" Quitta gushed.

"You know I do. Ever since Milan came to see you I've been a little spooked. But I'll be back to see you soon. And I'll try to get a room with no window so I can taste you again," he grinned lustfully.

"Come and eat up, Nate. I love cumming on your beard," Quitta replied as her phone dinged. It was a text message from her mother. The message made her mind go blank and took her breath away.

"And I love the way you moan. Sounds like music."

Quitta didn't respond to the comment. She was literally stuck, her body going numb.

"You good?" Nate asked when he seen the look on her face.

Quitta blinked a couple of times and her voice trembled. "My mother just sent me a text telling me my little brother died." Russo's mouth dropped open and eyes popped. "What? Just now?"

"Yeah. I gotta go. I'ma call you back later," she said, not giving him a chance to get in another word.

"Please, God. Don't let nothing have happened to my brother," she prayed, tears spilling down her face as she called her mom.

"Quitta! Oh, my God! Toogie dead!" Darlene cried.

Quitta closed her eyes as the worst pain she ever felt hit her in the chest. "No, mama! No! What happened?"

"He shot his self, baby. He committed suicide. I can't believe he dead. Oh, Lord, help me!"

Quitta heard what her mother said but couldn't believe it. "He killed his self? What you mean? How? Why?"

"At Ron's house. We on our way to Lacrosse right now. I can't believe my baby is gone."

Quitta was speechless. All she could do was hold the phone and cry with her mother.

"I can't even talk right now, Quitta. I'm a mess. I just need... Oh, God!"

Quitta's pain was increased by listening to her mother's grief. She needed to get off the phone. "Mama, I gotta call Ron. I need to find out what happened. I'ma call you back later."

"Okay, baby. I love you. I need you to come home. Please. I need my family together. Come home."

After ending the call, Quitta broke down, sticking her face in the pillow as painful sobs raked her body. Her little nigga was gone. She couldn't believe it. She would never see the young giant's smile or get another hug. And one question kept going through her head. Why? After a few minutes of grieving, she gathered herself to call her brother.

"Man, Quitta. He gone," Ron sobbed.

"What happened? Why the fuck would Toogie kill his self?"

When Ron answered, he sounded spaced out. "I don't know, my nigga. I don't know."

"Tell me what happened. Who was he with?"

"I was upstairs sleep. Heard the gunshot and somebody screaming. I ran downstairs and found that nigga face down at the table with the pistol still in his hand. White Boy Eddie was screaming. He was sleep on the couch but woke up when he heard the shot. Oh, my God. I can't believe my nigga dead."

"What was they doing? Was they high or drunk? What the fuck happened?" Quitta yelled, getting mad that nobody could tell her what happened.

"Quitta, this shit just happened like thirty minutes ago, my nigga. I'm standing in front of the house tryna figure this shit out. Its police and ambulances everywhere. I can't think straight right now, my nigga. Hit me back later."

After ending the call with her brother, Quitta lay down in bed at cried some more. Cried so much that her pillow case was wet like she dipped it in water. She needed to get the fuck out of jail. She needed to find out what happened to her brother. She needed to be with her family. So, she scrolled through her phone for the one person's number that could open the doors.

***

Nate Russo wasn't a bad cop. For as long as he could remember, being a cop was all he ever wanted. When he was a kid, he loved watching the TV show Cops and playing cops and robbers with his brother and friends on the farm. In high school, he was super excited when Sergeant Miles from the Lacrosse Police Department showed up for Career Day. While listening to Sergeant Miles explain what it meant to be a cop, young Nate made it up in his mind that he would join the academy as soon as he graduated high school. However, his father didn't like the decision. Papa Russo wanted his boys to keep up the family tradition running the farm. But Nate couldn't see himself milking cows, planting corn, and driving tractors for the rest of his life. He wanted action. High speed chases, drug busts, and shootouts with the bad guys is what he dreamed about. Following his dream and with the support of his mother, he enrolled into the Police Academy as soon as he graduated. He excelled at the academy, finishing near the top of his class. After graduating from the academy, the Lacrosse Police Department became his home. He would quickly work his way up the ranks with good police work. Unfortunately, life in the Lacrosse Police Department wasn't what he imagined it would be. There were no shootouts, major drug busts, and only a few high speed chases. Twelve years on the force and he still hadn't fired his gun at a suspect. The biggest drug bust he'd ever been on garnered nine ounces of coke. And the high speed chases were mostly drunk drivers trying to escape their third, fourth, or fifth DUI charge. The crime rate in Lacrosse was incredibly low as they only averaged about two homicides a year. For most people, easy work was good work. But not Nate. He yearned for something more. He wanted excitement. He wanted action. He wanted an adventure. He wanted more than the Lacrosse Police Department could offer.

Nate was also unsatisfied with his love life. He'd only been with one woman since high school. Shelly McIntosh. They met as freshmen and dated up until six months ago. When they graduated high school and the real world came calling, Shelly answered by becoming a Certified Nursing Assistant. She didn't make much money, was unhappy with her life, and her ballooning weight created severe self-esteem issues. When the scale tipped past 230 pounds, Nate stopped having sex with her. To quench his sexual urges, he whacked off to interracial porn of white guys fucking black girls with big butts. When Shelly complained about him working too much, he began working more, creating even more distance between them. When she finally left, he felt free. Free and lost. Since high school, all he'd known was Shelly and police work. Now that she was gone, his equilibrium had been thrown off. He needed to find something to do. He craved excitement and action. And then he got the call about the overdose.

The first time he laid eyes on Quitta, he did a double take. She looked just like his favorite black porn starlet, Amarie. While his colleagues interrogated her, trying to get her to confess to a crime they knew she didn't commit, Nate fantasized what it would be like to have her full lips wrapped around his dick. He'd never been with a black woman but if they were anything like he'd seen in the videos, he was missing out on a good time. A good time he really wanted to have.

She also showed a surprising strength by refusing to snitch on Steph. That was a rare quality that he hadn't seen in the women that entered an interrogation room. Most women confessed as soon as the door closed. But Quitta didn't. And it made him respect and want her even more. And since she was locked in a cell with no one to help, he knew she was desperate for compassion. A compassion that he would give.

A couple months later, Nate found himself thinking about how he would tell his parents about the girl from the hood that stole his heart in an interrogation room while being questioned for murder. Dad might be easier to get on board than mom. Once pop seen Quitta all dolled up, he would understand why Nate had to have her. His mother would be another story. She would probably fly off the wall and cry and beg him to leave her. But he wouldn't. Somehow, he would make them see what he sees in Quitta. Somehow, he would make his drug supplier's baby mama his woman. After all, she was the reason he began selling drugs. He imagined she lived a certain lifestyle and he wanted to be able to provide her the quality of life she was used to.

Thoughts of Quitta made him think about the text message he got from her last night. There was one word. Sorry. He wasn't sure why she was apologizing. Maybe it was because she hadn't answered the phone since she found out her brother died yesterday morning. The best he could figure was she unplugged from the world to grieve the loss of her brother. Maybe that's what the apology was for. For shutting the world out.

As he climbed out of bed, he thought about Quitta's brother's death. He had gone over to the scene to get a look. Toogie sat at the kitchen table, dead from a self-inflicted gunshot wound. He wanted to comfort the grieving family but had to remain professional in front of his colleagues. Plus, none of her family knew who he was. Yet. So, he gathered what information he could and waited on Quitta to call so he could answer as many questions as he could. After a yawn and stretch, he grabbed the phone to check for messages and the time. It was 5:47 am and there were no messages. He walked into the kitchen and opened the cabinet above the sink, grabbing the jar of Folger's. He sat it on the counter and popped the top when movement outside caught his eye. An armored vehicle was driving onto his lawn. Police in SWAT gear trotted next to the armored beast.

"What the fuck?" He cursed, frozen with fear. Then, he thought about the twelve ounces of cocaine in his bedroom along with the seventy thousand dollars in cash. His face on the news, the shameful look on his parents faces, and a prison cell flashed in his mind. When he realized what was about to happen, he panicked.

"Shit! Shit! Shit!" He yelled while running to his bedroom as the front door came crashing in.

"POLICE! POLICE!" The SWAT yelled.

Nate grabbed his service Glock before going into the closet for the drugs. He needed to get to the bathroom to flush the coke. After securing the drugs, he raced into the hallway, headed for the bathroom, and right into the path of four tactically dressed officers with semiautomatic rifles.

"Drop the gun and get on the ground, Nate!"

Nate froze, looking into the eyes of Sergeant Williamson, Michael Sigfrid, Amy Schaffner, and Donald Goldstein. They were all colleagues and friends. People he had known for many years. Shame, anger, and fear reflected in the eyes of his peers. Disgust shown on their faces. He couldn't let them take him in. He couldn't be locked in a cell that he had locked people in. He would take his case to God and hope the man upstairs showed him mercy.

"Fuck you!" Nate yelled, raising the gun a firing.

The four SWAT officers unloaded their weapons, filling Nate's body with bullets and killing him.

***

Dazè sat in the chair inside Jamaica's, playing in the food with his fork. The restaurant was one of the best places to eat in Milwaukee. They served authentic Jamaican food, but he wasn't hungry. He couldn't stop thinking about the altercation in Parklawn yesterday. Lines had been drawn in the sand. Junior banned Cee-Cee from the hood and said he would kill him if he returned. Dazè found that hard to accept. His nigga, that he spent the last five years going to war with in The Bay, had a green light on his head. A nigga that he shed blood for. A nigga that loved and looked up to him like a big brother. He couldn't let his nigga go out like that for a bunch of niggas that he barely knew.

"You not gon' eat to food?" Renae asked.

Dazè looked into his woman's eyes and seen the concern. "I'm not hungry. This shit good but I don't really got no appetite."

"What's wrong? Why you not hungry?"

Dazè shot a glance at Cee-Cee. He was sitting a table over with Patricia. "I don't know what to do. I fuck with yo' family, but I can't let them touch my nigga."

"All he got to do is not come back to Parklawn and he gon' be good. Junior not going out to look for him."

Dazè let out a heavy breath. "That ain't the point. The issue is niggas even threatening my nigga's life. If a nigga tell you he gon' kill you, you get him out the way first. That's just the way it go. You don't sit back and wait for a nigga to come at you. Junior put it on my nigga head. We gangstas. We don't accept that shit. If a nigga want it with me, I give that shit back. But this shit so tangled up that I can't just hit back. Junior is my nigga. You my girl. Cee-Cee fuck with y'all cousin. All this shit fucking with my head and my pride."

"Gimmie yo' hands," Renae said, reaching a hand across the table to interlock her fingers in Dazè's. "I know that this shit is fucked up right now, but I got to back, baby. I'm not going nowhere. We gon' figure this out together. I'm caught in the middle of all of this too. I love you and my brother—"

"You love me?" Dazè interrupted.

Renae didn't realize what she said until he pointed it out. For a moment, she didn't know what to do. Then, she owned it. "Yeah. I love you." She admitted, hoping he said it back.

Dazè stared at her and smiled. He knew that she loved him but to hear her say it felt different. It made everything realer. "I love you, too."

Renae smiled like somebody told her that she won tickets to be front row at a Chris Brown concert. "You love me, too?"

"Ain't that what I just said, nigga?"

Renae's smile grew wider. "Say it again. One more time."

"I said I love you too."

Renae giggled like a little girl. "Patricia, Dazè just told me he love me."

Patricia melted. "Awe, that's cute. They in love!"

"You in love, G?" Cee-Cee grinned.

"Real shit, brah. This my baby."

"Oh, my God! I'm so happy that I don't know what to do with myself." Renae smiled, dancing in the chair.

Dazè shook his head. "You crazy, baby."

"I know. But in a good way." She grinned. Then, something flashed in her eyes, and she got Patricia's attention as she got up from the table. "We need to go use the bathroom."

When the women walked away, Cee-Cee got up and sat in the seat across from Dazè. He wore a smile while shaking his head. "You in love, my nigga?"

"Yeah, fam. Renae is a good one. She all the way down for a nigga."

"She's your queen!" Cee-Cee sang in a high-pitched voice like the man on Coming to America.

"Fool ass nigga!" Dazè laughed.

"That's what's up, though. I'm happy for you," he said before becoming serious. "But that don't change the move, right? I'm still killing her brother."

Dazè matched his nigga's seriousness. "Ain't nothing changing. We gon' knock off both brothers and take over the Grinders. Ain't no nigga finna do nothing to you as long as I'm breathing. I already talked to the Folks in Chicago and their ready whenever I say go."

Cee-Cee grinned, murder in his eyes. "Junior mine, my nigga. Y'all can buss them other nigga's shit, but he mine."

"You already know."

Renae and Patricia popped up a moment later, interrupting the plot on Junior.

"Guess what?" Renae asked, the look in her eyes telling that she had a secret.

"What?" Dazè asked.

"My mother want to talk to y'all right now."

He looked at the phone in her hands. "Where she at? She on the phone?"

"We just got off the phone with her. She want us to bring you and Cee-Cee over. She want to talk to y'all."

"For what?"

"And you know Junior nem on that bullshit," Cee-Cee added.

Patricia spoke up. "We called her while we was in the bathroom and told her about everything. She said she want to talk to you, Dazè, and Junior. She want y'all to squash everything, so nobody don't get shot."

"Y'all shouldn't have got in the middle of this shit. This don't got nothing to do with y'all." Dazè said, getting a little irritated.

"Yes, it do. Y'all our niggas and Junior is my brother. We ain't finna sit back and wait until one of y'all get hurt before we say something. We tryna stop it before it get that far. Just talk to my mama and see what happen. It can't hurt nobody to have a conversation."

Dazè looked to Cee-Cee. "Let's go holla at Gail, fam. She might be able to talk to fam so we can go back to getting this money."

***

Junior lay the phone down and shook his head. He was sitting on the couch at Jeff's house watching Black Ink when he got the call from Darlene. Toogie was gone. Suicide. He couldn't believe the little nigga killed himself. Why would an eighteen year old, with his entire life ahead of him, end it early? It didn't make sense. He was also surprised that he hadn't heard from Quitta. Darlene said she talked to Quitta this morning, so she obviously knew about her brother. But why hadn't she called him to fuss, cry, and grieve? Did she establish an emotional connection with Russo, and he was comforting her? The thought of her building something with the cop burned in his chest, making him pick up the phone and call. It went right to voicemail. He checked her Facebook and seen that she hadn't been active all day.

Fifty walked into the living room and seen the frustration on Junior's face. "You good?"

"Nah, man. Quitta brother knocked his shit out yesterday but I still ain't heard from Quitta."

Fifty's eyes popped. "The nigga killed his self? On what?"

"Yeah. I guess the nigga got drunk and did it. I been tryna call Quitta since yesterday but it keep going right to voicemail. She ain't been active all day either."

"Shit, she probably in that bitch sick. It's fucked up when you lose niggas that's close to you while you locked up."

"Yeah, I guess. That shit gotta be rough. Now, I gotta figure out a way to explain this shit to Mooka. Toogie was his nigga."

"He still young so he gon' be aight."

Junior's phone vibrating grabbed his attention. It was a text from John.

CC at OG house with Dazè.

"What the fuck?" Junior cursed, jumping to his feet, and heading for the front door. "I told this bitch ass nigga not to come back to my hood!"

"What's good, brah?" Fifty asked.

"Cee-Cee by my mama house with Dazè. I'm finna kill this bitch ass nigga!"

"Oh, hell yeah! Think it's a game until them thangs come out." Fifty laughed, ready to get his gun dirty.

While they were walking through the projects, Junior got a call from his mother. "Hey, mama."

"Where you at?"

"I'm in Parklawn, what's good?"

"Come home real quick. I need to talk to you."

Junior got a funny feeling. Something was up. "You called Dazè and Cee-Cee over there?"

"I sure did. Now, get over here so I can talk to all of y'all. Y'all ain't finna be running around here shooting each other over some dumb shit."

"C'mon, ma. Why you getting involved in my business? This don't got nothing to do with you."

"You my son so whatever business you got is my business. Now get on over here. Bye."

Junior let out an angry breath as he dropped the phone in his pocket.

"She called them niggas over there?" Fifty asked.

"Yeah. She getting in my business, fam, and I ain't feeling that shit. I don't give a fuck what she say. That nigga dead. That's my word."

Junior and Fifty walked in the house and seen John, Gail, Renae, Patricia, Dazè, and Cee-Cee seated around the living room. After mugging Cee-Cee, Junior addressed his mother. "What is you doing, mama? Why you getting in my business?"

"I just told you that yo' business is my business. I'm the mama, not you. Now, what is the problem with you and Cee-Cee? Why you telling him he can't come to Parklawn?"

Junior stared at his mother angrily. He wanted to curse her ass out but then he would probably have to fight her, John, and Renae. He didn't think he could take them all, so he stood there fuming.

"Cee-Cee shot somebody, and the police think Junior did it," Renae blurted. "Plus, he got into it with Ebony the other night and hit her. Junior mad about it because Ebony part of his Parklawn Grinders clique."

"Shut up and stay the fuck out my business before I beat yo' ass, nigga!" Junior lashed out.

"Fuck you, bitch ass nigga! You ain't gon' do nothing to me." Junior moved like he was about to blaze Renae, but Dazè jumped in front of him. "Hold on, fam."

Junior tried to push by Dazè, "Move, nigga!"

The war ready gangsta didn't move. "Chill, fam."

They grabbed each other and began tussling. Cee-Cee stood like he was about to help. Fifty lifted a hand to stop him while John got between Junior and Dazè.

"Hey! Hey! Stop that shit, right now!" Gail screamed, jumping up and getting in everybody's face. "If anybody touch anybody else, I'ma start bussing y'all in y'all shit. Think I'm playing and try me! Try me!"

Threats from the matriarch made everyone fall back.

"Now, all of y'all, sit y'all asses down!"

The men sat down slowly.

Gail remained standing and addressed them all. "Now, I don't know what y'all problems is. I don't know nothing about no shooting or what happened between Cee-Cee and Ebony. But what I do know is that I knew Dazè since before he went to jail. I know yo' whole family, man. My kids grew up playing with you and yo' sisters. And now you and my daughter together. I want y'all to stay together. Cee-Cee, my niece like you and I hope y'all can figure out what y'all doing. This is deeper than just what you want, Junior. These people is in relationships, and they can't just pick sides. Just because y'all have a disagreement don't mean somebody got to get shot. Y'all need to use y'all words and talk about the problem. I ain't tryna see none of y'all in jail or dead over no dumb shit. Act like some grown men and figure out how to solve the problem without turning to violence. Darlene lost her son yesterday and now she got to bury him." She paused, getting emotional as tears began spilling down her face. "I don't want to have to bury nobody or go to nobody funeral. Y'all need to figure it out."

Junior felt bad when he seen his mother cry. He got up to wrap her in a hug. "It's all good, mama. Don't cry."

"It's not all good if y'all out there acting stupid and talking about killing each other. Y'all need to figure it out and quit the dumb shit."

Renae got up to hold her mother. "Move, nigga. I wanna hug my mama. You the one that made her cry."

Junior didn't move. Instead, he reached out to grab Renae, pulling her into the hug. Moments later, everybody in the living room were all wrapped around Gail in one big hug. As the love fest continued, Junior eyed Dazè and Cee-Cee. They were watching him watch them. All of the men's eye's reflected the same warning. The beef is squashed. For now.

"My bad for coming at you like that yesterday," Cee-Cee apologized, extending a hand to Junior.

"It's all good, fam. Er'body fuck up. Just can't make the same mistake."

"So, can I get another shot with the Grinders? Y'all niggas like my family."

Junior eyed him for a moment, assessing his worth. "This yo' last shot, my nigga. Like baseball. Three strikes and you out."

"It ain't gon' be no third strike. That's my word."

"I'll take that." Junior nodded before turning to Dazè. "What y'all niggas doing tonight? We can hit up a lil spot and get lit if y'all want."

"I'm down," Dazè grinned, flashing a deadly smile.

"Call it a celebration for getting the band back together."

***

Dark clouds in the sky covered the moon, making the night seem even darker. Rain poured in sheets from the sky like God and all the angels were crying. Lightening flashed every couple of minutes while thunder boomed and echoed in the background. Most people were inside shelter on a night like this, but the fractured Parklawn Grinders had scores to settle.

Instead of being at home wrapped in the arms of bad bitches, the Grinders were riding through the city in a Sprinter Van, armed and on edge. Dazè sat in the driver's seat, steering the van through traffic, sneaking peaks through the rearview mirror at his passengers in the backseats. He needed to keep an eye on them. Needed to make sure he seen it coming so that he could give them some of his own. The pistol sitting on his lap with the safety off would be Fifty's judge and jury. He had already sent a text message to D'shon in Chicago, putting a green light on Junior. He had even given them the addresses to his house and Gail's. If Junior didn't die from Cee-Cee's gun tonight, he would surely be dead before the sun went down tomorrow night. That was a guarantee. Cee-Cee's heart was beating like a kick drum. They'd smoked several blunts while riding around but the weed did nothing to calm his nerves. The energy in the van was electric and hairs stood up on his forearms and the back of his neck like a feral cat. Death was certain. He could feel it. He remained ready and on point, his hand wrapped around the gun on his lap. As soon as Dazè gave the word, he was going to spin around and blow Junior's face off.

Fifty sat behind Dazè, fantasizing about what a 357 bullet would look like entering the back of his head at close range. Would it come out of his forehead or stay lodged inside his skull? Would he slump forward and rest on the horn like dead people do in the movies? He had no answers to the many questions that flowed through his head but there was one thing that he knew for sure. Dazè was a dead man. No way would the snake leave the sprinter on two feet. He was leaving in a body bag and nothing or no one could prevent what was about to happen.

Junior figured it out. The reason Dazè agreed to kick it tonight was because they planned on killing him. They were setting him up. He had already caught Dazè sneaking looks at him through the rearview mirror. And he knew they had pistols in their laps. He and Fifty already planned to kill them as soon as the van parked behind Club Paradise, but it looked like Dazè, and Cee-Cee had the same plan. He leaned over to holla at Fifty, catching Dazè's eye in the mirror.

"They know. We gotta go now."

Fifty was game. "As soon as he stop at the next light."

When Dazè seen them whispering, he knew it was about to go down. The energy inside the Sprinter was tense. He leaned forward to change the song, getting Cee-Cee's attention. He mouthed *ready?* Cee-Cee gave a barely noticeable nod that he understood. Dazè clutched his pistol as *Vory's 'Not My Friends'* came through the speakers. The red light ahead was the signal. As soon as the van stopped, it was on. He just hoped Cee-Cee was ready.

Junior clutched the .38 Special, preparing to leave all six shots in Cee-Cee's body as the van began slowing down for the red light. He took his eyes off Cee-Cee for a moment to glance at Fifty. The seasoned killer clutched the chrome 357 in his fist, keeping it next to his thigh and out of view. When Junior looked back to Cee-Cee, the van was just about to come to a complete stop. It was go time. Junior moved first, bringing the .38 Special from his lap, and letting off. Cee-Cee tried to react but was too slow. Lead began slapping into the back of his head, propelling his body forward.

Dazè kept his eyes on the rearview mirror as he brought the van to the crosswalk. When Junior began shooting Cee-Cee, Dazè spun in the seat, taking aim at Fifty. While he was spinning around, Fifty had already upped the 357 and squeezed the trigger. The first bullet from the revolver flew by Dazè's head, missing his face by inches, and blasting through the windshield. The second bullet hit him in the neck, the third in his chest. But Dazè kept his word and didn't go alone. While he was taking slugs, he also dished them out. He got off three shots, all of them landing home. Fifty took one in the shoulder and two in the chest.

"Ahh shit!" Fifty groaned, falling back in the seat clutching his chest.

The driver's door opened and Dazè jumped out the van.

"Fif, you good, nigga?" Junior asked, looking over his at his nigga.

"Bitch ass nigga got me, my nigga. Fuck!" He groaned, breathing rapidly as blood began wetting his shirt, oozing through his fingers.

Junior looked out the window and watched Dazè fall into the middle of the street, the rain pelting his body. He didn't get up. Cee-

Cee was slumped against the passenger door, blood and brains seeping from holes in his head. "We gotta go, Fifty. Can you move?"

Fifty's breathing became raspy, and he tried to catch his breath, his chest heaving rapidly. "I- I c-can't b-breathe!"

Junior didn't know what to do. He didn't want to leave his nigga but Fifty wasn't going to make it. His eyes grew wide as he continued to struggle to catch his breath. Then, suddenly his eyes became clear, reflecting the realization that he was going to die. His lips curled into a smile and remained that way permanently.

"Fifty? Get up, nigga! Fifty?" Junior called, tears falling from his eyes.

Fifty didn't move. His eyes were open, but they were blank, the smile still etched across his face. He couldn't believe his nigga was gone. They survived countless shootouts and brushes with death but now it was over. When he realized his nigga wasn't going to get up, he left the Sprinter Van, disappearing into the rainy night.

CHAPTER 16

Junior dreamed he was getting some bomb ass head. He couldn't see the face of the woman sucking his dick because she kept her head down. But damn she was about to make him bust. It felt so real that he awoke to see if somebody was really sucking his dick. When he seen Quitta's naked frame kneeling between his legs with his dick in her mouth, he closed his eyes again. It had to be a dream because she was in jail. But the warmth and wetness around his dick didn't disappear when he closed his eyes. It actually started to feel better. When he opened his eyes again, Quitta stopped sucking to smile at him.

"Hey, baby daddy!"

He wiped his eyes and blinked a couple of times, not believing what he was seeing. "When did you get out? How?"

"Let's talk about it later. Right now, I want some dick," she said before crawling up his body and sticking her tongue in his mouth. His hands instinctively gripped her ass and hips as she grabbed his dick and eased her way down. Her pussy felt better than he remembered but not good enough to make him ignore her being home.

"Wait," he broke the kiss. "How did you get out?"

"Mmmmh!" Quitta moaned, continuing to work more of his dick inside of her. "I did what I had to do to put our family together. Damn, baby daddy, I missed you." She kissed him again, rocking her hips, taking what she wanted.

But Junior couldn't let it go. He broke the kiss again. "What the fuck do that mean?"

She stared him in the eyes while continuing to rock her hips, taking all of him deep inside her walls. "It means that—Oh shit! I would do anything to... Damn, baby daddy! To wake up fucking you. Now stop asking me questions. You —ooh shit. Fucking up my concentration."

Junior continued to stare in her eyes, trying figure out what she wasn't telling him. "Okay. One last question. Do I got anything to worry about?"

She lowered her head to kiss him again. "I love you, Junior, and I got yo' back. I would do anything for you. Anything."

He could see the truth in the browns of her irises. Whatever she did, she did it for him. If she didn't want to talk about it right now, that was cool. But she would definitely tell him everything after he fucked her brains out. "Okay," he nodded. "We gone talk later. Right now, I need you to put them titties in my mouth."

Quitta lifted her heavy milk engorged breasts to his lips, and he suckled the nipples while she continued to ride his pipe. He gripped her luscious booty cheeks, thrusting his hips to match the motions of her hips. When he slipped his middle finger into her ass, the moans told how much she loved it.

"Damn, baby daddy! That shit feel so fucking good! Stick another finger in my ass."

He brought the single digit from her rectum before going back in with two. When Quitta began bucking, he knew that her orgasm was close. He teased her nipples with his teeth, increasing the pleasure and pain, sending her over the edge.

"Oh shit, baby daddy! Oh, my God!" She cried as a powerful orgasm rocked her body.

Junior continued fingering her ass rapidly while thrusting up into her pussy, prolonging her orgasm. Quitta's body locked up, forcing her to sit down on him, unable to move until the orgasm passed.

"Damn, baby daddy. That shit way fiya!" She breathed, trying to catch her breath.

"We ain't done yet, nigga," he said before flipping her onto her back and opening her legs. He stared at her pussy for a moment. The lips were slick with cum and swollen with blood from her arousal. The thought of tasting her was crossing his mind. He had never ate her pussy before and she needed to be rewarded for keeping it a stack and taking the case for him. It was time. He moved the hand that he didn't stick in her ass between her legs to rub the swollen pussy lips. Then, he slipped two fingers inside and began fingering her.

"Oh, yeah!" Quitta moaned.

Right when it was getting good, he pulled his fingers out and put them in his mouth. Quitta's eyes grew wide as she watched him taste her pussy.

"Mmmh. You taste good. I should've done that a long time ago. You want some?"

Quitta nodded. "Yeah, let me taste."

He stuck his fingers inside her again and brought them to her lips. She sucked them slowly, looking into his eyes like she was sucking his dick. "I do taste good."

"You want me to eat that pussy?"

Quitta almost couldn't believe her ears. "Yeah. Eat it. Eat my pussy.

Junior went down slowly until he was laying on his stomach, her pussy a few inches from his face. He had never ate pussy before, but he watched enough porn to know the basics. Find the clit and lick it. He spread her pussy lips apart and found the hard little pink ball and began flicking his tongue across it.

"Oh yeah, Junior! Keep doing that! Stay right there!" Quitta moaned, arching her back and grabbing two handfuls of the sheets. Hearing her arousal and pleasure made him want to please her more so he slipped two fingers inside her as he licked. Quitta's moans got louder.

"Oh, shit! Damn nigga! Suck it, Junior! Suck my pussy!"

He sucked her clit between his lips like she asked and Quitta exploded a few minutes later, squirting in his face and mouth.

"Oh, God! Oh, God!"

Junior had no idea what the fuck he was doing but he didn't stop sucking her pussy until the orgasm passed.

"Damn, girl. You nutted in my fucking face," he grinned, wiping pussy juice from his face.

Quitta couldn't move. She sucked in deep breaths, eyes low like she smoked a fat ass blunt. "Damn, nigga. That shit just felt so muthafuckin good."

"And you know what the best part about it is?" He asked.

"What?"

He crawled up her body holding his dick like it was a dangerous weapon. "I still didn't get mine yet."

Quitta opened her legs wide, lifting them onto his shoulders. "What you waiting for?"

When he slipped his dick inside of her, he didn't stop until he was balls deep. Then, he began beating that pussy like he hated her. He drilled with long fast strokes. The sweat from their bodies was making a loud slapping noise every time their pelvises smashed together. When he finally reached his peak, he thrust inside her one last time and exploded.

"Ahhhh!" He groaned before collapsing on top of her.

The lovers lay there for a moment collecting their breath.

"I missed you," Quitta mumbled, kissing the top of his head.

He lifted his head to kiss her. "I missed yo' ass too. Now, tell me how the fuck you get out."

She stared in his eyes for a moment, afraid to tell the truth but knowing she had to. "I helped Milan get Nate."

Junior took a moment to think about what she said. "Russo in jail?"

She shook her head. "He dead."

His eyes popped. "Russo dead?"

"He died yesterday morning when they tried to arrest him."

Junior's mouth dropped open and he was speechless for a moment. Quitta snitched on Russo, and he died rather than go to jail. But what happened when the Lacrosse Police figured out he was doing business with Junior? He jumped out of bed and began to panic.

"You snitched on Russo! Nigga, is you crazy? What the fuck is wrong with you? I asked you if that shit could get back to me and you talking all that I love you ass shit. What the fuck, nigga?"

"I didn't have no choice. It was the only way I could get Milan to throw away the recording of us and not give it to Johnson. And I got my charges dropped. What else was I supposed to do?"

"I don't know, nigga, but you wasn't supposed to snitch. Now, what if this shit get back to me? What if they find some dope in his house or some kind of evidence that we been doing business? Then, what? Goddamn, Quitta!"

Quitta got mad at his reaction. "Nigga, I just stopped Johnson from getting his hands on a recording that could've got yo' ass locked up for murder and I got my own murder charges dropped and you mad? Seriously? Nate was the police. Fuck him. I just sat all that time in jail while you was out here living it up and going on trips and fucking who knows how many bitches. I'm pregnant with yo' muthafuckin baby, nigga. What, you wanted me to stay in jail and have it? Don't matter as long as yo' ass is out here free, huh?"

"That wasn't what I was saying, nigga. I'm saying that the Lacrosse Police might be finna come at my ass if they find something in Russo house or phone. Yeah, you got out that jam, but you might've jammed me up in the process. That's what the fuck I'm talking about."

"Would you rather for Johnson to have that recording and lock yo' ass up for murder and me still in jail charged with a murder I didn't do? It was a catch 22, baby daddy. I had to do something that would hurt us the least. Any way it went, we was gon' be in a jam. But now the jam is not as serious."

Junior stared at her for a moment thinking about what she said. On the one hand , he did get rid of a major piece of evidence that could've probably gotten him sent up north for murder. But she also exposed him to drug charges. She was right. It was a catch 22.

"You saying that the DA got rid of them recording? It's gone?"

"Henrik got the only copy and destroyed it. He knew about the deal and made sure it was good."

"Henrik knew, huh?" Junior laughed and shook his head. "Damn, Quitta. What the fuck?"

Quitta got up from the bed to stand before him and look in his face. She could see the confusion and conflict swirling in his eyes. She grabbed his hand a put it on her stomach so that he could feel the baby growing inside her. "I did it for us. I would rather you face a dope charge than a murder charge. And just like you had my back when I was locked up, I'ma have yours if they come for you. I love you, Junior. You the only nigga that I ever really loved. I would do anything for you."

He didn't know what to say. She had just sat in jail for him and turning in Russo did more to help him than hurt him. He didn't like that she snitched, but it was probably the best move for both of them. He owed her. He wrapped her in a hug, closed his eyes, and lay his head on her shoulder. "You did good, baby mama. Thank you."

The tender moment made her get emotional as tears slipped down her face. "You welcome."

The lovers continued to stand and hold one another until Junior's phone began vibrating on the bed. He checked the screen. It was Renae. He knew what she wanted. Dazè was missing and she wanted to question him on his whereabouts. He didn't feel like talking to her, so he denied the call.

"Who was that?" Quitta asked, suspicious that a woman called.

"Renae. I can't talk to her right now."

"Why you won't talk to yo' sister?"

He didn't answer right away.

"Junior, I know you heard me."

He checked the time on his phone. It was a little after six in the morning. It wouldn't be long before the homicide detectives contacted the families and the news got out that Dazè, Cee-Cee, and Fifty were dead.

"Dazè dead and I don't feel like talking to her about it."

Quitta's eyes grew wide with surprise. "What? Dazè dead? What happened? When he die?"

"He died last night. So, did Cee-Cee and Fifty."

Quitta stared at him for a moment, connecting the dots. Then, her eyes got even bigger. "You killed all of them?"

He shook his head. "Just Cee-Cee. Dazè and Fifty killed each other."

Quitta continued to stare at him. "Oh, my God, Junior! Oh my, God!"

He lay back in bed and closed his eyes. "I don't know what to do. I got a feeling that everything gon' come back to me. Renae knew we was all together. She loved that nigga. I got to tell her to keep my name out that shit when the D's come and talk to her. But the whole hood seen me and Cee-Cee tussling in the street so I'ma automatically be a suspect. If Johnson get on the case, I'ma really be fucked. Then, on top of that, I watched my nigga Fifty die last night. That shit ain't gon' never leave my head."

"Damn, baby daddy," Quitta mourned, sitting on the bed next to him. "I think it's time for us to leave. It's too much. We gotta go." Junior just lay there, his eyes closed, thinking about everything that he'd been through the last few months. He'd gained so much but the things he lost seemed to weigh more. And if he lost had freedom, that would erase everything that he gained. Quitta was right. It was time to go. If he didn't leave now, he might not ever get another chance.

"Okay. I think it's time for me to leave. Where you want to go?"

Quitta couldn't believe that he agreed but was happy as hell that he was finally ready to go. "I don't care. Somewhere where nobody know us. Let's just get in the car and drive. Let's leave everything and go."

"Okay. But first, I gotta go see my family. I need to talk to Renae, so she don't give the police no information on accident. And I gotta tell John that he in charge of the Grinders."

"And we need to stop in Lacrosse. I want to stay until Toogie funeral."

He sat up to kiss her. "Let's wake up Mooka and leave."

Quitta packed them some bags while Junior went to wake and dress Mooka. The family jumped in the Subaru, headed for Parklawn. Junior was so distracted by thoughts of talking to John and Renae that he didn't notice the black Monte Carlo that had been following him since he left home. When he parked in front of his mother's house and jumped from the Subaru, the Monte Carlo's tires screeched, getting his attention. He turned and seen three niggas with pistols climbing out of the coupe. He looked to his pregnant baby mother and son. They stood a few feet from him. If he didn't do something, they would be killed. He had to protect them. So, he charged at the niggas with guns, taking all of the fire. He could hear Quitta and Mooka screaming as the hot bullets filled his body. A montage of important moments in his life flashed through his head as he fell to the ground. When the Monte Carlo sped away, Junior lay on the sidewalk in front of his mother's house with twenty-seven bullets in his body.

THE END.

Lock Down Publications and Ca$h Presents assisted publishing packages.

BASIC PACKAGE $499
Editing
Cover Design
Formatting

UPGRADED PACKAGE $800
Typing
Editing
Cover Design
Formatting

ADVANCE PACKAGE $1,200
Typing
Editing
Cover Design
Formatting
Copyright registration
Proofreading
Upload book to Amazon

LDP SUPREME PACKAGE $1,500
Typing
Editing
Cover Design
Formatting
Copyright registration
Proofreading
Set up Amazon account
Upload book to Amazon
Advertise on LDP Amazon and Facebook page

***Other services available upon request. Additional charges may apply

Lock Down Publications
P.O. Box 944
Stockbridge, GA 30281-9998
Phone # 470 303-9761

Submission Guideline

Submit the first three chapters of your completed manuscript to ldpsubmissions@gmail.com, subject line: Your book's title. The manuscript must be in a .doc file and sent as an attachment. Document should be in Times New Roman, double spaced and in size 12 font. Also, provide your synopsis and full contact information. If sending multiple submissions, they must each be in a separate email.

Have a story but no way to send it electronically? You can still submit to LDP/Ca$h Presents. Send in the first three chapters, written or typed, of your completed manuscript to:

LDP: Submissions Dept
Po Box 944
Stockbridge, Ga 30281

DO NOT send original manuscript. Must be a duplicate.

Provide your synopsis and a cover letter containing your full contact information.

Thanks for considering LDP and Ca$h Presents.

NEW RELEASES

OUL OF A HUSTLER, HEART OF A KILLER 2 by
SAYNOMORE
SOSA GANG by ROMELL TUKES
PROTÉGÉ OF A LEGEND 2 by COREY ROBINSON
BRONX SAVAGES by ROMELL TUKES
A GANGSTA'S PAIN 3 by J-BLUNT

A Gangsta's Pain 3

Coming Soon from Lock Down Publications/Ca$h Presents
BLOOD OF A BOSS VI
SHADOWS OF THE GAME II
TRAP BASTARD II
By **Askari**
LOYAL TO THE GAME **IV**
By **T.J. & Jelissa**
TRUE SAVAGE **VIII**
MIDNIGHT CARTEL IV
DOPE BOY MAGIC IV
CITY OF KINGZ III
NIGHTMARE ON SILENT AVE II
THE PLUG OF LIL MEXICO II
CLASSIC CITY II
By **Chris Green**
BLAST FOR ME **III**
A SAVAGE DOPEBOY III
CUTTHROAT MAFIA III
DUFFLE BAG CARTEL VII
HEARTLESS GOON VI
By **Ghost**
A HUSTLER'S DECEIT III
KILL ZONE II
BAE BELONGS TO ME III
TIL DEATH II
By **Aryanna**
KING OF THE TRAP III
By **T.J. Edwards**
GORILLAZ IN THE BAY V
3X KRAZY III

225

J-Blunt

STRAIGHT BEAST MODE III

De'Kari

KINGPIN KILLAZ IV

STREET KINGS III

PAID IN BLOOD III

CARTEL KILLAZ IV

DOPE GODS III

Hood Rich

SINS OF A HUSTLA II

ASAD

YAYO V

Bred In The Game 2

S. Allen

THE STREETS WILL TALK II

By Yolanda Moore

SON OF A DOPE FIEND III

HEAVEN GOT A GHETTO II

SKI MASK MONEY II

By Renta

LOYALTY AIN'T PROMISED III

By Keith Williams

I'M NOTHING WITHOUT HIS LOVE II

SINS OF A THUG II

TO THE THUG I LOVED BEFORE II

IN A HUSTLER I TRUST II

By Monet Dragun

QUIET MONEY IV

EXTENDED CLIP III

THUG LIFE IV

By **Trai'Quan**

226

THE STREETS MADE ME IV
By **Larry D. Wright**
IF YOU CROSS ME ONCE III
ANGEL V
By **Anthony Fields**
THE STREETS WILL NEVER CLOSE IV
By **K'ajji**
HARD AND RUTHLESS III
KILLA KOUNTY IV
By **Khufu**
MONEY GAME III
By **Smoove Dolla**
JACK BOYS VS DOPE BOYS IV
A GANGSTA'S QUR'AN V
COKE GIRLZ II
COKE BOYS II
LIFE OF A SAVAGE V
CHI'RAQ GANGSTAS V
SOSA GANG II
BRONX SAVAGES II
By **Romell Tukes**
MURDA WAS THE CASE III
Elijah R. Freeman
THE STREETS NEVER LET GO III
By **Robert Baptiste**
AN UNFORESEEN LOVE IV
BABY, I'M WINTERTIME COLD III
By **Meesha**

QUEEN OF THE ZOO III

J-Blunt

By **Black Migo**

CONFESSIONS OF A JACKBOY III

By **Nicholas Lock**

GRIMEY WAYS III

By **Ray Vinci**

KING KILLA II

By **Vincent "Vitto" Holloway**

BETRAYAL OF A THUG III

By **Fre$h**

THE MURDER QUEENS III

By **Michael Gallon**

THE BIRTH OF A GANGSTER III

By **Delmont Player**

TREAL LOVE II

By **Le'Monica Jackson**

FOR THE LOVE OF BLOOD III

By **Jamel Mitchell**

RAN OFF ON DA PLUG II

By **Paper Boi Rari**

HOOD CONSIGLIERE III

By **Keese**

PRETTY GIRLS DO NASTY THINGS II

By **Nicole Goosby**

PROTÉGÉ OF A LEGEND III

By **Corey Robinson**

IT'S JUST ME AND YOU II

By **Ah'Million**

BORN IN THE GRAVE III

By **Self Made Tay**

FOREVER GANGSTA III

A Gangsta's Pain 3

By Adrian Dulan
GORILLAZ IN THE TRENCHES II
By SayNoMore
THE COCAINE PRINCESS VII
By King Rio
CRIME BOSS II
Playa Ray
LOYALTY IS EVERYTHING III
Molotti
HERE TODAY GONE TOMORROW II
By Fly Rock
REAL G'S MOVE IN SILENCE II
By Von Diesel

Available Now

RESTRAINING ORDER I & II
By CA$H & Coffee
LOVE KNOWS NO BOUNDARIES I II & III
By Coffee
RAISED AS A GOON I, II, III & IV
BRED BY THE SLUMS I, II, III
BLAST FOR ME I & II
ROTTEN TO THE CORE I II III
A BRONX TALE I, II, III
DUFFLE BAG CARTEL I II III IV V VI
HEARTLESS GOON I II III IV V

J-Blunt

A SAVAGE DOPEBOY I II

DRUG LORDS I II III

CUTTHROAT MAFIA I II

KING OF THE TRENCHES

By **Ghost**

LAY IT DOWN **I & II**

LAST OF A DYING BREED I II

BLOOD STAINS OF A SHOTTA I & II III

By **Jamaica**

LOYAL TO THE GAME I II III

LIFE OF SIN I, II III

By **TJ & Jelissa**

BLOODY COMMAS I & II

SKI MASK CARTEL I II & III

KING OF NEW YORK I II,III IV V

RISE TO POWER I II III

COKE KINGS I II III IV V

BORN HEARTLESS I II III IV

KING OF THE TRAP I II

By **T.J. Edwards**

IF LOVING HIM IS WRONG…I & II

LOVE ME EVEN WHEN IT HURTS I II III

By **Jelissa**

WHEN THE STREETS CLAP BACK I & II III

THE HEART OF A SAVAGE I II III IV

MONEY MAFIA I II

LOYAL TO THE SOIL I II III

By **Jibril Williams**

A DISTINGUISHED THUG STOLE MY HEART I II & III

LOVE SHOULDN'T HURT I II III IV

A Gangsta's Pain 3

RENEGADE BOYS I II III IV

PAID IN KARMA I II III

SAVAGE STORMS I II III

AN UNFORESEEN LOVE I II III

BABY, I'M WINTERTIME COLD I II

By **Meesha**

A GANGSTER'S CODE I &, II III

A GANGSTER'S SYN I II III

THE SAVAGE LIFE I II III

CHAINED TO THE STREETS I II III

BLOOD ON THE MONEY I II III

A GANGSTA'S PAIN I II III

By J-Blunt

PUSH IT TO THE LIMIT

By **Bre' Hayes**

BLOOD OF A BOSS **I, II, III, IV, V**

SHADOWS OF THE GAME

TRAP BASTARD

By **Askari**

THE STREETS BLEED MURDER **I, II & III**

THE HEART OF A GANGSTA I II& III

By **Jerry Jackson**

CUM FOR ME I II III IV V VI VII VIII

An **LDP Erotica Collaboration**

BRIDE OF A HUSTLA **I II & II**

THE FETTI GIRLS **I, II& III**

CORRUPTED BY A GANGSTA I, II III, IV

BLINDED BY HIS LOVE

THE PRICE YOU PAY FOR LOVE I, II ,III

DOPE GIRL MAGIC I II III

J-Blunt

By **Destiny Skai**
WHEN A GOOD GIRL GOES BAD
By **Adrienne**
THE COST OF LOYALTY I II III
By Kweli
A GANGSTER'S REVENGE **I II III & IV**
THE BOSS MAN'S DAUGHTERS I II III IV V
A SAVAGE LOVE **I & II**
BAE BELONGS TO ME I II
A HUSTLER'S DECEIT I, II, III
WHAT BAD BITCHES DO I, II, III
SOUL OF A MONSTER I II III
KILL ZONE
A DOPE BOY'S QUEEN I II III
TIL DEATH
By **Aryanna**
A KINGPIN'S AMBITON
A KINGPIN'S AMBITION **II**
I MURDER FOR THE DOUGH
By **Ambitious**
TRUE SAVAGE I II III IV V VI VII
DOPE BOY MAGIC I, II, III
MIDNIGHT CARTEL I II III
CITY OF KINGZ I II
NIGHTMARE ON SILENT AVE
THE PLUG OF LIL MEXICO II
CLASSIC CITY
By **Chris Green**
A DOPEBOY'S PRAYER
By **Eddie "Wolf" Lee**

232

A Gangsta's Pain 3

THE KING CARTEL **I, II & III**
By **Frank Gresham**
THESE NIGGAS AIN'T LOYAL **I, II & III**
By **Nikki Tee**
GANGSTA SHYT **I II &III**
By **CATO**
THE ULTIMATE BETRAYAL
By **Phoenix**
BOSS'N UP **I , II & III**
By **Royal Nicole**
I LOVE YOU TO DEATH
By **Destiny J**
I RIDE FOR MY HITTA
I STILL RIDE FOR MY HITTA
By **Misty Holt**
LOVE & CHASIN' PAPER
By **Qay Crockett**
TO DIE IN VAIN
SINS OF A HUSTLA
By **ASAD**
BROOKLYN HUSTLAZ
By **Boogsy Morina**
BROOKLYN ON LOCK I & II
By **Sonovia**
GANGSTA CITY
By **Teddy Duke**
A DRUG KING AND HIS DIAMOND I & II III
A DOPEMAN'S RICHES
HER MAN, MINE'S TOO I, II
CASH MONEY HO'S

J-Blunt

THE WIFEY I USED TO BE I II
PRETTY GIRLS DO NASTY THINGS
By Nicole Goosby
TRAPHOUSE KING **I II & III**
KINGPIN KILLAZ I II III
STREET KINGS I II
PAID IN BLOOD **I II**
CARTEL KILLAZ I II III
DOPE GODS I II
By **Hood Rich**
LIPSTICK KILLAH **I, II, III**
CRIME OF PASSION I II & III
FRIEND OR FOE I II III
By **Mimi**
STEADY MOBBN' **I, II, III**
THE STREETS STAINED MY SOUL I II III
By **Marcellus Allen**
WHO SHOT YA **I, II, III**
SON OF A DOPE FIEND I II
HEAVEN GOT A GHETTO
SKI MASK MONEY
Renta
GORILLAZ IN THE BAY **I II III IV**
TEARS OF A GANGSTA I II
3X KRAZY I II
STRAIGHT BEAST MODE I II
DE'KARI
TRIGGADALE I II III
MURDAROBER WAS THE CASE I II
Elijah R. Freeman

234

A Gangsta's Pain 3

GOD BLESS THE TRAPPERS I, II, III
THESE SCANDALOUS STREETS I, II, III
FEAR MY GANGSTA I, II, III IV, V
THESE STREETS DON'T LOVE NOBODY I, II
BURY ME A G I, II, III, IV, V
A GANGSTA'S EMPIRE I, II, III, IV
THE DOPEMAN'S BODYGAURD I II
THE REALEST KILLAZ I II III
THE LAST OF THE OGS I II III
Tranay Adams
THE STREETS ARE CALLING
Duquie Wilson
MARRIED TO A BOSS I II III
By Destiny Skai & Chris Green
KINGZ OF THE GAME I II III IV V VI
CRIME BOSS
Playa Ray
SLAUGHTER GANG I II III
RUTHLESS HEART I II III
By Willie Slaughter
FUK SHYT
By Blakk Diamond
DON'T F#CK WITH MY HEART I II
By Linnea
ADDICTED TO THE DRAMA I II III
IN THE ARM OF HIS BOSS II
By Jamila
YAYO I II III IV
A SHOOTER'S AMBITION I II
BRED IN THE GAME

235

J-Blunt

By S. Allen
TRAP GOD I II III
RICH $AVAGE I II III
MONEY IN THE GRAVE I II III
By Martell Troublesome Bolden
FOREVER GANGSTA I II
GLOCKS ON SATIN SHEETS I II
By Adrian Dulan
TOE TAGZ I II III IV
LEVELS TO THIS SHYT I II
IT'S JUST ME AND YOU
By Ah'Million
KINGPIN DREAMS I II III
RAN OFF ON DA PLUG
By Paper Boi Rari
CONFESSIONS OF A GANGSTA I II III IV
CONFESSIONS OF A JACKBOY I II
By Nicholas Lock
I'M NOTHING WITHOUT HIS LOVE
SINS OF A THUG
TO THE THUG I LOVED BEFORE
A GANGSTA SAVED XMAS
IN A HUSTLER I TRUST
By Monet Dragun
CAUGHT UP IN THE LIFE I II III
THE STREETS NEVER LET GO I II
By Robert Baptiste
NEW TO THE GAME I II III
MONEY, MURDER & MEMORIES I II III
By Malik D. Rice

A Gangsta's Pain 3

LIFE OF A SAVAGE I II III IV
A GANGSTA'S QUR'AN I II III IV
MURDA SEASON I II III
GANGLAND CARTEL I II III
CHI'RAQ GANGSTAS I II III IV
KILLERS ON ELM STREET I II III
JACK BOYZ N DA BRONX I II III
A DOPEBOY'S DREAM I II III
JACK BOYS VS DOPE BOYS I II III
COKE GIRLZ
COKE BOYS
SOSA GANG
BRONX SAVAGES
By Romell Tukes
LOYALTY AIN'T PROMISED I II
By Keith Williams
QUIET MONEY I II III
THUG LIFE I II III
EXTENDED CLIP I II
A GANGSTA'S PARADISE
By **Trai'Quan**
THE STREETS MADE ME I II III
By **Larry D. Wright**
THE ULTIMATE SACRIFICE I, II, III, IV, V, VI
KHADIFI
IF YOU CROSS ME ONCE I II
ANGEL I II III IV
IN THE BLINK OF AN EYE
By **Anthony Fields**
THE LIFE OF A HOOD STAR

J-Blunt

By Ca$h & Rashia Wilson

THE STREETS WILL NEVER CLOSE I II III

By K'ajji

CREAM I II III

THE STREETS WILL TALK

By Yolanda Moore

NIGHTMARES OF A HUSTLA I II III

By King Dream

CONCRETE KILLA I II III

VICIOUS LOYALTY I II III

By Kingpen

HARD AND RUTHLESS I II

MOB TOWN 251

THE BILLIONAIRE BENTLEYS I II III

REAL G'S MOVE IN SILENCE

By Von Diesel

GHOST MOB

Stilloan Robinson

MOB TIES I II III IV V VI

SOUL OF A HUSTLER, HEART OF A KILLER I II

GORILLAZ IN THE TRENCHES

By SayNoMore

BODYMORE MURDERLAND I II III

THE BIRTH OF A GANGSTER I II

By Delmont Player

FOR THE LOVE OF A BOSS

By C. D. Blue

MOBBED UP I II III IV

THE BRICK MAN I II III IV V

THE COCAINE PRINCESS I II III IV V VI

A Gangsta's Pain 3

By King Rio
KILLA KOUNTY I II III IV
By Khufu
MONEY GAME I II
By Smoove Dolla
A GANGSTA'S KARMA I II III
By FLAME
KING OF THE TRENCHES I II III
by GHOST & TRANAY ADAMS
QUEEN OF THE ZOO I II
By Black Migo
GRIMEY WAYS I II
By Ray Vinci
XMAS WITH AN ATL SHOOTER
By Ca$h & Destiny Skai
KING KILLA
By Vincent "Vitto" Holloway
BETRAYAL OF A THUG I II
By Fre$h
THE MURDER QUEENS I II
By Michael Gallon
TREAL LOVE
By Le'Monica Jackson
FOR THE LOVE OF BLOOD I II
By Jamel Mitchell
HOOD CONSIGLIERE I II
By Keese
PROTÉGÉ OF A LEGEND I II
By Corey Robinson
BORN IN THE GRAVE I II

J-Blunt

By Self Made Tay
MOAN IN MY MOUTH
By XTASY
TORN BETWEEN A GANGSTER AND A GENTLEMAN
By J-BLUNT & Miss Kim
LOYALTY IS EVERYTHING I II
Molotti
HERE TODAY GONE TOMORROW
By Fly Rock
PILLOW PRINCESS
By S. Hawkins

BOOKS BY LDP'S CEO, CA$H

TRUST IN NO MAN

TRUST IN NO MAN 2

TRUST IN NO MAN 3

BONDED BY BLOOD

SHORTY GOT A THUG

THUGS CRY

THUGS CRY 2

THUGS CRY 3

TRUST NO BITCH

TRUST NO BITCH 2

TRUST NO BITCH 3

TIL MY CASKET DROPS

RESTRAINING ORDER

RESTRAINING ORDER 2

IN LOVE WITH A CONVICT

LIFE OF A HOOD STAR

XMAS WITH AN ATL SHOOTER

J-Blunt

www.ingramcontent.com/pod-product-compliance
Lightning Source LLC
Chambersburg PA
CBHW060550260626
47161CB00003B/1133